W9-BGU-155

Contents

Dedication

This book is lovingly dedicated to:
my husband
Rob
You are my inspiration.
Song of Solomon 5:16

and

my son
Joshua
The cutest baby on earth.
Isaiah 9:6

Appreciation

Extra Special Thanks to:

Marvin Moore — for the idea, the encouragement, and the support.
Mom and Dad — for Solomon (my computer) who made writing this book so much easier.
Rob — I love you! Thanks for your support.
My sister, Aimee (the teacher) — who proofed the copy for me.
Dorie Mirucki — for her valuable advice on my proposal and for being my cheerleader.
My wonderful Jesus — thank You for giving me the strength to grasp Colossians 1:29 even when my mind was oatmeal.

CHAPTER

1

Moving

Sherrie Raines cast one last, longing glance around the bare house . . . searching. For what? She was positive she hadn't left anything behind. Memories maybe, hiding here where the boys had grown up.

She could hear them tossing a football around on the front lawn and pictured her husband Jack outside by the moving van getting impatient as he waited for her. Still, she was reluctant to leave. When she stepped out the door, it would be for good. It would be like putting her seal of approval on their move to Maine, and she wasn't sure she was ready to do that. Yet.

"Just a minute," she called out the window to Jack. He was leaning against the fender of the van, watching the boys with a rare smile. She wished she hadn't packed the camera. "I'm just going to check upstairs again. Then I'll be right out."

He nodded indulgently, and she closed the window, unconsciously locking it too. Against what? Robbers? She lingered in the hallway, in the stairwell, in each of the bedrooms upstairs. Scott's room, Caleb's room, both spotless. Sherrie wouldn't have considered leaving a mess for the next owner to clean up. What would they think of her?

She leaned against the windowsill and watched them through the sparkling glass. Caleb tossed the ball to Scott, who ran for it as if his life depended on it. Caleb followed Scott's progress with his eyes, but his face never lost its impassive, sullen expression.

Sherrie knew he didn't want to leave Tennessee, his friends, and all their relatives. Ever since Jack announced they'd be moving and had the house built in Maine, Caleb had become

7

withdrawn. A few times she'd caught him scribbling in a note-book and decided he'd taken to journaling as a way to express himself. Jack said it was healthy, but she wasn't sure.

Scott, on the other hand, was ecstatic about the move. But then, she mused, he was ecstatic about everything from broccoli to math homework to chores. It didn't seem to matter to him. She waved when he saw her in the window and grinned. Jack pointed to his watch. She nodded vigorously.

Time to go. Time for the final goodbye. She ran her hand gently along the windowsill, picturing Caleb's tousled five-year-old head bowed there saying his prayers. Shaking herself, she hurried from the room before the threatening tears could spill.

All the lights . . . off. Windows . . . closed. She pulled the big outside door shut behind her, turned the key in the lock one last time, and marched briskly down the steps. She dropped the key in Jack's outstretched hand.

"Ready?"

She nodded and attempted a businesslike smile. "Ready."

"Do you have the map?"

She patted her purse. "Right here. I'll give it to Caleb. I've got the route marked in red. We shouldn't have any trouble. I'll drive slowly anyway."

She scooted into the car and buckled up, glancing in the rear-view mirror to be sure Scott did too. Caleb reached into the back for his things. He was going to sit up front with her and read the map. As he picked up his notebook, she saw him swat at Scott.

"Knock it off," she warned. "I don't want to have to spend the whole trip watching you two. You're not babies anymore."

"Aw, Mom," Caleb protested in that hoarse, squeaky, high-low voice that kept making her do a double-take whenever he spoke lately. She stifled a grin. "Tell him to stop making fun of me."

"I'm not."

Sherrie rolled her eyes. "Get in, Caleb. Hurry up; your father's waiting." He sat down and buckled up. On his lap was the yellow notebook. She jerked her head at it as she pulled out in front of the van and waved at Jack.

"What are you writing about, Caleb?"

He squirmed uncomfortably. "Nothing."

"Well, you must be writing about something," she probed.

"Just stuff," he replied evasively.

Sherrie let the subject drop, but she wondered why he wouldn't talk to her about it. Lately, she was seeing a new side of Caleb. One she was very uncomfortable with. This Caleb didn't want her around, moped around the house, and wrote about "stuff" in a notebook that had "PRIVATE PROPERTY OF CALEB RAINES" written across the front in big letters.

"Someday," she promised herself, "I'm going to read it." She'd never seen the book except when Caleb was writing in it, so she was pretty sure he hid it somewhere in his room. She toyed with the idea of demanding to read it but decided that it would probably make him stop writing in it, and she wouldn't learn anything except what he'd already written. Better to read it sometime when he wasn't around so he wouldn't know.

"Anyway," she argued to herself, "there isn't anything in there that I shouldn't be able to read. He is my son, after all." They bumped softly along the highway, and Caleb's pen scratched without pause. Sherrie eyed the scrawling words uneasily. What was he writing about? Her? The move? Scott? What?

She bit her lip in frustration. She'd find out sometime, she determined. Sometime soon. She tried to take her mind off the notebook by mentally unpacking the boxes. Most of their belongings had already been shipped up to Maine the week before. All that was left was in the van Jack drove.

A big sign welcomed them to Virginia. "We just left Tennessee, boys," she informed them, forcing herself to sound cheerful. "Say goodbye to the old home state."

"Goodbye, Tennessee!" whooped Scott obligingly. Caleb looked up briefly, then returned to his scribbling. Sherrie spent some more time worrying about his writing and mentioned it to Jack that night as they tried to sleep at a plush hotel in Pennsylvania where they stopped for the night.

"Oh, don't worry about it." Jack yawned. "It's probably just a phase."

"But I want to know what he's writing about."

"Nothing. Stuff. He's fourteen years old. What can he have to write about?"

"I don't know," she replied, still suspicious. "Did you ever have a diary when you were his age?"

"No. I can't write. Why do you think I became a doctor?"

Sherrie giggled. "Stop. I'm serious. I've been thinking of reading it sometime when he's not around," she confided. Then added hastily, "Just to see what it says."

She felt Jack shrug. "So? Read it. What harm can it do? I'm telling you he writes about nothing."

Sherrie relaxed, glad that Jack thought it was OK too. The nagging objection in the back of her mind retreated into silence. Now she just needed the right opportunity. She sighed deeply and snuggled into Jack's shoulder.

The next morning, everyone was irritable. Around lunchtime, Sherrie decided she'd rather jog the rest of the way than be cooped up in the car with her whiny offspring. At a rest stop, she made Scott ride the rest of the way with his father. Jack shot her a questioning glance, but a quick glare dared him to ask why.

The remainder of the trip was made in a silence broken only when Sherrie commented on the seascape passing fleetingly on the right. Once she rolled the window down and was surprised to smell the ocean, briny and thick. The air seemed to invade the car and settle over them like a cool, moist blanket.

As the sun was about to dip behind the rolling hills that Maine called mountains, they pulled into their driveway. Sherrie sat behind the steering wheel feeling the stillness for a moment before climbing wearily out of the car.

Piles of fresh dirt were mounded in the yard. Jack reminded her that the builders would be back to grade the lawn later in the week. She regarded them uneasily.

"How soon?"

"How soon what?"

"How soon will they be back? I don't like those piles."

"By Wednesday. They've got a few things to finish in the house too, remember?"

Sherrie groaned. "No, I'd forgotten. How am I supposed to unpack with builders messing everything up?"

Jack pulled the doors of the van open. "Grab an armload, boys," he instructed. "Don't worry about it, Sherrie. It's little stuff."

He grunted as he took a box off the van and began to carry it into the house. Caleb followed him, notebook tucked under his arm. Jack stopped and swung around to face him.

"Caleb, didn't I ask you to grab something from the van?"

Caleb held up his notebook. "I've got something, Dad."

"From the van, Caleb. Go back and get something."

Caleb turned sharply and almost ran into Scott, who had so much in his arms that he couldn't see where he was going. Scott whistled as he staggered up the steps into the house and dropped his armful with a crash on the bare living-room floor.

Sherrie glared at him as she set her load down on the tarp covering the sofa. "Gently, Scott."

He picked everything up and stacked it neatly on the sofa. "Want me to go get some more, Mom?"

Sherrie nodded absently. Where was she going to put all this stuff? Especially if she couldn't unpack everything. Finally, she decided it didn't matter, since she wasn't up to unpacking anything tonight anyway.

That night they ate supper using the biggest box for a table and smaller ones as chairs. Sherrie tried to ignore the wrinkled noses when she brought the two-day-old sandwiches out of the cooler. The homemade whole-wheat bread was soggy, and the avocado, onion, and lettuce inside had all blended together with onion as the predominating flavor.

"All right, I'm sorry," she said defensively. "I'll go to the store tomorrow. Is there a decent store around here?"

Jack thought a minute. "I think there's a health-food store right in downtown Pawlet. If I'm right, it's small. There's also a grocery store."

Caleb crunched a carrot stick. "Do you think we could have some potato chips?" he asked hopefully. "Or maybe some nachos?"

Sherrie frowned. "You aren't serious?"

Caleb ducked his head. "Guess not," he mumbled, but Sherrie didn't believe him. Lately he was making quite a number of cracks about the food she cooked, and worse, he was requesting junk food every time she went to the store. This time she decided to confront him.

"Do you know what potato chips would do to you?" she demanded. Caleb didn't answer, and Scott appeared thoughtful. "They'd fill you up with a lot of grease and calories and salt. You wouldn't want that, would you?"

"Guess not."

"Well, I hope not anyway. I hope I've brought you up better than that. Your body is the temple of the Holy Spirit, you know. It's sinful to dump toxic waste like potato chips into it."

"Your mother's right, Caleb," Jack agreed. "We spend extra

money to buy healthful foods because we believe that's something God wants us to do. You understand that, don't you, son?"

A hot flush crept up Caleb's downcast face. "Yes, sir."

Jack nodded and took another bite of his sandwich. "That's good. I'm glad we got that all cleared up."

Sherrie was thankful that at least the carob cookies had survived the moisture in the cooler. Jack and Scott helped themselves liberally, but Caleb skipped dessert. Getting up from the "table," he went to sit on the tarp-covered sofa with his notebook. Soon his pen was scratching vigorously.

Sherrie raised her eyebrows. Jack shrugged as if to say, "Too bad, more for us." Sherrie bit thoughtfully into a cookie, wishing she could understand this change coming over her son. She didn't like it, not at all.

The rest of the week passed uneventfully. If she hadn't been so busy trying to get the house in order, she would have been much more nervous about meeting the members of their new church.

After the first three days, she decided that she just might like Maine after all . . . eventually. The builders, with their funny accents, were considerate and managed to finish everything in time for her to get most of the house in order by Sabbath. Neither of the builders was an Adventist, she discovered, and seemed stumped that there was a church in their town that they'd never heard of. Jack, who was taking the week off to help her and the builders, was just as puzzled as Sherrie at this news.

Sabbath evening, as they gathered for sundown worship, Sherrie looked around her new home with a deep sense of satisfaction. Almost everything was done. The Harry Anderson painting they gathered around for worship hung in an honored corner of the living room. They knelt around it, each picturing themselves as one of the children gathered around Jesus.

Jack led out in prayer, and Sherrie tried to encourage the boys to be more vocal by inserting a reverent Amen whenever he paused. Sometimes Scott ventured a timid echo to her loud, firm Amen, but his sounded so unsure that it whistled off into nothing. Caleb never opened his mouth during worship. Instead, he rocked back and forth from one knee to the other, shifting and shuffling until she was sure he'd be across the room by the time they finished.

Scott played his harmonica while they sang a few songs; then

Jack pronounced a Sabbath blessing on each of them. It was a family tradition, passed on by Sherrie's folks, and Jack made up a new blessing each week or found one in the Bible. Then one of the boys offered a closing prayer, usually in a voice so soft they had to lean forward to hear it. When worship ended, Sherrie and Jack sent the kids to bed and decided to turn in too.

"Nervous about tomorrow?" Sherrie asked as she shuddered into her nightgown. Maine nights were cold!

"Why should I be?"

Sherrie shrugged. "You know, meeting all those new people. First impressions."

"No, not really. I am nervous about starting work on Monday, though."

"Well, let's not talk about that on Sabbath," Sherrie reminded him as she slipped in between the frosty sheets.

"Sorry," he grunted. She knew he had to be nervous to mention work on the Sabbath. She felt bad for him.

"It'll be fine, Jack. Everything will be fine. Go to sleep."

"Sure. Good night, Sher," he murmured.

Sherrie rolled over and watched the moon climb steadily until it looked like a ball caught in the skinny branches of the tree outside her window. It was the last thing she remembered before falling asleep.

CHAPTER

2

New Members

"Caleb? Hurry! We're going to be late for church." Sherrie ran a wet sponge over the already-clean countertop and cast a quick glance around her spotless kitchen. She inhaled deeply; fresh paint and newly stained wood. It seemed to satisfy her, and she turned toward Jack, who stood near the door tapping his foot impatiently.

Scott, hair still slick from his shower, sat calmly at the kitchen table. His Bible tucked beneath his arm, he was whistling the song about Noah and the Arky, Arky, loudly and off-key. The sound grated on Sherrie's nerves.

"Go on," she said irritably. "Wait in the car."

Scott jumped up as if he'd been catapulted and, still whistling, went out the door to the car. Jack frowned.

"Should I go get him?" he asked, glaring up the stairs. "I told him last week he'd be punished if he couldn't be ready on time." As he turned to go up the stairs, Caleb rushed down. His hair was tousled, his tie awry, and, Sherrie noticed, his socks didn't match.

"What have you been doing?" she demanded.

The boy's face darkened. "Getting ready," he muttered.

"This time, you're in hot water, mister," Jack said ominously. "We'll talk about your punishment after Sabbath is over."

Caleb's angry eyes avoided his parents'. He shuffled out to the car, and they followed him. Sherrie watched his stiff back and fought the urge to make him stay home. It wouldn't do him any good. Besides, it was probably what he was hoping for so he could lie around the house doing nothing. Besides, there would be uncomfortable questions.

14

Sherrie got in the car, balancing the casserole dish on her knees, and pulled down the visor to check her hair. Finding something she didn't like, she fooled with it for a few minutes as they rolled down the road. As she flipped the visor back up, she asked over her shoulder, "Are you boys excited?"

Scott nodded vigorously. Caleb grunted noncommittally.

"Do you want to hear my memory verse?" Scott asked hopefully. Sherrie nodded absently, and he repeated it, beaming afterward like an eager-to-please puppy who knows he's done a good job. Caleb shot him a dirty look.

"Caleb?" Sherrie asked. "Your memory verse?"

Caleb shifted uneasily within the confines of his seat belt. "I'm, uh, not quite sure."

"About what? Your memory verse? Either you know it, or you don't," Sherrie snapped.

"I don't," Caleb mumbled.

"Well, then, get out your Sabbath School lesson and learn it before we get to church." She shook her head. "What will your teacher think?"

Caleb pulled out the ragged quarterly and flipped to the week's lesson. Sherrie watched his lips move as he silently repeated the verse to himself. She wondered how much of a difference it would make in the end. By tomorrow, he'd have forgotten every word of it.

She stared out the window and watched the rolling Maine landscape pass. The woods were a brilliant patchwork of scarlet, orange, and yellow leaves, like the old crazy quilt on Grandma Raines's bed back in Tennessee. Despite the cheerful colors, she couldn't seem to shift the anxiety she felt about their impending first church experience here.

Scott strained forward so hard he almost seemed cut in half by his seat belt. "Ten points to spot the church first," he said, studying each passing structure with a discerning eye.

As the colorful countryside gave way to the old town buildings, Sherrie searched for the stately church building they'd been told about. When Jack pulled the car around the sharp corner into a crowded parking lot, she realized, with keen disappointment, that their idea of stately was not the same as hers.

"There it . . ." Scott's exultant cry was choked off as they drew up to the building.

The old church may indeed have been called stately sometime in the past, but it could hardly be thought of as anything but rundown by present standards. Although most of the buildings in Pawlet were well kept up, some even historic, the outside of the Seventh-day Adventist church building was sadly neglected.

Jack climbed slowly out of the car and eyed it passively. He straightened his tie and glanced at his wife. Sherrie gawked openly at the flaking exterior, mentally calculating how many cans of paint it would take to make it look presentable. She gave up, and her shoulders drooped.

"Do you think we could talk them into fixing up the outside?" she whispered to Jack as they walked across the parking lot. Inside, the faint sound of singing floated out to them.

"Don't you think we ought to at least meet them before we start painting the building?" Jack joked. "After all, it is Sabbath."

Sherrie didn't answer but walked a little ahead of him and entered the church. The inside was almost as bad as the outside. Faced with two doors, Sherrie opened the one directly in front of her and peeked in. It was obviously the pastor's study. She didn't need to open the one on the right to know it was Cradle Roll because she could hear the children singing.

Having no other choice, she descended the stairs on her left. Jack and the boys followed. The stairs led to the basement, a dingy affair with stone walls and a kitchen on one end, which seemed to be the fellowship room. Off to the side was a door marked "Junior/Earliteen," which Scott headed for the second he spotted it.

"Wait," Sherrie hissed. "Jack, shouldn't we introduce them to their teachers?" Jack nodded, and they followed Scott as he rapped on the door. Caleb trailed unenthusiastically behind. A smiling young woman whom Sherrie guessed to be in her mid-twenties answered their knock. She held out her hand.

"Hi, I'm Caren Nason. Are you visitors?"

"No, we just moved here," Scott said.

"From Tennessee," Jack added hastily, taking her hand and giving it a brisk shake. "We're the Raineses. Perhaps you were expecting us? I'm Dr. Raines. This is my wife Sherrie. Our boys, Scott and Caleb."

"Oh, yes!" Caren's eyes brightened in recognition of the name. "Both of the boys will be in my class. You'll find the adult class upstairs in the sanctuary."

"How do we get there?" Sherrie asked. "We're rather lost . . ."

"Upstairs." Caren pointed in the opposite direction from where they'd entered as the boys brushed past her and into the classroom. "To the right. You'll see it. And you can leave your casserole on the shelf." She smiled once more before closing the door and leaving them in the empty fellowship room.

Sherrie deposited her casserole on a shelf crowded with similar offerings. Jack took her hand and squeezed it as they headed in the direction indicated. Up a flight of steps and to the right, they were greeted by a short woman whose dress was the color of a newly minted gold piece and almost as shiny. Her honey-colored hair, which paled in contrast to the dress, was pulled back with a gaudy, ribboned banana clip that looked, Sherrie thought, like the kind kids bought at a dime store.

She held out a bulletin in one hand and offered the other to be shaken. "Hello," she said, smiling brightly. "Happy Sabbath."

"Thank you," Sherrie murmured, taking the bulletin and shaking her hand, startled by the woman's firm grasp. She turned to Jack and stood by his elbow as he looked through the window in the door at the Sabbath School class. They were kneeling while someone on the platform offered a prayer. Jack and Sherrie bowed their heads until the members rose and seated themselves.

"Did they just start?" Sherrie asked quietly.

"Oh, they haven't really started yet," the woman replied. "They still have to have the mission story, if someone's got it this week. Then the superintendent will talk for a while before they separate for classes."

"Are you just visiting?" she asked, after a long pause.

"No, we've just moved," Jack replied.

"You must be the Raineses," the woman exclaimed, causing a few heads inside to turn toward the door. "Welcome! I'm Tammy Merrill. My two boys have been dying for you to get here."

"You have two boys?" Sherrie asked politely, her eyebrows arching slightly.

"Oh, yes, the boys are fourteen and ten, and Anne, our daughter, is nine. You will put them in church school, won't you? Your boys? Dave and Brian will be so disappointed if you don't."

Jack nodded. "Yes, we plan to send the boys to the church school."

"I'm so glad," Tammy gushed. "The school is small, mind you, but it's a good one. My kids just love it here. The teacher is great. He came highly recommended."

Jack began to nudge the door open. "Yes, that's good. Maybe we can talk to you about it some more after the service."

"Sure, sure. You're going to stay for potluck, aren't you? Yeah? Great. Wonderful. I'll see you then," she called after them as they pulled themselves firmly away and entered the sanctuary. A few curious eyes turned to follow their progress up the aisle to a seat.

Jack folded his arms and watched the remainder of the Sabbath School program critically from beneath lowered eyebrows. The superintendent had forgotten to assign the mission story to someone to be read, so it was skipped. She talked about the nice weather, the leaves, showers of blessings, and other things in a disjointed fashion. Finally, they separated for classes.

There was an additional adult class offered in the basement, but Jack and Sherrie remained in their seats. A tall, thin, soft-spoken man stood up and began to teach the sanctuary class. His low voice seemed to hover in the air above her head, and try as she might, Sherrie couldn't seem to concentrate on what he was saying.

Instead, her eyes flitted discreetly around to each member's face, and her thoughts followed, wondering who they were and what they were like. When the teacher finally closed with prayer, Sherrie realized she hadn't heard a word he'd uttered. Guiltily she closed the quarterly, which lay open on her lap, and tucked it under her Bible.

She was about to send Jack to find the boys when Caren Nason, their young teacher, led them into the sanctuary and pointed to where Sherrie and Jack sat. Directly behind them was Tammy Merrill, dwarfed by her two lanky sons and flanked by her daughter, who wore a banana clip that was an exact replica of her mother's. A sober-looking man, who had to be her husband, tagged along behind. Propelling husband and children ahead of her, Tammy managed to squeeze her entire family into the pew with the Raineses.

"How are you folks enjoying the service so far?" she asked, smiling. She twisted and turned, trying to find some room on the crowded seat to set her Bible. Finally, she tucked it behind her.

"Fine, fine," Jack assured her, leaning in front of Sherrie so he could see her. "This must be your husband?"

"Oh, yes, this is Bob."

The man took Jack's hand and shook it firmly but didn't say anything. Jack leaned back as the pastor and elders made their way onto the platform. Tammy tilted her lips toward Sherrie's ear.

"That's our pastor, Ron Hawley," she whispered hoarsely. "His wife died last year of cancer. Poor man. He was just devastated. He hasn't been doing much in the church ever since.

"And that man on the left," she tried to point without pointing, "that's the church schoolteacher."

Sherrie nodded politely, wishing Tammy would keep her running commentary to herself. The Sabbath School teacher had special music, and according to Tammy, it was a miracle that he could even sing, having had laryngitis the week before. She went on to say, somewhat proudly, that he was a *Listen* literature evangelist, one of the only ones in the state.

Sherrie's smile curdled. Why couldn't this woman keep quiet? She'd never remember all these names, faces, jobs, and illnesses anyway. She wanted to ask her nicely to keep still, but she couldn't bring herself to break her own rule of not talking once the service started.

Jack shot Sherrie a stern look, and she glared at him. It wasn't her fault! Then Tammy seemed to settle down and pulled her Bible out from behind her back, opening it up on her lap. She asked Bob in a loud whisper for the text they were on.

As they filed out after the service, Tammy introduced them to anyone who would listen. By the time they had gotten through the potluck line and sat down with their food, Sherrie had a pounding headache and realized she couldn't remember a single name. Tammy, seated strategically opposite her, kept up an endless stream of chatter.

"Is that something you would be interested in?" she was asking.

Sherrie squinted at her, wondering what the question had been. "Interested in what?"

"Being in charge of the women's committee next year," Tammy repeated. "I'm in charge of it this year, but I just haven't had the time to do anything with it. If you'd be interested, I'll pass the word along to the nominating committee when it forms in a couple of months. They love to have volunteers. It makes their job a lot easier."

"Maybe we ought to make sure that the transfer of our membership is passed first," Sherrie said, trying to smile. "But it's certainly something I'd be interested in."

"Great," Tammy responded. "That's great. I hope you folks will take a lot of the jobs next year. We sure need all the help we can get. Most of our members are tired of trying to get the other ones enthusiastic about any program they try to start. To tell you the truth, our church hasn't been very active lately. We're all kinda tired of trying. Still," she finished cheerfully, "somebody's got to do it, right?"

Sherrie nodded. "I'm sure Jack and I will be willing to help in any way we can."

Riding back home that afternoon, nursing her headache, she felt overwhelmed by this new church. There was so much to do. Though she was quiet on the trip home, her mind raced ahead, planning and organizing. After listening to Tammy, she was sure that the church would be more than glad of her help. Her imagination, thus fueled, completely remodeled the church and revitalized its members by the time the car pulled up in the driveway of their new home.

CHAPTER

Joggers

Four o'clock Sunday morning came early. Sherrie fumbled with the alarm and shook Jack's shoulder. He muttered something and rolled over. Forcing her legs over the side of the bed, her bare feet brushed the floor before she could yank them back up. Brrrr! She searched tentatively for her slippers with one foot.

"Come on, Jack. Get up." She shook his shoulder again.

Jack moaned and pulled himself up. "Let's have devotions downstairs by the woodstove," he suggested, yawning.

"Good idea," Sherrie agreed. Her bathrobe felt almost stiff from the cold as she shivered into it. Grabbing her Bible off the night stand, she went down the hall to wake the boys. Scott, a light sleeper, was almost always pulling on his bathrobe by the time she opened the door. Caleb was another story.

"Caleb, time to get up," she instructed, shaking his shoulder.

"I'm up. I'm up," he muttered thickly.

"Get out of the bed." She knew from experience that it took more than a little shake to completely wake him up. She flipped on the light switch. Scott blinked at her. Caleb rolled over and pulled the covers over his eyes.

"Oh, no, you don't," Sherrie said. Grabbing the covers, she yanked them off the bed. Caleb sat up immediately to get them back, his eyes only half open, filled with sleep and confusion.

"Are you awake enough now to get up?" Sherrie asked.

"I'm awake."

She hung on to the covers and tossed him his bathrobe. She could hear Scott shuffle into the adjoining bathroom to brush his teeth. Out of the corner of her eye, she caught a glimpse of yellow. The notebook! The very edge of it poked out from behind Caleb's dresser. Now at least she knew where he hid it.

"You've got five minutes to get downstairs. Don't make me send your father up here to get you," she warned before leaving the room.

Downstairs, Jack had stoked the dying fire in the woodstove and added some wood to it. It was just beginning to throw some heat when Sherrie came down. She rubbed her hands over it while she waited for the boys to join them.

"I told Caleb to be down in five minutes, or I'd send you up to get him," she informed Jack. He nodded. "I don't know why that boy has so much trouble getting up in the morning. It isn't as if we just started getting up at four o'clock. We've been doing it all our lives."

Scott padded quietly down the stairs, his Bible in hand. He sat expectantly at the table. Jack glanced at his watch.

"Caleb coming?"

Scott nodded. "He's putting on his bathrobe. But," his eyebrows shot up smugly, "he says he won't brush his hair even if a reporter was going to be down here to take his picture."

Sherrie rolled her eyes, and Jack shrugged. "Just as long as he's here," he reminded her. As he was checking his watch, Caleb made his way down the stairs.

"Sit down," Jack barked. "We haven't got all morning." As the woodstove warmed the frosty Maine air, they gathered around the table and bowed their heads. After a short prayer, they opened their Bibles. Jack had decided that if they each read a chapter out loud every morning for worship, it would be a good way to read the Bible through.

By the time they finished reading, the woodstove was blazing, and the temperature in the kitchen had risen to a comfortable level. Jack said the prayer and asked a blessing for each one.

"I'm going to work for a while today," he announced as he rose and stretched. "You boys will have to wait for the shower."

"What do we need the shower for anyway?" Caleb muttered.

Jack stopped with his foot on the bottom stair and turned toward Caleb slowly. "What did you say?"

Caleb swallowed slowly. "I meant, we're not going to school today . . . or anything."

"You know, Jesus wasn't ever smart-mouthed, Caleb. Keep pushing it, and the rest of us won't see you in heaven. Is that what you want?" Jack warned. Caleb lowered his eyes.

"No, sir."

"I hope not," Jack said, continuing up the stairs. "I hope I haven't raised a son who doesn't want to go to heaven."

"Anyway, don't be too sure you're not doing anything today," Sherrie said dryly as she pulled bowls and utensils from the cupboard. "It just so happens that we're going to do some yardwork."

"Yardwork? Aw, Ma," Caleb whined.

"I like yardwork," Scott informed him. "Besides, the weather forecaster said it would be one of the last beautiful days this fall, so we'd better enjoy it."

"That's right," Sherrie agreed. "They say we're in for a week or two of rain. And I want to get that yard raked and my bulbs planted before it hits."

Caleb glowered darkly as he took the bowls and laid them out on the tablecloth Scott had just laid down. Sherrie shot him a quick look and wondered what he was thinking. Surely he didn't want to stay inside and write in that notebook all day long.

She stirred the cereal briskly. Slowly, she and Jack were losing their control over Caleb. It was a frustrating feeling. Well, she'd show him whose house he was living in. There were responsibilities involved in being part of a family. It was about time he learned that.

"Caleb," she said sharply. "Smile."

He didn't respond but managed to screw his frown into a grimace as he began slicing the fresh fruit they always had for breakfast. Scott stood behind Sherrie, watching the cereal over her shoulder.

"Can we have dates and walnuts in the oatmeal this morning?" he asked.

Sherrie nodded. "If you chop them."

Scott pulled out the chopping block and a large knife. He had almost finished when Jack came downstairs trailed by a faint breeze of Sherrie's favorite cologne. He gave her a quick hug before sitting down at the table.

"Looks good," he observed. Sherrie served as the boys quickly took their places. After a quick blessing, they ate.

"What do you need to do at your new office today that can't

wait?" Sherrie asked.

Jack shrugged. "Just want to check the place out. I'm a little nervous about tomorrow, I guess. I shouldn't be gone long."

Sherrie nodded. "The boys and I are going to do some yard-work."

"Great. The yard could sure use it before winter sets in. I'll give you a hand when I get back."

While Caleb and Scott did the breakfast dishes, Sherrie went up to her room to study. As she passed the boy's room, she glanced in, checking for the little splash of yellow that indicated the notebook was still behind the dresser. It was.

Once she got the boys busy outside, she planned to come back in and read it. Her stomach knotted in a sudden panic, sending goose bumps coursing along her arms.

"This is silly," she told herself. "He's my son. I have a right to know what he's writing about. It shouldn't be a secret." She shook herself a little, trying to loosen the apprehension that clung to her.

She sat at the table where she studied her Bible every day and tried to concentrate, but her prayers seemed to fall flat. She opened her Bible but found her mind had wandered, and at the end of a chapter, she didn't know what she had read. Finally, she skimmed her lesson, said a quick prayer, and hurriedly got dressed in her oldest clothes.

She knocked on the boys' door as she passed. "Finish up your lessons. It's time to work."

Scott crashed down the stairs as Sherrie was pulling her gloves on. Caleb followed close on his heels.

"Mom," Scott said breathlessly and with a look of triumph in his eyes. "Caleb didn't study his lesson. He wrote in his note-book instead."

"Tattletale," Caleb hissed.

Sherrie squinted at him. "Is that true, Caleb?"

Caleb hung his head but didn't say anything. Sherrie was half-tempted to make him stay inside until he'd finished his lesson, but that wouldn't really accomplish anything. Besides, it would be more of a reward than a punishment. She chewed her lip.

"Well, Caleb, I guess you'll just have to catch up on your lesson while Scott and I have lunch. Now, let's get going. We don't have the whole morning to waste."

"I said I'd tell on him if he didn't study his lesson, and I did," Scott told Sherrie, his breath catching in excitement.

"Thanks, Scott," Sherrie said without emotion. "Sometimes we have to do things that will hurt other people when it's for their own good."

Outside, she handed him the rake, and he began attacking the fallen leaves with an enthusiasm that almost sickened her. Caleb put a religious tape in his Walkman and began to rake slowly and methodically. Sherrie gathered up her bulbs and gardening tools and sank onto the soft dirt of the flower bed, her back to both of them.

Her hands shook as she wiped them on the legs of her baggy gardening pants. A fresh start. That's what they needed. To go back to the beginning and erase the rebellion that was creeping into their home. As she caught a ragged breath, she thought she knew a little of what God felt like when Lucifer rebelled. It wasn't a nice feeling.

Slowly, as she worked in the garden, she began to feel better. After all, it wasn't over yet. Caleb was only fourteen. He'd just gotten off track. He'd get back on. They'd raised him with biblical principles since he was a baby. Soon he would see that rebelling wasn't the answer and would begin to cooperate again.

She hardly noticed the sun creep over a nearby mountain and begin to warm the crisp air. The warmth on her back and a faint whiff of balsam tugged her back to reality. She sat back on her heels and looked around.

The boys had been having a leaf fight, but as she watched, a relaxed smile on her lips, they suddenly stopped. She was about to call to them not to stop when she saw the reason. Jogging down the road was a tall, well-built woman. She had on fluorescent, skin-tight leggings and a tight-fitting jacket. Her honey-brown hair was tied up in a ponytail. Next to her was a slightly shorter replica, except that the daughter's hair was bleached blond, almost white. The two were talking gaily and waved to Sherrie and the boys.

Sherrie turned her head quickly, pretending not to see them. Out of the corner of her eye, she saw Scott looking studiously at the ground. Caleb waved back, gawking openly, watching them until they were out of sight.

"Caleb," Sherrie hissed. "What are you looking at?"

"Nothing," he said defensively, quickly picking up his rake and pulling the scattered leaves back into a neat pile.

"They go to our church, Mom," Scott informed her quietly.

"What?!" Surely not!

"That girl was in our class. She came in later than we did, and I don't think they stayed for church. I don't remember her name."

"Trista," Caleb said suddenly. "Her name is Trista."

Sherrie pulled off her glove and wiped a clammy hand across her forehead. Those people at church? And Caleb remembered the girl's name. She must have made quite an impression on him. Sherrie felt desperate enough to writhe on the ground in agony.

"You boys finish raking those leaves into piles. I'm going to go in and make lunch. Don't come in until I call you." Quickly, Sherrie made her way into the house. Closing the door behind her, she leaned heavily against the wall, her breath coming in ragged gasps.

Before she could collect herself, the phone rang. She reached out and picked it up reluctantly. "Hello?"

"Hi, Sherrie! I'm bringing the troops over to give you a hand with the yard."

The voice was familiar. She could almost place it. "The troops?" she asked uncertainly.

"Oh, don't worry about feeding us. We'll bring our own lunch . . . like a picnic. You haven't eaten yet, have you?"

"No, I was just getting . . ." The voice cut her off.

"Terrific! Great!"

Sherrie groaned. It was Tammy Merrill. And just when she wanted to be alone. "When did you say?"

"We're on our way right now. See you in a couple."

"Sure." Sherrie tried to sound cheerful as the phone went dead in her hand. She sank into a nearby chair and cradled her head in her arms.

Tight bands of pain clamped around her forehead. She sat up suddenly and clenched her fists. This had to stop. She couldn't get a migraine now. She'd worry about Caleb later. Tammy Merrill was on her way over, and she had to pull herself together before Tammy arrived.

She took a few deep breaths before standing up. Methodically, she began to pull out the ingredients needed for lunch. Since they were going to have company, Caleb would have to eat with them and miss supper later.

She was putting the finishing touches on the sandwiches when she realized with a start that since Tammy was coming, there was no way she was going to be able to read Caleb's notebook. She slammed her hand down on the counter in a quick flash of anger. Well, she'd just have to be patient, that was all.

Gravel crunching in the driveway and a horn tooting wildly announced the Merrills' arrival. Sherrie opened the door and waved with as much enthusiasm as she could muster.

"Hey, here come the troops," Tammy shouted, bounding out of the station wagon. She had on cat-eyed sunglasses and, Sherrie could hardly believe it, a white sweat suit. Was she planning on working or directing?

She pulled an enormous picnic basket out of the back seat, and her kids tumbled out of the car, swatting at each other good-naturedly. Scott walked up to them completely at ease, and they engulfed him eagerly, but Caleb hung back, following along at a safe, nonthreatening distance like a satellite.

"Hello, hello," Tammy squealed, throwing her arms around Sherrie's neck and giving her a squeeze. "When Jack said you were doing yardwork today, I just said to myself, 'Oh, no, yard-work. I'll bet she needs help.' And so here we are."

"Jack?"

"Oh, sure. We live just two houses down from his office. I saw him working in there this morning when I brought Taffy for her walk."

"Taffy?"

"My poodle. So anyway, I just stopped in to see if he needed anything, and he mentioned that you and the boys were doing yardwork today. I know you probably haven't had time to make many friends yet, so you wouldn't have anyone to ask for help. So, I decided to volunteer. And, *voilá*! Here we are. Where do you want me to set this up?"

Sherrie waved toward the table, where she had already set out the lunch she'd made for herself and the boys. Her eyes widened in surprise as Tammy pulled soda, chips, and cookies from the cooler along with the sandwiches.

"There we go." Tammy smiled, setting the cooler on the floor. "Want me to go find the kids?"

Sherrie shook her head and forced a return smile. "No, that's

OK. I'm sure they're nearby."

She opened the front door and found them crowded around Tammy's oldest son, who had managed to catch a garter snake. He was giving them an encyclopedic description when she interrupted him.

"It's time for lunch." The boy let the snake loose in the garden as the others pushed by her and into the house. She stopped Caleb as he passed her.

"Since we have company, you'll have to eat with us and skip supper to study your lesson." Caleb nodded curtly and walked on as if he hadn't heard her.

The kids all seated themselves quickly. Sherrie took the empty seat next to Tammy, who said a quick grace. The kids wasted no time, and soon all dialogue ceased. Sherrie tried to analyze Tammy's sandwich without being noticed. It looked like some type of fake meat and loads of mayonnaise.

She nibbled on her sprout-tomato-and-cucumber sandwich. Tammy didn't let the food stop her and kept up a constant stream of chatter. Sherrie tried to nod politely at appropriate intervals, but her mind was a million miles away.

"Do you want a soda, honey? We brought plenty. Have some chips."

Sherrie returned to the present with a thud. Scott was looking skeptically at the proffered soda, but Caleb's eyes had lighted up.

"No, thank you, Tammy," Sherrie said firmly. "The boys are fine. We don't encourage them to eat junk food. Water and carrots are fine."

"But they don't have any water," Tammy observed quizzically.

"We don't drink with our meals." Sherrie felt as if her smile was getting stiff.

"Oh," Tammy said, then brushed the incident off. "So, I saw Lauren and Trista jogging. Did you see that outfit Lauren had on? Wild!"

Sherrie sat up, instantly alert. She coughed a little as she inhaled a small piece of sandwich with a startled gasp. "You know them?"

"Know them? Of course," Tammy laughed. "They go to our church. Well, not regularly. They were just baptized a little while ago. Maybe a year."

"They're members?" Sherrie struggled not to let the shock she felt show on her face.

Tammy nodded. "Not real strong, from what I gather. They don't come to church all the time, and I heard they go to the movies and they still wear their wedding rings. The daughter, Trista, goes to public school and seems to do what she wants."

"She listens to rock music and eats meat," Tammy's younger boy piped up.

Tammy waved an irritated hand at him. "Brian, you don't know that for sure. Don't spread rumors."

Brian nodded vigorously. "I do too. Trista told us so last week. She had a tape with her. And she even said she smokes sometimes."

Tammy sniffed. "Well, it isn't the kind of thing you should be repeating. Anyway, as I was saying, they aren't exactly pillars of the church community, but they are members."

"She's nice," Caleb said, chewing contemplatively.

"Well, of course, they're both nice," Tammy stammered. "I didn't mean to imply that they weren't. You don't need to pick up that stuff, Sherrie. Anne will get it. Won't you, honey?" She smiled at her daughter and gave her a quick hug.

"Sure, Mom," the girl chirped.

"Thanks. Now point me to the work." Tammy stuffed the remains of her last cookie into her mouth and stood up. "I'm going to have to work for hours to get rid of those calories," she groaned. "Lead me to it."

The Yellow Notebook

Contrary to Sherrie's first opinion, Tammy Merrill was all the help she claimed to be. She worked with an enthusiasm that electrified not only her own kids, but Caleb and Scott as well. By the time Jack pulled into the driveway, as the sun was sinking behind the mountains, the work was done.

Sherrie was able to return Tammy's hug with a genuine squeeze as Tammy gathered her things, rounded up her kids, and packed them into her car.

"From now on, don't hesitate to call me if you ever need anything. OK?" Tammy called as she hopped into the car, her sweat suit somehow still immaculate. Sherrie nodded as Tammy tooted and roared out of the driveway. A tangle of hands waved from assorted open windows, and they all waved back.

Jack watched Tammy pull out with an amused smile. "Did she help you out much?"

"You wouldn't think so, but yes. She was a big help."

"She stopped by the office this morning with her dog." He laughed. "She certainly gets around, doesn't she?"

Sherrie nodded. "Hungry?"

"Starved. I didn't have a very big lunch. Come to think of it, I'm not sure I ate lunch. How soon will it be ready?"

"Shouldn't take me long. You boys can go for a bike ride if you want before supper," she called to Caleb and Scott as they wrestled on the lawn. Jumping up, they whooped and ran happily for the garage.

"They worked awfully hard today too," she told Jack as they walked toward the house. Then she sighed. "By the way, Caleb won't be joining us for supper."

"Oh?" Jack's eyebrows shot up. Not in surprise exactly, Sherrie noticed. More curiosity. It was as if they were getting accustomed to Caleb's deviant behavior.

"He wrote in his notebook instead of doing his lesson this morning."

"I suppose Scott told you?"

"Yes, and you know, I wanted to throttle them both. Caleb, for trying to get away with it, and Scott, for telling on him."

"I know what you mean," Jack agreed. "Sometimes I wonder which one of them is acting more normal."

"Don't say that," Sherrie said irritably. "We both know Caleb is starting to test us. Scott is just acting responsibly. And it's a good thing too; otherwise, how would we know what Caleb's up to? He never talks to us anymore." As the words came out of her mouth, she remembered the notebook behind the dresser in Caleb's room. What a perfect opportunity to read it.

As Jack settled into his favorite chair in the living room with a medical book, Sherrie stared into the refrigerator. She had planned on making a casserole, but then she wouldn't have time to read Caleb's notebook before he got back. The leftover stew sat temptingly on the bottom shelf.

In one swift movement, Sherrie scooped it up and poured it into a pot. Turning the temperature to medium, she set the table quickly and laid out the bread. Then, slowly, nonchalantly, she went up the stairs.

As she felt the boys' door push inward a sudden panicky fear gripped her. A hot pain seared her chest, and she realized she was holding her breath. This is silly, she told herself.

Tentatively, she inched her hand behind the dresser. The cool cover of the notebook startled her for a moment when she touched it. She made a grab for it and sank weakly onto Caleb's bed. The notebook seemed to glare up at her accusingly as she held it gingerly on her lap. She sat for what seemed like a long time without opening it.

Finally, she flipped it open, and her eyes skimmed the page. Caleb's messy scrawl was hard to make out, and she tried to pick out only the pertinent items. There was a lot about his old school and moving. Then she found something.

"Dan didn't believe me when I told him that Mom and Dad make us go to bed at seven and get up at four. He said he'd give me the potato chips and cookies out of his lunch if I could prove it. I told him to show up at our house at seven and see if there were any lights on. The next day he gave me his chips and cookies and just shook his head."

Sherrie felt a hot flush sweep over her. She'd taught him to eat healthfully. What was he doing, bargaining for chips and cookies? She didn't have time to think about it because another entry caught her eye.

"We went to our new church for the first time today. What a downer. The place is real old. But, I met a nice girl named Trista. She doesn't let her parents push her around. She said she just tells them the way it's going to be and that's it. She gets to do whatever she wants. Someday I'm going to do just what I want to. Nobody will make me eat that awful food and go to bed early and get up early and go to church. I'll stay up late and eat junk food and sleep until twelve. Trista says she'll loan me a tape sometime."

Sherrie sucked in a mouthful of air, making her teeth tingle. A tape! What was it Brian said the girl listened to? Heavy metal? Satan music? Suddenly the room seemed to be spinning around. A blinding anger gripped her. What was Caleb thinking of?

Her first thought was to confront him with the notebook. *No, I can't do that*, she reasoned shrewdly. *If I confront him, he'll stop writing or hide the notebook somewhere else. He hasn't done anything yet compared to what he could do. It would be better to bide my time and wait for something really big.*

Otherwise, she thought wryly, *I may never know.*

She was engrossed in the next entry when Jack's voice boomed upstairs, seeming to cut right through the walls and expose what she was doing.

"Something's boiling down here."

"Coming," Sherrie yelled back, her hands shaking slightly as she closed the notebook with a snap and slid it back behind the dresser. She smoothed the bedspread before going downstairs.

"Well?" Jack asked, as if he could read her mind.

"Well what?" Sherrie asked innocently, wondering if she was that transparent.

"Did you find out anything?"

"Yes, but we'll talk about it later."

From the kitchen window, she could see the boys ride up the driveway. She rapped on the window to catch their attention and mouthed the word *dinner*. They waved and wheeled their bikes toward the garage.

"Caleb?" Jack called, as the boys stomped in the front door. "Would you come here a minute?" Caleb's smile fled as he walked over to stand in front of his father. Scott lingered by the door, taking off his boots.

"Go wash your hands, Scott," Sherrie instructed. She could hear Jack and Caleb's low voices as she spooned stew into the three bowls on the table.

"I understand you preferred to write in your notebook rather than study your lesson this morning," Jack was saying.

"Yes, sir," Caleb replied in a hushed voice.

"Why?"

"Well, I just, the lesson's so . . . boring," Caleb finished lamely.

"So you thought you'd deceive your mother and me by pretending to study it?" Jack pressed.

"No, I mean, yes, I mean, I didn't mean to deceive you. I just didn't want to study it."

"But you realize that you were deceiving us?"

"I guess so." Caleb hung his head miserably.

"You know, son," Jack said gently. "Your mother and I don't always find studying the lesson fascinating either, but we still study it. If we didn't study our lesson, we wouldn't get to know Jesus, and then we wouldn't be in heaven. And we want to be in heaven more than anything. Don't you?"

"Yes, sir."

"And you understand that studying your lesson is a law while you live in this house, and since you broke that law, you must pay the penalty. Right?"

"Yes, sir."

"Now, we're going to eat supper. What are you going to do?"

"Go to my room and study my lesson," Caleb recited.

"That's right." Jack smiled. "And after supper you can bring your quarterly down, and I'll review the lesson with you to be sure that you understand it. All right?"

Caleb nodded. "May I go upstairs now?"

"Go ahead." Jack turned to the kitchen as Caleb brushed

past him. "Everything ready?"

"Come get it while it's hot," Sherrie replied with forced cheerfulness.

Supper was quiet. Scott shifted uncomfortably in his chair, shooting occasional glances at Caleb's empty place. He cleared the table and dried the dishes without comment. As soon as he was finished helping Sherrie clear the table, he slipped upstairs.

Sherrie sank onto the sofa with a groan. Jack set his medical book down and grinned at her.

"What was that for?"

"Just tired, I guess." She closed her eyes and rubbed her temples. "What are we doing wrong, Jack?"

"Wrong? Nothing. This is a natural phase for kids. He's just testing his boundaries. It'll pass. You'll see."

"I hope so," Sherrie muttered. "You wouldn't believe some of the things he wrote in that notebook. He is so against us and everything we stand for. Why?"

"He's not really. He just wants to see if the world's way is better than our way. He'll straighten up soon. Don't worry."

"I hope you're right. I pray for him every day, but sometimes I wonder if it does any good at all."

"Where's your faith, woman?" Jack chided gently.

Sherrie smiled wanly. "You're right. I'll get some more right away."

"We just have to be strict and not let down our guard. That's what he's waiting for. If we're lax in our discipline even once, Caleb will see that we're really not totally committed."

"You're right," Sherrie agreed. "But sometimes it's tiring. Do you want to talk about what I found in his notebook?"

Jack shook his head. "It's not necessary, really. I know what's going on in his head."

"Well, I'm going to continue reading it anyway," Sherrie returned defensively. "Just to keep track of what he's doing."

Jack shrugged. "Suit yourself. But he'll straighten out soon. You'll see."

"I sure hope so." Sherrie pulled herself out of the chair. "I think I'll read a little before I go to bed. Are you coming up now?"

Jack glanced at his watch. "What time is it? Six-thirty? In a minute. As soon as I get done with Caleb."

"All right. I'll send him down."

Sherrie knocked on the boy's door as she passed. "Caleb? Your father wants to see you now."

She flipped the light switch in her room and closed the door softly behind her. Walking absently around the room, she unconsciously picked up stray pieces of clothes, straightened dresser tops, and smoothed the comforter on the bed. Finally, she changed into her nightgown and slipped between the cool sheets, propping the pillows up behind her.

She picked up her favorite copy—the hardcover edition of *Steps to Christ*—from her night stand and flipped it open to the bookmark. Her eyes moved down the page without seeing it, her mind not on the words. Finally, the book slipped from her fingers, and she sat staring out the window. It seemed like she could always see the moon rising from this window, she mused.

Inside, she felt like a ball of yarn all knotted up and tangled. She clutched the front of her nightgown as if she could physically remove the tangle.

"Why, God?" she whispered. "I do all the things I'm supposed to. I'm involved in Your work. I read my Bible, do my lesson, and I've read almost every book Ellen White ever wrote. Why are You letting my son slip away from me? From You?"

She slammed a fist onto her lap angrily. "Why can't he be more like Scott? I never have trouble with Scott. Why are You letting this happen?" She glared accusingly toward the bright moon as if it were to blame. She listened to her own ragged breathing in the quiet room, waiting, but no one answered her.

"Well, I'm not going to let it happen," she said firmly. "I can be with those kids almost all the time, and I will. I'll watch them so closely they won't even blink without my knowing it. You'll see, he'll straighten out. He'll have to. He can't very well get away with anything right under my nose."

She took a deep breath. Satisfied. That's exactly what she'd do. Suddenly she felt at peace with herself. The tangled ball inside rolled neatly up and slipped away. Now that she had a plan of action, she could sleep easy.

Setting the book on the night stand, she fluffed the pillows and rolled over to watch the moon climb up the tree trunks.

"I'm sorry I was angry with You, God," she whispered. "Thank You for showing me what to do. I'm sure Caleb will straighten out soon, and it will all work out according to Your will. Amen."

CHAPTER

5

School

Monday morning, Sherrie was surprised to see steam coming from the hall bathroom when she went to wake the boys up. Scott was searching in his night stand for his Bible.

"Caleb?" Sherrie asked incredulously, glancing from the steam in the hall to Caleb's rumpled, but empty, bed.

Scott nodded. "He said he wanted to be ready for school."

"Guess he must be pretty excited, huh?"

"Nah," Scott replied. "Scared, I think."

"Of what?" Sherrie couldn't think of one thing in a small school to cause this much terror in her elder son.

Scott shrugged. "Girls?"

Although it was more a question than an answer, she didn't reply. She tried to remember whether there had been any other girls Caleb's age at church on Sabbath besides Trista, but she couldn't think of any. She tried to quell the uneasy feeling that Caleb was this nervous about the possibility of seeing Trista again. Then she relaxed. Tammy had said that Trista went to public school.

"Be down in ten minutes," she told Scott. Then she rapped on the bathroom door as she passed it. "Ten minutes," she called.

"Coming," Caleb yelled back. "I just have to dry my hair."

"He's in the shower," Sherrie reported when she saw Jack downstairs.

"Who? Scott?"

"No, Caleb. Can you believe it?"

Jack chuckled. "No, but I guess we shouldn't complain."

Ten minutes later, to the second, Caleb dashed down the stairs perfectly dressed and groomed. He tried to ignore the astonished looks of his parents, and for her part, Sherrie tried not to gawk.

They were the first people in the church parking lot. As they sat in the car, Sherrie drummed her fingers nervously on the steering wheel. Scott was reading a book, and Caleb's pen scrawled relentlessly across a page in his yellow notebook.

"The school is in the church, right?" she asked.

Scott looked up for a minute. "That's what Brian told me."

"And school starts at eight-thirty?"

Scott nodded. "But it's only five after eight right now."

"I know that, Scott," Sherrie snapped. "But shouldn't the teacher at least be here getting things set up? What kind of school is this? I hope we'll be able to let you boys stay here."

At this, Caleb looked up with a worried frown. "Maybe the teacher got up late," he suggested hopefully.

"Then he's not a very responsible person, is he?"

Five minutes later, the Merrills' big station wagon careened into the parking lot and pulled up beside them with a squeal of the brakes and a puff of oily smoke. Tammy waved and bounded out of the car.

"Hi! You haven't been waiting long, have you? I passed Don and Sara on the way. They had a flat, but they should be here soon. Isn't that awful? The first day of school, and they have a flat. But they had it under control, so I told them I'd open up the school for them and let anyone in who happened to be here. Did you say you'd been here long?" Tammy didn't wait for a reply this time either, but barged on without even seeming to take a breath.

"Dave, don't forget those hamsters Mr. Wagner asked you to bring for the class project. Brian, grab their food. Here's your lip gloss, Anne." She smiled broadly at Scott and Caleb as they stood silently watching her. "And how are you boys this morning? Anxious to start school?" A chorus of groans from her own breed followed her words.

"Oh, stop. You know you love school."

Loaded down, they trooped into the school. Sherrie scanned the room with a practiced eye. The furniture wasn't new, but it wasn't ancient either. The teacher's desk was ugly, but that didn't matter. The room had been tastefully decorated with vibrant pictures of nature.

The boys were all huddled together attempting to set up the

hamsters' cage. Anne had plastered herself in front of the mirror on one wall and was playing with her hair. Several young children came in with their mothers and clung tenaciously to their skirts. Tammy introduced her to each of them as they came in, but after the first few, Sherrie couldn't tell one from the other.

As the hand on the clock crept closer and closer to eight-thirty, the noise level in the room steadily rose. Still, no teacher made an appearance. Tammy looked out the window a few times, muttering about maybe going back to check on their progress. Finally, she recognized their car and was immediately all smiles again.

"So, are you going home?" she asked.

Sherrie's eyebrows arched like frightened caterpillars. "Home? Do I have to? I mean, I thought I'd stay and watch. At least for the first few days."

"No, you don't have to go home. Don and Sara are usually happy for the extra help. I'll tell you what, though. When you get sick of watching what goes on in school, would you like to help me?"

"Do what?" Sherrie assumed that this meant Tammy didn't plan to go home either, and she relaxed visibly.

"I have to clean the church up some. Get rid of some stuff we don't use anymore. I finally convinced the board that it needs to be done, and guess who they elected to do the dirty work."

Sherrie felt a rush of excitement. "I'd love to help you." She leaned closer to Tammy as if she were afraid of being overheard. "Between us, this place could sure use some cleaning up."

"You think so too?" Tammy exclaimed. "Well, you can help me. I've been trying to do it single-handedly for years, and I can't seem to get anywhere. This is the first time the board even considered it, and I had to fight long and hard just for the opportunity. We've got a lot of older members who just don't want to see one particle of dust moved. Oh, but here are Don and Sara. I'll introduce you."

A tall, sandy-haired man, practically hidden by all that he carried in his arms, pushed through the front door and wove between the milling children trying to reach his desk. He was followed by a tall, athletic-looking woman and a boy who was taller than either of them.

A girl trailed them all, but it was hard for Sherrie to believe that she was part of the family, although Tammy assured her later that she was. She wore a dress that was covered with an almost ridiculous amount of lace and ribbon. Every square inch of her head was curled, frizzed, or teased.

"Don? Don?" Tammy followed him to his desk, where he was trying to set his load down without losing anything. Finally, he had the pile stable, and he straightened up with a relieved sigh. "Don, this is Sherrie Raines. She's enrolling her two boys, Caleb and Scott. You remember I told you about them? Her husband is a doctor?"

Don smiled. It was a smile that didn't quite reach his eyes, Sherrie noticed, and she had the distinct impression that his day had already been too much for him to handle. "Mrs. Raines. Yes, I remember. Nice to meet you. And the boys? Are they here as well?"

Sherrie pointed them out. As she did so, she unconsciously searched the room for any girls Caleb's age. There weren't any, but she didn't have time to decide if she was relieved or worried about it.

"Great," Don was saying. "I'm sure the boys will like it here. Have you met my wife? This is Sara. Sara, this is Sherrie Raines."

Sherrie turned to face Don's wife. Short, jet black hair framed a face almost severe in its angles. She took Sara's proffered hand and was surprised by the strength in her grasp. There was no doubt in her mind that this was a strong woman.

"Nice to meet you," she found herself saying.

"And it's nice to meet you too," Sara returned, smiling. Sherrie was amazed at how much it softened her face.

"Sara helps me out in the classroom, so there are always two of us present."

"And parents are welcome to stay?" Sherrie asked.

"Well. . . ." Don seemed reluctant to answer her question. It was clear to Sherrie by the look on his face that he preferred that parents *didn't* stay. "Some parents prefer to stay for an hour or two the first couple of days, but it really isn't necessary."

"Oh, Don," Tammy chided him, laughing. "You know you love having us underfoot."

Don's smile seemed strained. "There are times when I like to have parents accompany the class as chaperons."

"Don't worry; we won't get in the way." Tammy gave his shoulder a little push. "Besides, we've got work to do today. And when we don't, you always manage to find something for us to do."

"I won't get in the way," Sherrie promised. She thought she

saw relief in Don's eyes. No doubt he sometimes had trouble maneuvering Tammy. Well, he wouldn't have the same problem with her. She'd stay far, far out of his way. "I'd just like to observe for a little while, and then Tammy has asked me to help her. But please don't hesitate to put me to work if you have things that need to be done."

"I appreciate your willingness to help." Don shook his finger playfully in her face, successfully breaking the tension surrounding the conversation. "Don't think I won't take you up on your offer," he warned.

"Please do," Sherrie insisted.

She found a seat in the corner, almost obscured by shadows, and watched everything intently. In all, she counted fifteen kids, most of them grade-school age. She watched with wry amusement as Tammy continued to roam about the classroom like a penned animal keeping things stirred up. She couldn't imagine Don and Sara putting up with that for too long.

Sure enough, after about twenty minutes, Sara pulled Tammy off to a corner of the room and gave her something to do while Don took attendance. Sherrie smiled softly to herself. "That must be how they 'manage' Tammy. Very clever." It probably accounted for why she felt they always needed her to do something.

After a while, Sherrie forgot all about Tammy as she watched Don interact with the class. She had to admit that he was dynamic. The kids hung on what he was saying, even the little ones. Sara floated around the room silently, checking on this one and helping that one. She was like an extension of her husband, his omnipresent eye checking on their progress and understanding. And according to Tammy, she didn't even get paid.

After what seemed like just a few minutes, Don suddenly announced that it was time to clean up and get ready for lunch. Sherrie sat back and checked her watch in amazement. It couldn't be! Not yet. She realized that she'd been so engrossed in the work herself that she'd lost track of time.

"Well, what do you think so far?" Tammy asked, from near her elbow.

Sherrie jumped. "Sorry, I guess I was daydreaming."

"What do you think?"

"He's a very good teacher," Sherrie admitted. "Excellent. They work well together," she observed, her eyes following Sara as she boosted a small child up to reach the water fountain.

"Did you bring a lunch?"

"Actually, I did," Sherrie admitted sheepishly. "Just in case."

"Good; then you won't have to go home to get something, and I won't have to eat alone."

They followed the kids down to the fellowship room, which the school used like a cafeteria. Tammy found a spot away from the bulk of the kids so they wouldn't have to shout to hold a conversation. Don and Sara chose to sit right in the middle of the action, and a lively debate issued from their table throughout the entire meal.

Sherrie was pleased to see Caleb sitting with Tammy's older son Dave and Don and Sara's boy Jay. Maybe he would make some strong Christian friends who would help to anchor him.

"You eat pretty healthfully, huh?" Tammy observed as she took stock of Sherrie's zucchini sticks and the sprouts poking out from the middle of her sandwich.

"It's our responsibility to eat healthfully," Sherrie replied. Without really meaning to, she cocked a reproachful eye at Tammy's chips, soda, and a luscious-looking slice of apple pie in its own pie-shaped container. "Our bodies are the temple of the Holy Spirit, and the health of our bodies affects the health of our minds. The only way that God can communicate with us is through our minds. If we pollute our bodies and minds with greasy or sugary foods, then not only are we corrupting God's temple just as surely as if we trashed the sanctuary, but we're also blocking the only way He can communicate with us."

Tammy seemed to take a moment to process this long explanation, then waved it aside. "Well, of course, it would be nice if everyone could live that way, but I mean, it's impossible. For me, anyway. I hate all that rabbit food. I'm a vegetarian and everything, but I could no more give up sugar and butter and all that than I could fly to the moon."

"But it's our responsibility," Sherrie insisted. "And if we don't live up to the light we've been given in the area of health, then it will be counted against us as sin."

Tammy neatly bypassed the implied warning. "Maybe, but if we're not convicted, then it isn't sin for us."

"It's sin for everybody," Sherrie insisted darkly, but Tammy appeared to ignore her comment.

"Do you think the church could use a coat of paint?" she asked abruptly.

Sherrie struggled to switch gears mentally. "Huh? Paint? Well, yes, of course," she stammered. "It needs paint desperately."

Tammy nodded emphatically. "You're right. I'm going to bring it up to the board immediately. I don't suppose you know any good painters? Did you have anybody do your house?"

Sherrie thought a moment. "As a matter of fact, I think I could recommend some local carpenters." She laughed without any real amusement. "It's funny, but they'd never even heard of the church until I told them about it. They seemed kind of surprised that there could be a church in town that they hadn't heard of."

"I was thinking white. What do you think?" Tammy ate quickly as she talked, hardly seeming to chew.

Sherrie nodded slowly. "I think white would be fine."

"Great. Terrific. I'll get it passed right away. We have to, anyway. There won't be many nice days left this fall, and it's got to be painted before winter. All done?" She picked up the scraps of her lunch and tossed them into the sack she carried her lunch in.

Sherrie finished up quickly, more rushed than she liked to feel when she was eating, and packed her garbage up as well.

"Great. Let's start cleaning."

Sherrie wasn't sure exactly what she'd been expecting, but whatever it was, the condition of the church's innards didn't match it. There was furniture—old, old, furniture—stashed away behind doors of rooms that human eyes couldn't have seen for at least twenty years. And boxes of books, literature, and teaching aids that were laughingly outdated. Cobwebs clouded the corners and hung eerily from the ceilings.

"What *is* all this stuff, anyway?"

Tammy shook her head. "I told you it was bad."

"Bad? This is awful. Where do we start?"

Tammy handed her a bottle of cleaning spray and a sponge. "Go for it."

Sherrie began to clean. Tentatively at first, then with a vengeance. Wash, spray, dust, bag, and throw away became the rhythm to which she worked. When she came up for air later, she could hardly believe the progress they'd made. Bags and boxes of stuff to throw away were lined up against the wall near the door.

"Oh, no," Tammy cried. "I forgot. Anne has a dental appointment at two o'clock. Do you think you could finish up here until school lets out?"

"Sure, don't worry about it."

"Oh, and . . ." she suddenly seemed hesitant to ask.

"That's OK. What?" Sherrie prompted her.

"Well, if it's not too much bother, do you think you could drop the boys off at my house on your way home?"

"Of course. They can help me bring all this stuff out to the dumpster. I could really use their help, and I don't mind dropping them off at all."

Tammy seemed relieved. "Great. I'll see you tomorrow, then."

After Tammy left, Sherrie surveyed the rest of the room. It was pretty clean, but some old junky furniture cluttered up the corner where Tammy had painstakingly arranged it. When Sherrie examined it, she found broken legs and shelves, missing nails, and chipped finish, and she couldn't see one good reason to keep any of it.

"This stuff's no good," she muttered to herself as she pulled it over to the pile headed outside for the dumpster. By the time the boys came down looking for her, she'd established quite a large pile for them to carry out.

It was dirty work, and after they'd dragged it all out to the large dumpster, she wiped her hands on her skirt and wished she'd worn older clothes. "Thank you, boys. Get your stuff and hop in the car," she called.

Don and his family had left them alone with strict instructions to be sure the door was closed tightly when they left. Sherrie slammed it hard and double-checked. She sighed heavily as she looked at the peeling paint on the old building. Well, it had been a very profitable day. Soon she'd be looking at fresh new paint. She tingled with the knowledge that the inside and outside of the church would soon be clean, upstanding representatives of the Seventh-day Adventist Church.

CHAPTER

Prayer Meeting

Sherrie dropped Tammy's kids off at her house and waved at Bob, who was outside stacking wood. He scrubbed his perspiring face with one of his leather gloves, leaving a dark smudge, and walked over to the car. Sherrie rolled down her window.

"In for a big winter, I think," he observed.

"What makes you think so?" Sherrie asked, more to make conversation than from actual curiosity.

"The animals are starting to get their winter coats already," he explained, "and it looks like they're going to be pretty thick."

Sherrie realized he must be referring to the two ancient nanny goats they kept in the few acres behind their house. They were just pets, Tammy had told her, and had never been milked in their lives.

"Think I'm hokey, do you?" Bob chuckled at the skeptical look on her face. "You'll see. We're going to have a lot of snow this year."

"If you say so," Sherrie laughed. "I guess I'd like to see a lot of snow at that. It's been a long time since I've seen enough to ski on. It'd be a nice change."

"I've never skied," Scott volunteered, leaning across the seat so he could look up at Mr. Merrill.

"These kids," Bob said, waving a hand broadly behind him to indicate Brian, Dave, and Anne, who were engaged in a pickup game of dodge ball, "they do it all, ski, skate, sled, snowboard, you name it." He winked at Sherrie. "Keeps them out of trouble."

"Better they're doing that than lots of other things," Sherrie agreed. She shifted into reverse. "We'd better get home and make supper before Jack gets there. It was nice talking to you." She backed the car out slowly, waving to Bob while Scott and Caleb waved to the kids.

That evening, as she washed the grime from her limbs in a hot shower, she mentally prepared a to-do list for the next day. There were several rooms they hadn't gotten to and piles of old literature left that Tammy insisted must be sorted through. Secretly, Sherrie hoped to persuade her to throw out the whole mess. After all, new literature would be more effective, and the cost had to be minimal. If it came down to it, she was willing to pay for the new literature herself.

One of her health practices was to finish her shower off with a blast of cold water to close her pores, but as her hand reached out to grasp the knob, she hesitated. It was chilly tonight, and the cold air seeping in under the door lent a frigid note to the steam-filled bathroom. Still, health principles were something one either abided by or not. Reminding herself of Tammy's chips and soda gave her the resolve she needed to quickly jerk the knob to cold.

As she shivered out of the shower and into a fluffy towel, she fleetingly thought that some of the requirements of a practicing Christian were hard to abide by. She was instantly horrified at the thought and sent up a quick prayer for forgiveness as she wrapped herself in a thick robe. Nowhere, she reminded herself, did it say that the Christian walk would be easy. If it were easy, then more people would probably be Christians.

Jack and the boys were already in bed when she stepped out into the dimly lighted hallway at 7:15. She padded quietly to the bedroom and hopped into bed beside Jack. She was grateful that he had warmed up the sheets, and she snuggled up close to him.

Before she fell asleep, her thoughts flitted back to the cold shower. She'd been finishing up her shower with cold water ever since Jack had read it was good for health. It wasn't that she liked taking cold showers. Actually, she'd had to force herself to do it at first. Then it became easier, and finally she felt a pious sort of pleasure every time the cold water coursed over her body.

Face it, she thought drowsily as her body slowly heated up, *there are some things that are hard to do. Narrow is the way that leads to heaven, remember? That's what they mean when they talk about the Christian life being a battle and a march*, she reminded herself. *Well, that's what makes the goal worth reaching.* With that thought, she drifted off to sleep.

The next day, they were the first ones in the parking lot again. Annoyed, Sherrie hunched against the door, sourly tapping her fingers on the steering wheel. Scott finally looked up from the book he was reading.

"It's all right, Mom," he assured her. "They'll be here soon. Probably our watches are fast."

Sherrie stifled a smile. "You think so?"

"Sure, Mom. Anyway, not everyone can be on time all the time."

"Oh, yeah?" Sherrie muttered under her breath. "We always are." Finally she took out her Bible and began memorizing Psalm 91. Before she was half through, the Wagners pulled up beside them. Although they walked through the doors of the school twenty minutes before it actually started, Sherrie felt tense because of the wait.

Tammy soon made her forget all about the tardy teacher by dragging her to the basement and pulling out books, magazines, and posters that were absolutely ancient.

"You can't mean to keep all this," Sherrie exclaimed as Tammy made two piles—"throw away" and "keep." So far, the "keep" pile was far bigger.

"Sure I'm going to keep it. It's still good stuff. Just because it's old doesn't mean it isn't valid anymore."

"But it can't reach today's audiences," Sherrie protested.

"Of course it can," Tammy objected. "The teaching is still the same. Just because the pictures look old is no reason to waste it."

Sherrie threw up her hands. "You can't keep it. Look, why don't we just throw it all away and start fresh? I'm sure the board will see the advantages of timely, on-the-edge literature that will really speak to people today, not their grandparents."

"They'll never go for it." Tammy shook her head resolutely. "No way."

"Then I'll pay for it myself," Sherrie said firmly.

Tammy's eyes widened in surprise. "You really feel that strongly about it?" Sherrie nodded. "All right. We'll throw it all away . . . after you find some to replace it. Then if we need any in the meantime, we'll use this."

Sherrie groaned inwardly. "Fair enough."

"Good. We have a health fair coming up in a few months at the mall, and we need to put some kind of literature on the table."

"Well," Sherrie said skeptically. "Maybe I can find something before then that you could use instead of this stuff. I taught a nutrition class at our old church. Maybe I have some literature left that we can use."

"Where is the furniture I left in the corner?" Tammy asked suddenly, looking around her as if she expected it to materialize before her eyes.

"That old junk? I threw it in the dumpster. Why?"

"Threw it away? Oh, no!" Tammy wailed, her face paling. "Those were antiques. They've been in the church for years. We were going to set up a room to display our history in."

"Antiques? I didn't know. They looked like junk. I'm sure they weren't worth much anyway."

"Monetarily, no," Tammy agreed resignedly. "But they had a lot of historic and sentimental value."

"I'm sorry," Sherrie said simply, not quite understanding why Tammy seemed so upset. "I didn't know they were that important."

Tammy smiled, but it seemed forced. Her eyes avoided Sherrie's. "No, of course not. I'm not blaming you. It's just that I don't know what I'm going to tell the board. Well, I guess it's nothing they need to know about right away, huh?"

The rest of that afternoon and the next seemed to drag by. Tammy seemed preoccupied about something and continually cast worried glances at the empty corner where the precious furniture had been. Sherrie decided that Tammy was over-reacting and tried to ignore her silences.

"Painters," Tammy suddenly exclaimed. "I almost forgot about getting the church painted. Who did you say did your house?"

Sherrie pulled off a rubber glove and rummaged in one of her pockets for a slip of paper, which she handed to Tammy. "Here. I wrote their names and phone number down for you. Were you able to get the board's approval?"

"I can get that tomorrow," Tammy assured her. "Right after prayer meeting tomorrow night, we'll have an emergency board meeting. You're coming to prayer meeting, aren't you?"

Sherrie nodded as she pulled her glove back on, picked up her sponge, and returned to wiping down the walls. They never missed a prayer meeting at their old church, and Jack often led the group. She had been anticipating this one since the Sabbath before. It would be interesting to see how different it was from their old church. For one thing, she told herself, it'll be a *lot* smaller. At the time, she had no idea just how small.

The following evening, when she and Jack walked into the sanctuary with two freshly groomed boys, well, young men, in tow, it was so quiet she could have heard a mosquito buzzing around outside. There were six people in all, if they included themselves in the count.

Jack ushered her into a pew right in front and maneuvered the boys between them. Sherrie could tell by the look on Caleb's face that he'd rather be anywhere but here. No doubt she'd get a full account of it in his journal later.

She sent Jack a sharp look and arched her eyebrows significantly toward the empty expanse behind them. He shrugged. The pastor stood—she couldn't remember his name and wished now that she'd paid more attention to Tammy's running member-by-member commentary. He began leading them in song . . . a cappella, since there was no pianist.

Caleb's lips were clamped tightly shut. When Sherrie elbowed him, he mouthed the words, but she was sure there was no sound coming out. By the end of the song, more people streamed in until, at the end of the song service, the first four pews were filled up. Sherrie didn't need to turn around to know that Tammy and her family were two pews behind them. She could hear them.

The pastor led out in prayer as the members knelt in the pews. Halfway through his prayer, which Sherrie was particularly interested in, she became aware of a heady fragrance drifting over her. She suppressed an almost uncontrollable urge to sneeze, and her eyes wandered down the row toward Jack, where the smell seemed to emanate from.

Beside her husband, a pair of bare legs, covered only in black fishnet stockings, reached up and ended in the shortest skirt she had ever seen. She felt a rush of emotion—anger?—grip her. Immediately, she recognized who it was. Lauren Pelton. Kneeling beside her was the perfect little replica Sherrie had seen by her side as they jogged past her house.

She whispered an echoing Amen to the pastor's prayer without being conscious of it and slid into the pew. As she did so, she snuck covert looks at Lauren. Jack seemed oblivious of Lauren and Trista's presence, but Caleb was eyeing them with interest.

Besides the fishnet stockings and miniskirt, Sherrie noticed that Lauren wore a body-hugging knit blouse and spike-heeled boots. *What an outfit*, she thought angrily, *and for church*! It was unthinkable. Beside her, Trista's clothing echoed her mother's. A siren red minidress hugged her body like plastic wrap. Sherrie noticed her tugging the dress down as she scooted back into the seat.

A wry snarl tugged at the corners of Sherrie's mouth before she could stop it. How hypocritical! *Don't feign modesty if you're going to wear an outfit like that*, she informed Trista haughtily in the recesses of her mind, wishing desperately that she could say it out loud.

Lauren's Bible lay open on her lap, and she appeared to be listening to the pastor as he spoke. What was it he was talking about? Sherrie realized she hadn't been paying any attention. Before she could force herself to focus on his words, movement at the end of the pew caught her eye.

A tall man dressed in shorts and a T-shirt pushed in beside Trista, forcing everyone in the pew to move down a little. Jack, his concentration shaken, turned and seemed to notice them for the first time. He smiled politely and murmured something Sherrie couldn't make out. She noticed that he pointedly avoided looking down and realized that he had probably already seen what Lauren and Trista were wearing and was making a conscious effort not to see it again.

Caleb, on the other hand, practically had his eyes glued on Trista. Sherrie gave him a quick jab in the ribs, and he blushed hotly. His eyes sought the pages of his open Bible as he made an effort to look like he was interested in something there.

"But how do you account for differences, Pastor Hawley?" a voice behind Sherrie asked.

What differences? Sherrie asked herself, waiting for the answer.

"We all have different gifts," Pastor Hawley replied slowly, "because we are all different people. Life would be pretty dull if we were all the same in every area, don't you think?" He smiled wanly. "And we're different in other areas too. Each of us is at a different place in our walk with the Lord."

"But," the voice behind Sherrie argued, "what about things

that we know are wrong?"

"Things that *we* are doing? Or things that we know *others* are doing?" Pastor Hawley asked pointedly, not seeming entirely happy with the way the questioning was progressing.

"Well, if we know they're wrong, and we still do them, isn't that sin?" Sherrie snuck a quick glance backward and saw that the voice belonged to Caren Nason, the boy's Sabbath School teacher. Caren's husband, sitting beside her, was staring intently at her face as she spoke.

"Yes," Pastor Hawley replied slowly. "Yes, if we do something we know is wrong, then that is sin. However, just because we know something is wrong doesn't mean that we can stop doing it the instant we realize it is a sin. It may take time for Jesus to change our hearts enough that we can claim His strength to overcome the sin in our lives. Sanctification is the work of a lifetime, remember? No one is perfect in everything. We all have stumbling blocks. And what is sin to you may not be sin to someone else who hasn't been convicted of it yet by God."

"But, Pastor, what about the really simple things? Like how we eat and keeping the Sabbath and paying tithe . . ."

"And dressing modestly," Sherrie blurted out before she could stop herself. Instantly she regretted it, then changed her mind. If Lauren and Trista took it as an assault on themselves, then they must have guilty consciences and should reevaluate their standards. After all, since she knew more than they did about the church requirements, she was responsible in part for their salvation . . . or lack of it. It was her *duty* to speak out. And if they were lost because of her silence, then she would be responsible for that. Pastor Hawley's eyes rested on Sherrie for a moment. He looked sad, but she couldn't bring herself to wish she hadn't let the words slip out.

"What seems like a simple thing to some of us is a stumbling block to another," Pastor Hawley finally answered. "Some sins take time and much prayer to overcome, even if they seem silly or simple to others who may have had an easier time overcoming them."

"But aren't we responsible for helping a struggling brother . . . or sister," Sherrie's eyes wandered unconsciously down the pew toward Lauren, "and admonishing them?"

"In love," Pastor Hawley stressed. "If we don't love them and approach them with a loving spirit, we can drive them from the very salvation we hope to bring them to."

"But we are responsible?" Sherrie persisted.

"In Galatians, Paul says, 'Brothers, if someone is caught in a sin, you who are spiritual should restore him gently,'" Pastor Hawley replied guardedly. "Then he goes on to say, 'But watch yourself, or you also may be tempted. Carry each other's burdens, and in this way you will fulfill the law of Christ.' That's in Galatians, chapter six, verses one and two, for those of you who want to look it up."

Jack's hand jabbed the air for attention. "Pastor? I'm following along in the New International Version and there's a note here that says the emphasis on 'burdens' is on moral burdens or weaknesses. So, that does support what my wife was saying earlier. Correct?"

"Yes, that is correct," Pastor Hawley explained patiently. "However, notice that the first verse uses the word *restore*, which is the same verb used in other texts for setting bones, mending nets, or bringing factions together. The object here is to unite the Christian body, not to bring more division into it."

"Of course," Jack agreed. "That's what I had in mind, and I'm sure Sherrie did also. There would be no purpose in trying to help someone else if in the end you drove them away from the very help you were trying to offer."

"Exactly," Pastor Hawley said, trying to smile. He didn't quite make it. "I'm sorry, but our time is just about up, and I like to remain faithful to those who have appointments elsewhere following the prayer meeting. Will someone have our closing prayer?"

Someone behind Sherrie, she suspected it was Caren Nason's husband, apparently volunteered, and they all knelt. A man's deep voice pleaded with God for unity in the church and in the world, thanked Him for blessings, and asked Him to go with each person throughout the remainder of the week. When he finished with a reverent Amen, it was echoed loudly. Everyone shuffled to their feet. Before Sherrie could even close her Bible, Tammy's hand was on her arm.

"Sherrie!" she exclaimed. "You came. So? What did you think?"

"Very . . . enlightening," Sherrie managed, not sure the word was entirely accurate. "Much smaller than what we're used to, of course."

"Oh, I'm sure. It must be great in a big church. I envy you," Tammy said wistfully. "Pastor Hawley! Over here!" She waved her hand to get his attention, and he made his way toward them.

"This is Sherrie Raines and her husband Jack and the boys, Caleb and Scott. They just moved here from Tennessee."

Pastor Hawley greeted them warmly, but Sherrie detected a sadness in his smile. Then she remembered Tammy saying that his wife had passed away.

"I'm so glad you folks could come," he was saying. "I noticed you last week, but I had to hurry out to make it to my next congregation. I hope we'll be seeing a lot of you."

"Oh, you certainly will," Jack agreed. "We plan to be very active in the church."

"Wonderful!" Then he was called away, and Tammy was introducing them to the Peltons.

"Lauren and Mark and their daughter Trista." Tammy pointed to each one as she said their name.

"Hello," Sherrie said coolly, extending her hand for a stiff shake. Before they could say anything, she took Jack's arm and turned away, missing the confused, hurt flush that swept over Lauren's face.

CHAPTER

7

The Women's Prayer Breakfast

Sherrie woke up early one morning about a month after they'd been in Maine. She tried not to toss and turn so she wouldn't wake up Jack, but after lying in bed watching the color outside her window turn from black to a hazy gray, she slipped quietly out of bed and pulled on her thick bathrobe.

She grabbed her Bible and crept quietly out to the porch. The air was chilly, almost nippy. She pulled the robe more tightly around her and inhaled deeply, closing her eyes.

In the early-morning fog, the trees seemed to brood eerily on the edge of the lawn. Their scarlet and yellow leaves were barely noticeable through the gray mist. The moisture in the air had seeped into the bark, turning it jet black, like an artist's ink drawing.

"It's beautiful, God," Sherrie whispered, looking up into the sky. A few thin ribbons of blue were visible, telling her that the fog would burn off, leaving another of the gorgeous Indian summer days they'd been enjoying for the past few weeks.

She sat down on the porch bench and opened her Bible, turning to Psalms, her favorite book. Usually she could find comfort in the beautiful words, but this morning they seemed to lie flat on the page. Her mind kept going back to Caleb. After struggling with her conscience for the better part of an hour, she decided that she had better take another look at his journal.

"It's for his own good," she kept repeating to herself. Sounds from inside the house warned her that the rest of the family was beginning to stir. She closed her Bible with a sense that she'd missed out on something and went inside to fix breakfast.

Later, when Caleb and Scott were downstairs helping Jack load some equipment into his car, Sherrie slunk into the boys' room. Furtively her hand darted behind Caleb's dresser, in search of the yellow notebook. She was determined to see if Caleb had written anything about Trista. She had to know what it was.

Her fingers brushed the smooth wallpaper behind the dresser, and her hand came out empty. Gone. He must have moved it. No, maybe he had it with him. Her eyes scanned the room quickly. Could it be that he was getting wise? That he knew she had been reading it?

No, of course not. How could he know? No one knew she'd even cracked the covers except Jack, and he surely wasn't about to tell Caleb about it. Still, she couldn't shake the feeling that he'd changed hiding places. Well, she didn't have time this morning to look more thoroughly. It would have to wait.

Frustrated, she went downstairs and prepared for school. This time, she didn't head for the basement immediately as she had been doing to help Tammy work on odds and ends. Instead, she found a seat near the rear of the class and decided to watch Don's teaching techniques. If Don Wagner was surprised, he didn't show it.

Tammy was, and she signaled for Sherrie to come with her. Sherrie shook her head firmly. There would be plenty of time for cleaning later. She wanted to see how the class was progressing. Tammy, however, wouldn't be ignored. Quietly, she made her way to where Sherrie sat.

"What are you doing? I thought we could talk this morning. I have something on my mind. Can't you observe tomorrow?"

One look at Tammy's face told Sherrie that she did, indeed, need to talk. Inside she groaned, *What could she possibly want to talk about? Not the junky old antiques again, hopefully*. She got up and followed Tammy down to the fellowship room.

"Want some tea?" Tammy asked. "I've got some water on."

"Sure. What was it you wanted to talk about?" Sherrie prepared herself to be bored.

"Actually." Tammy seemed nervous. "I really wanted to talk about prayer meeting."

"Prayer meeting?" Sherrie questioned guardedly.

"Sort of. Remember the first prayer meeting you came to? I've been thinking about that discussion, and I kinda wanted to talk about it and . . ." she hesitated, then plunged on, "Lauren Pelton."

Sherrie was instantly alert. She toyed with the mug Tammy handed her and shielded her eyes, hoping Tammy wouldn't notice her sudden interest. "What about Lauren?"

"Well, I'm sure you noticed how she was dressed that night."

Sherrie snorted derisively before she could stop herself. "How could I help it?"

Tammy's smile was weak. "I know, I know. The problem is that it's getting worse. At first, when she began coming to church and she and her husband started studying, she was very careful about what she wore. Probably she felt uncomfortable around all us long skirts." She allowed herself a rueful chuckle before continuing.

"After a while it was a short skirt here, a low-cut shirt there. Then the wedding bands went back on. And now and then she'd wear a pair of earrings. But that prayer meeting, well, there is just no excuse for it. I mean, short skirts are one thing, as long as no one asks me to wear one. I'm really worried about her. About them. I don't want to see them slip out the back door because of the things she wears and what it makes people say and think about her."

Sherrie studied the countertop for a full minute before answering. It was a strange pattern, like someone had dribbled gold paint all over it. She tried to collect her thoughts. Tried to dissect Tammy's words to see where she was really coming from. How to be the most tactful? She cleared her throat and sipped some tea. It was just beginning to cool.

"Of course, I know what you mean. I was certainly shocked when I saw what she was wearing. I mean, a member. There's no excuse. And her daughter was a carbon copy." She paused before going on, tracing one of the designs on the countertop with her finger. "I think that what we talked about at that prayer meeting was valid."

"You mean about us being responsible for others?" Tammy asked. "I believe that. I really do. But we can't just go up to her and say, 'Sorry, Lauren, but you can't wear those clothes to church here anymore.' We'd drive her out of the church."

"Well, there is a time and place for every type of confrontation.

In this case, though, I believe that a subtler approach would work much better."

"Such as?"

"What about a women's prayer group?"

Tammy's eyes lighted up. "You mean instead of prayer meeting?"

"No, in addition to it. We could hold it here in the fellowship room one morning a week. We could get speakers, have tea and muffins, prayer and singing."

Tammy seemed skeptical. "Where would we get speakers?"

"Everywhere. You could let me take care of that. What do you think of the idea?"

"I really like it. But what does it have to do with what we've been talking about?"

"Don't you see? It would give the stronger Christian women a chance to minister to the younger ones. Isn't that what Paul tells us in Titus? 'Then they [the older women] can train the younger women to love their husbands and children, to be self-controlled and pure, to be busy at home, to be kind, and to be subject to their husbands, so that no one will malign the word of God' (Titus 2:4, 5, NIV)."

"That," Sherrie said pointedly, "is what worries *me*. What kind of a witness do you think Lauren Pelton is when she tells people she's a Seventh-day Adventist while tugging her skirt down? What does that tell people about Seventh-day Adventists?"

Her thoughts immediately went to Caleb. "And what do you think it says to our children? Our boys especially? Children are easily impressionable. They look at her and think, 'Well, she's a Seventh-day Adventist, and she does it. Why can't I?' Someday your little Anne could say just that to you. What are you going to tell her?"

Tammy stirred her tea absently. "I hope I never have to deal with that," she whispered.

"The women's prayer group is one way we can help Lauren and others to see their mistake without actually pointing fingers at them," Sherrie said, slapping her hand down on the counter to emphasize her words. Tammy jumped guiltily as if she were ashamed of what they'd been talking about. She looked around furtively to be sure no one had snuck down the stairs while they'd been talking.

"You're right," she admitted simply. "When do you want to do it?"

"Well, it'll take some time to get everything organized and have it announced. I'd say a couple weeks at least. The best day would probably be a Monday or Tuesday, say, at about eight-thirty. Do you think many of the women will be able to come?"

"Yes, most of them, actually. I can only think of two or three who work outside the home."

"Good. We'll call it a women's prayer breakfast. Do you think the board would approve refreshments like muffins and herbal tea?"

"I guess," Tammy stammered, confused. "You mean you . . . eat . . . muffins?"

"Of course. They have great muffins at the food co-op. They're all natural, no sugar, no fat. I love muffins."

Tammy groaned. "Oh, those kind. Maybe I could pick up a few at Dunkin' Donuts for those of us who like our muffins with sugar."

Sherrie bristled. "If you must," she said coolly.

"I must," Tammy assured her. "Maybe we can integrate the natural muffins over time, but to start out with, we should give people a choice. Anyway, that's not important. Who do you think we should get for a speaker?"

"I'd speak for the first meeting if you'd like me to," Sherrie offered casually. "I'm sure I could think of an appropriate topic. It would serve as an introduction. Next time we could get someone from the community. What about a nutritionist? Do any of the women who are coming have areas of specialty? I'd like to see someone have a talk about herbal remedies, children's crafts, back care. There are a lot of topics we could cover."

"Actually, we do have a few professional women and some who are really creative with children. This could turn out to be a really big group."

Three weeks later, after the women's prayer breakfast had been announced for a few weeks during announcement time before church, the fellowship room was packed. Some of the women had brought friends with them. Tammy was positive they would run out of muffins and kept herself busy in the kitchen to hide her nervousness.

Sherrie sat in one of the metal folding chairs they'd set up

and reviewed her notes. She'd chosen the topic of dress. She hid
a smile behind her hand as she glanced around the room eyeing
the long hemlines and conservative styles. For most of these
women, it would be a review of the basics. Then she caught sight
of Lauren Pelton.

In her hands was a box of muffins she'd brought. From a
bakery, Sherrie noted. Probably loaded with sugar. She wore
a cable-knit sweater and jeans that she must have painted on
that very morning.

"The paint still looks fresh," Sherrie muttered under her
breath. Well, the significance of her topic wouldn't be lost on at
least one of the listeners. She returned to her notes with satisfaction until the church organist made her way to the front to call
the meeting to order with a short song service.

Sherrie waited, almost impatiently, for it to be time for her to
speak. After the song service, each of the women seated named a
blessing or asked for a special prayer request. Someone led out in
prayer, and a few of the women joined in.

"Ladies," Tammy was saying, having made her way to the front
and looking uncomfortable, "some of you have probably met Mrs.
Sherrie Raines by now. Sherrie recently moved with her family
from Tennessee, and we're happy to have her here with us in
Maine. This breakfast prayer group was Sherrie's idea, and she
deserves a lot of credit for making it all happen. This morning,
she will also bring us our talk."

Having made it completely through the introduction of the
speaker, Tammy let out a loud sigh of relief and sank into the
nearest chair. Sherrie passed her on the way to the front of the
room and gave her a fleeting smile, wondering if Tammy had
guessed the topic of her talk, which she'd decided to keep a secret
until the meeting.

She set her notes down on the polished wood of the podium
and smiled pleasantly. The sea of faces before her blended into
one as she began. No nervous butterflies fluttered around in her
stomach, her mouth wasn't dry, and her palms weren't wet.
Compared to the groups she had spoken to in Tennessee, this
was like a small living-room-sized gathering.

She let her eyes wander over the individual faces, noting interest on most. She was surprised that she knew so few of the
women in the crowd. Caren Nason's earnest face, illuminated

with the kind of light that suggested she was hearing truth and wanted to shine with the brilliance of it, encouraged Sherrie, and she felt a surge of power in what she was saying.

These women felt the same way she did, she told herself. They were relying on her to speak up, to say what they were too shy or afraid to say on their own. As her voice rose in pitch, reaching the clinching point in her talk, her eyes fell on the blanched white face of Lauren Pelton.

Two spots of cherry red stood out on her cheeks. It was as if she knew, instinctively, that Sherrie was talking about her and her alone. She shifted uncomfortably in her seat, glancing to each side to see if anyone was glaring accusingly at her. She tried to cover her jeans with the Bible she'd brought along, opening it as if she were looking up a text.

She knows, Sherrie thought, not skipping a beat in her talk. *She knows I'm talking about her. Please, Lord*, she shot up a silent prayer, *help it to encourage her to dress more modestly*.

"In closing, sisters, I would admonish you as Paul when writing to Timothy, 'I also want women to dress modestly, with decency and propriety, not with braided hair or gold or pearls or expensive clothes, but with good deeds, appropriate for women who profess to worship God.' That's in First Timothy two, nine and ten, if you want to look it up. May each one of us here today go and do likewise."

A chorus of Amens followed Sherrie to her seat. Someone she didn't know closed the meeting with prayer, and then it was all over. *A success*, she thought happily as she looked around her. Groups of women clustered together in little knots discussing her talk. Little snatches of conversation she overheard confirmed that they mostly agreed with her speech.

"Sherrie? Look who came today. Lauren Pelton." It was Tammy's voice . . . behind her. Sherrie turned slowly. Lauren's face was pasty and mottled. Unspilled tears shone in her eyes. Tammy's eyes pleaded with Sherrie to say something nice.

"Lauren, yes, we met at prayer meeting." Sherrie stuck her hand out to shake Lauren's, putting as much warmth as she could into her voice.

"I enjoyed your talk," Lauren said shyly. "The more I hear, the more I realize there is to learn." She laughed without any joy. "There's so much to remember, isn't there? Sometimes I wonder if I'll ever be able to do it all."

"You will," Sherrie said confidently. "It's just a matter of will-power, you know, strengthened, of course, by the Holy Spirit. We all want to be able to call ourselves Christians and be worthy of the name, don't we? Just lean on Him, and He'll give you the power to do what you know is right and convict you in other areas where you're lacking."

Lauren swallowed hard. She glanced self-consciously down at her jeans and tugged at the hem of her sweater. "Yes, I'm sure He will. If you'll excuse me, I have to go. Will you be doing this again next week? Fine, I'll be here."

She turned and made her way slowly through the crowd. No one greeted her or stopped her to talk.

"Doesn't have too many friends, does she?" Sherrie observed.

"No, I guess not," Tammy agreed. "I felt bad for her. I think she realized that your talk was aimed at her. I guess she needed to hear it, but I don't want her to get discouraged. Maybe it wasn't such a good idea after all."

"It was a great idea," Sherrie objected. "Look at how well it went over with everyone else. You just wait. After she's been coming for a while, she'll change. It will just take some time. Right now, our biggest problem is who we're going to get to speak next time. Any ideas?"

They sat down together at one of the tables and planned the following meeting before all the participants of the first had drifted out the door. Sherrie looked around the room with a feeling of contentment and accomplishment, eagerly anticipating the next women's prayer breakfast.

CHAPTER

Trista

That evening, Sherrie discussed the success of the meeting with Jack. He closed the big medical book he'd been reading and gave Sherrie his full attention.

"I could just feel the Holy Spirit filling me," Sherrie told him, reliving again her powerful speech. "I know Lauren was convicted. She was upset, but it'll be a long time before she wears another short skirt. You'll see."

"You've convinced me." Jack smiled. "I'm really glad it all went well, honey. And I'm proud of you. There's no excuse for Lauren and her daughter to dress the way they do. Especially for church."

"Her daughter?" Sherrie whispered hoarsely. "I'd forgotten about Trista. Do you suppose Lauren will be able to enforce her new dress code on Trista too? Do you suppose she'll even think of it?"

"Oh, I'm sure she will."

"But right away?"

Jack shrugged as he picked his medical book back up. "I don't know. I guess so. Why?"

"It's Caleb. I'm worried about Caleb. Jack, you should have seen the way he was ogling her at prayer meeting a few weeks ago. I meant to see what he'd written about her in his journal, but when I looked, I couldn't find it. I guess he moved it, but I'll find it soon."

Jack closed the book with a loud crack. "Caleb what?" There was a dangerously low tone in his voice that boded no good for Caleb and his wandering eyes. It was almost frightening.

"At that first prayer meeting, you saw what they were wearing. Caleb was staring at Trista. I'm sure he must have written about it."

"I'll have a talk with him." He said no more, but Sherrie could tell by the expression on his face that Caleb wasn't going to enjoy the "talk."

She didn't have an opportunity to even look for Caleb's notebook until a week later, after school. Scott approached her as the kids rushed around collecting their bags, books, and coats.

"Mom?" He licked his lips nervously. "Could we go home with Mrs. Merrill? Dave wants to show us his butterfly collection."

Sherrie opened her mouth to say No, but before she could get it out, Tammy rushed over to her.

"The boys will be OK with us for a few hours. They're welcome to come. I know Dave and Brian would really enjoy it. If you want, I can call Jack and have him run them home when he leaves his office. That way, they'll be home for supper."

"Well, I . . ." Apparently she was outnumbered. Scott and Caleb just stared at her silently, hoping. But the Merrill kids clustered around her, whining.

"Can they come, Mrs. Raines? Please?" Anne tugged impatiently on Sherrie's sleeve, and she wondered vaguely why Anne should even care.

"It will be very educational. I promise," Tammy assured her. "It couldn't help but be with all Dave's animals. It'll give him the chance to tell the boys all about them."

"I guess so," Sherrie finally said, weakening. She wasn't thinking so much about the boys as she was the opportunity of returning to an empty house and having a little time to herself. And a little time to read Caleb's notebook without having to worry about someone discovering her. "I don't want you boys eating anything at Mrs. Merrill's. Understand?

"It'll spoil their supper," she explained aside to Tammy.

"Thanks, Mom," Scott said gratefully, giving her a quick hug.

"Go on," she said, laughing. Caleb said nothing but gathered his books and trooped out with the Merrill kids. Sherrie followed them slowly.

"Looks nice, doesn't it?" Tammy asked, walking beside her. Sherrie turned to view the paint job Tammy was referring to.

"It's beautiful. They should be done in a few days." The new paint glistened, making the building look fresh and clean.

When Sherrie pulled up in her driveway and stepped out of the car, she inhaled deeply of the pine-scented air. The sun was close to the tops of the mountains, and she realized with a jolt that the days were getting shorter. She shivered involuntarily. Summer was almost spent. Already the leaves had dropped from the trees and lined the woods with a thick carpet.

She wandered over and gazed sorrowfully down at her flower bed. A few marigolds, sheltered somewhat by the house, clung tenaciously to life. Their frost-blackened leaves drooped dismally around their worn orange faces. Sherrie absently pulled out a few straggling weeds and wondered why she had bothered to plant anything so late in the season.

The sound of voices floating clearly through the thin air caught her attention. Movement by the edge of the woods near the road revealed two people on mountain bikes riding past the house. They waved when they saw Sherrie, and their talk ceased abruptly. Sherrie waved back without thinking. It was only after they had disappeared down the road that she realized the helmeted cyclists had been Lauren and Trista. She dusted her hands off on her slacks and headed inside.

It seemed strange walking in the front door of a silent house. Sherrie took off her coat and hung it up in the closet. She was anxious to get upstairs and search for the notebook, but she knew it would be better to start dinner first.

The fire had died down, but there was a good bed of coals, which flared up when she jabbed them with the poker. She filled the stove, then headed for the kitchen, where she'd left beans simmering in the slow cooker all day. Quickly, she retrieved the ingredients she needed to mix with the beans while she fried an onion on the stove. Fifteen minutes later, she mixed everything together and popped the beans into the oven to bake.

Now, she thought as she wiped her hands hastily on a towel hanging from the refrigerator, *I can read Caleb's notebook.* A quick look behind the dresser confirmed that it wasn't there. *Probably Scott caught him hiding it, and that forced him to move it,* she thought. Her eyes darted around the room. It had to be there somewhere. At the bottom of a drawer?

She opened each drawer of Caleb's dresser and carefully moved the clothes. Nothing. In his desk? A quick search of his desk proved equally fruitless. The mattress! Her fingers, groping beneath the mattress of Caleb's bed, hit something hard and smooth. She pulled it out, her heart pounding. Success!

She sat on the side of the bed and tried to calm her nerves. She could hear every beat of her heart in the whoosh of blood pounding in her ears. "This is for his own good," she told herself firmly.

When the thundering had died down, she opened the notebook, quickly flipping to where she'd left off the last time. There had to be something about Trista. Her eyes scanned the scrawling handwriting for the name. Finally she found something.

"Mom and Dad made us go to prayer meeting here last night. I don't like it. I wish we had stayed in Tennessee. In Tennessee prayer meeting was a little interesting, and there were lots of kids. Trista Pelton was at prayer meeting, but I didn't get to talk to her. I don't think Mom likes her very much, probably because she looks like someone you'd see on TV. At least, she looks like the actresses I saw on TV at Dan's house once."

Sherrie cringed. TV? He'd watched TV? They'd made such an effort to protect the boys from television. So, he thought Trista looked like an actress. Well, the comparison didn't elevate her in Sherrie's mind. Her eyes sought the next entry.

"I wish Trista went to school with us. There aren't any girls my age in school at all. Scott thinks Anne Merrill likes him, but I told him he doesn't know what he's talking about. He says he'll probably marry her someday because he wants to marry a nice Christian girl and have a family. He's crazy. If he did that, he'd live just like we do now. Not me. Things are going to be different when I'm on my own."

A shiver slipped down Sherrie's spine. What was happening to all the things they'd pounded into Caleb's head for fourteen years? Were they really gone? Or was it like Jack said? Just a phase that would wear off? A scribbled note that wasn't really an entry caught her eye.

"Dad told me that he'd better not ever catch me looking at Trista 'that' way ever again. Mom must have told him. She poked me at prayer meeting. But I couldn't help looking! I HATE them."

The entries went on, but Sherrie closed the notebook and sat in the darkening room, thinking. He'd written in anger, she realized, and didn't really mean what he'd said. Still, it wasn't easy to look at the words and know that he'd felt hatred for her and Jack, even in anger.

Funny, she thought as she replaced the notebook under the mattress, *Jack didn't say he'd spoken to Caleb. Probably wanted to forget he'd ever had to.* The sound of car wheels crunching the gravel in the driveway hurried her down the stairs to the kitchen. She'd spent more time than she'd intended to reading the notebook. She hoped the beans weren't burnt. It would be hard to explain.

That Sabbath, Sherrie decided she'd like to see firsthand what happened in Caleb and Scott's Sabbath School class. Instead of following Jack up to the adult class, she explained to him in hushed tones what she was going to do and then headed for the boys' class. Caren Nason looked surprised to see her.

"Can I do something for you, Mrs. Raines?"

"Yes," Sherrie smiled, trying to break the ice. "You can call me Sherrie. I'd like to observe your class. If that's OK?"

"Certainly," Caren agreed and refrained from asking why. "I'm sure one of the boys can find a chair, and you can sit in the back or right up here with the kids if you'd like."

"I'll just sit in the back. I don't want to disrupt anything."

Five minutes after she'd settled in at the back of the class, Sherrie was sure the kids had forgotten about her, until she caught one of them glancing back worriedly. None of them seemed too anxious to answer Caren's questions either. Were they afraid she was there to spy on them for their parents?

A quick glance around the room confirmed her initial suspicion that Trista wasn't even there. Caleb seemed to realize the same thing and slumped in his chair, refusing to answer any questions. When Trista slipped through the door ten minutes later, he sat up and tried to appear oblivious that she chose the seat next to him.

Sherrie was disappointed to see that her talk on modesty in dress hadn't carried over well from mother to daughter. Trista had on a pair of jeans, ripped in strategic places, and a V-necked T-shirt that dipped precariously low.

"We're glad you could make it, Trista," Caren Nason said coolly. As Caren eyed Trista's clothes, Sherrie could almost guess what she was thinking. "Would you recite our memory verse for us, please?"

"I don't know it," Trista replied sarcastically. "Why do you ask me to say it every week? You know I don't study the lesson."

A thin smile played on Caren's lips. "I keep hoping that maybe this time you'll know it. Aren't you at all interested in going to heaven when Jesus comes back?"

The rest of the kids shifted uncomfortably in their seats. Trista shook her head slowly. "No. Why would I want to go to heaven? I couldn't listen to my music, none of my friends would be there, and I'd have to float around on a cloud playing a stupid harp."

"There's nothing in the Bible that tells us we're going to float on clouds strumming harps all day," Caren corrected her. "And, no, you wouldn't be able to listen to your music, and I dare say that your friends won't be there. But the most important person is Jesus. He'll be there."

"What do I care?" Trista asked bitterly. "I don't know Jesus, and I don't want to. Then I'd have to give up a lot of stuff that I like to do, just like my mom and dad did."

Sherrie wondered just what Trista's parents had given up, but she didn't have time to dwell on it. Caren seemed to realize that pursuit of the conversation was a waste of time, and she moved on. When she asked Caleb a question, he denied knowing the answer, and Sherrie was positive that he did know it. She made a mental note to question him about it later.

After the class was over, the kids raced each other for the door. Caren gathered up her materials, and Sherrie noticed that none of the kids lingered to talk to her.

"Did you learn anything?" Caren asked, smiling wearily. "They're a tough bunch."

"Yes," Sherrie agreed. "I don't envy you your job. You have a way with them, though."

"Thank you. I really like kids. Someday maybe I'll even have some." She smiled again and made her way out the door. Sherrie followed her out and headed into the kitchen for a drink of water before the service. She filled her glass and let her eyes wander around the kitchen as she drank it slowly. Voices around the corner caught her attention.

"Is that a real tatoo, Trista?" a girlish voice asked in awe.

"Nah," Trista's voice laughed. "It comes off with baby oil. That way I can have lots of different ones."

"Do you ever skip school?" asked a voice.

"That's kids' stuff," Trista scoffed. "We cut class all the time and go into the woods to drink. The teachers never catch us," she bragged.

"Drink what?" asked one innocent.

"Beer. What else is there to drink?"

"You mean you drink real beer?"

"Yes, I drink real beer," Trista mocked. "And I smoke real cigarettes too."

"I don't believe you," a voice challenged in a whisper.

"Then what are these?" Trista asked.

"Those are cigarettes," someone exclaimed, only to be shushed by the rest. Sherrie wondered where all the adults were.

"That's what I said. Why don't you guys go upstairs? I want to talk to Caleb for a minute." Caleb? What did she want with Caleb? Panic gripped Sherrie's heart. Maybe she should stop them. No, better to hide and find out what they talked about. She could hear the other kids head up the stairs, grumbling. She ducked farther back into the kitchen, realizing that if they came around the corner, they would see her. The sound of their footsteps walked closer.

"Still want this?" she heard Trista ask.

Want what? Sherrie thought desperately. *What does Caleb want?*

"Yeah." His voice was eager, frightened. "Are they your favorite?"

Was what her favorite?

"Nah. I like the Black Rattlesnakes. They're more my style." What was she talking about? "Look, I gotta get outside and have a smoke before I have to sit through that boring service. Why don't you sit with us? We can pass notes."

"Sure, yeah. I'll ask my mom."

"Oh, then I won't hold my breath."

She heard one set of footsteps head up the back stairs and one move toward the front. After waiting for a long time, she bolted from the kitchen into the bathroom, where she locked herself in a stall to settle her nerves. Several deep breaths later, she felt well enough to go up to the service.

At the top of the stairs, she found Caleb waiting nervously. There was no sign of whatever Trista might have given him.

"Mom, can I sit with the Peltons for church?"

Sherrie didn't hesitate. "Absolutely not," she replied, steel lacing her voice. "Why aren't you in there now? Come on." She held the door open, forcing him to precede her to the pew where Jack and Scott sat. Caleb walked like a condemned man, and as she sat next to him, she could feel hatred spilling out of every pore.

"You'll thank me one day," she muttered under her breath.

CHAPTER
9

Church Officers

Sherrie had just settled down in her favorite armchair when the phone rang. She groaned and began to lay her tea down on the table next to her when Jack hopped up.

"I'll get it," he announced.

Sherrie sank back into the chair and carefully cradled her cup of herb tea. She picked up the latest *Adventist Review* but hesitated before flipping to the table of contents. Sipping her tea, she listened to Jack's monotone responses.

"Yes, yes, yes," he was saying. "That will be fine. Yes."

Who could that be? The magazine fell onto her lap.

"I appreciate the recommendation. Certainly, I don't mind. That will be fine. I'm glad to help where I can."

The office? Nah, the hospital?

"Sherrie? Phone."

Sherrie set her tea down gingerly. Jack covered the receiver and mouthed the words *nominating committee* before handing her the phone. Oh, the nominating committee. She tried to quell the rush of nervous energy that immediately coursed through her.

"This is Sherrie." Her voice sounded tinny in her ears. Fake. She didn't recognize the voice on the other end but was told that she was speaking to Josh Nason. Caren's husband, she realized.

"You've done such a wonderful job setting up the women's prayer breakfast," Josh was saying when Sherrie focused in on his words. "The nominating committee would like to know if you would be willing to lead the women's committee?"

"I would be happy to," Sherrie murmured, picking up a pen and absently drawing circles on the pad of paper beside the phone.

"And also the head deaconess and personal ministries assistant? And would you be on the school board?"

"Certainly."

"I'm sure you're already aware of the responsibilities, but if you have any questions, I would be happy to answer them for you."

Sherrie laughed. "Actually, I've held all of those positions at one time or another."

"I know we're all looking forward to your input and leadership," Josh told her. "My wife Caren was very impressed with the women's prayer breakfast. She's very eager for the next one."

"I appreciate that, and I'm glad she received a blessing."

"As I told your husband, the church will approve your nomination when they vote on Sabbath. Then you'll be stepping into your new positions after the first of the year."

"I'm looking forward to it," Sherrie assured him.

"Thank you again, and please thank your husband for me. He's taking on a lot of the Lord's work too. Take care."

Sherrie hung up the phone and returned slowly to her chair. Picking up her tea, she took a small sip and raised her eyebrows at Jack.

"Well?"

"Well, what?" he asked innocently.

"What did they ask you to do?" Sherrie probed. "Come on, don't be so modest."

"Well," Jack drew the word out as if it were a long spaghetti noodle. "They asked me to be an elder and the personal ministries leader and the community services leader as well as being on the school board. And they'd also like me to lead out in prayer meeting sometimes and hold a few Bible studies."

Sherrie gasped. "Do you have time for all that?"

"I'll make time," Jack replied firmly. "There is no more important work than the Lord's work. I must be about my Father's business."

"But your job . . ."

"I'll make time," Jack repeated. "What did they ask you to do?"

"Head deaconess, women's committee leader, personal ministries assistant, and school board. I can't believe they asked us to do so much. I wonder why?"

"Josh said that the members who had these positions last year aren't filling them. Nothing is being done, and the nominating committee doesn't really have a lot of people to pick from. None of the members are willing to do anything. Some of the leaders we're replacing asked to be removed months ago, and no one has taken their places."

"There's something strange about this church, Jack," Sherrie mused, running her finger around the rim of her mug. "Don't you think so?"

"It's dead," Jack stated simply. "The pastor isn't very vital and, in my opinion, he's terribly liberal. That's why this church is in the condition it's in now. There is no one to push people, to straighten out the members, and to make them pull their weight. It seems to me that there are a few members who do all the work, but most don't do anything."

"You're right." Sherrie nodded. "Most of them seem content to sit back and let things slide. You know, I think God led us here to help these people. They need leadership, and neither one of us is a stranger to leadership."

Jack held his hands out in front of him and flexed his fingers. "I know we've got a few months to go, but I'm itching to start planning the first meeting. Where did we put all my records and notes from our old church? You know, from the offices I held there?"

Sherrie managed to locate the papers, plus a pile of her own notes and meeting outlines, in the hall closet. They sat down together on the living-room floor like a couple of kids and sifted through the papers. An hour past their normal bedtime, they had straightened everything out and tentatively planned their first meetings, pending the final church approval, which was to be voted on Sabbath.

The shrill piercing ring of the phone exploded into the early-morning quiet, wrenching Sherrie from a sound sleep. She bolted out of bed not completely aware of what was happening or what exactly had woken her up. Jack stirred and groaned as the phone rang again. Sherrie stumbled across the dark room and fumbled for it.

"Hello?" she croaked. Clearing her throat didn't seem to help the hoarseness. She shook her head, trying to clear it. "Tammy? What . . ."

"I hate to wake you this late, Sherrie, I really do." Tammy's voice seemed strained, unnatural. "But I need your help. I don't know if you remember meeting the Grants? They have several small children. Anyway, Pastor Hawley called me and said their house just burned to the ground. They weren't able to salvage anything, and one of the little girls is hurt pretty badly."

"I can't believe . . ." Sherrie choked, feeling as though someone had dumped ice water on her. "That's awful. What do you need me to do?"

"Pastor Hawley went with Mrs. Grant and the little girl, Sylvia, to the hospital; that's where he called me from. Mr. Grant is planning to join his wife at the hospital as soon as they can find someplace for the two boys to stay for the night. I told him they can stay here and gladly, but Bob is working the late shift tonight, so I don't have a car. Could you . . . would you pick Mr. Grant up and drive him to the hospital?"

"Certainly," Sherrie assured her. "Just give me a minute to get dressed, and I'll be right there."

"Thanks, Sherrie, I knew you'd do it." Tammy sounded relieved. "He's here at my house. We're getting the boys settled. We'll see you in a little while."

Sherrie replaced the phone gently on its cradle and crept over to her dresser. Jack was still sleeping, and she couldn't see any reason to wake him. She hunted blindly for a pair of slacks and a top, hoping she'd come out with something color coordinated. She dressed in the bathroom and ran a brush quickly through her hair.

As she drove through the still town to Tammy's house, she prayed silently for the Grants and especially for little Sylvia. She tried to remember them, to place the name with faces, but she came up blank. The Grants could be any number of young families in the church.

Every light in the Merrills' house was blazing as Sherrie pulled up in the driveway. Tammy threw open the door before Sherrie's car even came to a complete halt, spilling light onto the frozen lawn. The cold air caught her breath as she jumped out and hurried up the walk. In her haste, she'd grabbed a thin jacket. Now she regretted it.

"How are they?" It was a stupid question. *How would I be if my house had just burned to the ground and my child was in the hospital?* she berated herself.

Tammy's face looked haggard in the harsh light. "The boys are settled in now. I woke Brian up and had him get them interested in some of his bugs and stuff. They were running on a lot of adrenaline, but they seem to be pretty played out now. Duncan is waiting in the living room."

Sherrie recognized Duncan Grant the moment she saw him. When she'd seen them at church on occasion, she'd had the impression that they were a very godly, if somewhat poor, family. Their children were extremely well behaved. Annette, his wife, was always cheerful when she brought the children to school.

Duncan had a tattered trench coat wrapped around him to cover the pajamas that he wore. As Sherrie approached him, she became aware of the acrid odor of smoke that was clinging to him. His face was pale and drawn, and there was a cut above one eye that looked like it had bled profusely. Dried blood flecked his face.

"Duncan, are you sure you don't want me to clean up your face before you go to the hospital?" Tammy pleaded. "At least let me get you some of Bob's clothes to wear."

"Thank you, but no. I just want to get to the hospital. Can we leave right away?" To Sherrie, he seemed dazed.

"Certainly." She shot Tammy a questioning look that asked if Duncan was really all right. Tammy shrugged, looking helpless. "Come on, I'll take you to the hospital."

Duncan followed her out to the car. When he got in, he reached automatically for the seat belt and fastened it. Then he stared blankly straight ahead. With one hand, he kept smoothing the material of the trench coat over his knees in an agitated fashion.

Sherrie kept a close eye on him as she drove to the hospital. The only time he spoke was to give her directions when she was unsure of where to go. He was out of the car before she even turned it off. Sherrie bolted out of the car after him.

She followed him up to the pediatric ward, where he found his wife Annette. They held each other close for a long time, and Sherrie hung back in the shadows, afraid to disturb them. Finally, Duncan broke away and asked a few terse questions about Sylvia before bending over her bed to see for himself.

The little girl was sleeping. Her hands and arms were bandaged, and she was hooked up to an IV. Duncan brushed the damp hair off her forehead. Bending down, he gave her a light kiss. As he turned, he became suddenly aware of Sherrie.

"I'm sorry, I forgot to thank you for the ride." In the semidarkness, the shadows under his eyes and the dried blood on his face made him look hideous.

"There's no need to thank me," Sherrie replied shortly, feeling self-conscious. "I was happy to do it, but shouldn't you have that cut looked at while you're here?"

He nodded wearily. "Maybe I should."

"Go, Duncan," Annette insisted. "We'll be fine here. Sylvia is sleeping anyway. You'll be back in a minute."

Duncan gave his daughter one final tender look before pulling himself away to go back down to the emergency room. Annette rubbed her bare arms and turned to Sherrie.

"Thank you for bringing Duncan. How are the boys?"

"They're fine," Sherrie assured her. "They're sleeping at Tammy Merrill's house." She eyed the flimsy nightgown Annette was wearing. The hospital staff had given her a thin cotton robe to wear over her nightgown, but she looked cold. Sherrie silently pulled off the sweat shirt she'd thrown on over her turtleneck and handed it to Annette. "Here, take this. It will keep you warmer than that bathrobe."

Annette hesitated, as if she was afraid to take it. "Are you sure?"

"I'm sure. I wish I could offer you my pants too, but I'd look kind of ridiculous going home without them. I'll get some things together for you in the morning, though, so don't worry about not having anything to wear."

Annette blinked back tears as she pulled the sweat shirt on right over the bathrobe and hugged herself. "It's even warm," she managed, smiling through her tears. "Thank you. I don't know how we'll ever repay you . . ." Her voice trailed off into a whisper.

"Repay me? You don't have to repay me. I want to help you. Lots of people will want to help you. Let them. You'd help if it was someone else." She patted Annette's arm awkwardly. "Just let us help."

Sherrie dearly missed her sweat shirt as she drove home in the cold car. She could feel every frozen ridge of vinyl in the seat beneath her right through her thin jacket and shirt. But inside she glowed with the warmth of giving.

The next morning, after an hour and a half of sleep, she

dragged herself out of bed. She managed to tell Jack the whole story as she got breakfast together and made his lunch.

"Now I've got to find some things for them." She yawned. "I'm not even sure where to start."

"If I were you," Jack suggested, "I'd get the list of church members and just start calling to find out what people can bear to part with. But, before you do that, why don't you go through the stuff we still have packed and see if we've got anything they can use."

Sherrie's eyes lighted up in spite of her lack of sleep. "That sounds like a great idea."

Jack nodded and smiled slyly. "I know. I'm full of great ideas. I'll tell you what. I'll drop the boys off at school today so you can stay here. And I'll let Tammy know what you're doing and ask her to scare up that list and come over here. You can run your little campaign from here."

"You're smarter than I give you credit for," Sherrie joked.

An hour later, when Tammy came, Sherrie was searching frantically through boxes of things they'd brought from Tennessee but had never taken out because they didn't have room for any of it. She found an almost complete set of dishes, some Tupperware, two chairs, a lamp, and lots of clothes.

Tammy's face was gray, and there were dark circles under her eyes. "You're industrious," she remarked. "I wish I had your energy. Those poor kids were up at the crack of dawn crying for their mother. There wasn't anything I could do. This morning, Bob drove them to the hospital." She chuckled. "I guess Annette told them they had to be brave and go to school, or something like that, because they came back about a half-hour later and seemed pretty content. Bob says little Sylvia is going to be fine. The doctors don't even think she'll have any scars."

"That's wonderful," Sherrie exclaimed. "That's the best news I've heard all morning."

Between the two of them, they managed to get everything boxed and bagged up for the Grants. Tammy had brought a list of all the members, and she called each one in turn, asking what they thought they could donate for the Grants and arranging a pickup time.

By the time they were finished, they'd even found a place for the Grants to stay while their house was being rebuilt. At two o'clock, Tammy heaved herself to her feet and made for the door.

"I've got to go home and get a few minutes' sleep before I have to pick the kids up at school. I'll see you tomorrow, OK? Thanks for all your help." She gave Sherrie a hug, but it lacked her usual intensity.

As soon as the door closed behind her, Sherrie collapsed on the couch with one arm flung over her eyes. She was so exhausted that the room seemed to be spinning all around her. Within minutes, she was sound asleep.

CHAPTER
10

Sledding Social

When Sherrie padded down the stairs early one Friday morning, the week before Christmas, she was surprised to see how bright the house was. At first she thought it must be illumination from the remains of a full moon, until she peeked out the window and realized that the world was positively buried in snow.

Rubbing frost off the glass, she stared out in disbelief. She pressed her nose up against the pane, gently fogging it up. There had to be two feet of snow out there!

"Eight inches," Tammy corrected her when she arrived, somewhat late, to bring the boys to school. "Hardly anything, really, but I hear we're going to get dumped on tomorrow and again on Sunday. The weather forecasters are saying we should have eighteen or nineteen inches before we're through."

"It's days like this that I wish we had a hot-lunch program here," Don griped as he stomped through the door, trying to shake the clinging snow from his heavy boots.

"Why couldn't we?" Sherrie asked suddenly. "Tammy and I are always here. Why couldn't we make lunch for the kids? It wouldn't have to be anything fancy. Maybe just soup and a sandwich, but it would be nice to serve them something hot on days like today."

Don regarded her quizzically. "You would do that?"

"Sure, why not?" Sherrie returned quickly.

"Why not?" Tammy shrugged in agreement. "She's right. We're always here. We might just as well make ourselves useful."

"You're hired," Don replied promptly. "Do you think you could get something going by Monday?"

"We'll try," Sherrie promised.

"Maybe we should go check out the equipment before we get too hasty," Tammy suggested.

The kitchen, like the rest of the little church, was a mishmash of old and new. There were two ovens to accommodate all the dishes brought to potluck. One was an ancient relic with questionable wiring and broken knobs. The second was a relatively new model that one of the church members had donated.

Pots and dishes of all sizes filled plywood cupboards. Tammy informed her that the late Mrs. Hawley had painted and stenciled the cupboards herself. Sherrie admired the stenciling for a moment, then reached out to open the refrigerator door. She drew her hand back quickly with a yelp.

"Zapped?" Tammy asked nonchalantly. Sherrie nodded. "There's something wrong with it. It doesn't give you a shock every time you touch it, but I guess we've all gotten zapped once or twice. Not a pleasant feeling, is it?"

Sherrie decided the refrigerator would do without bothering to examine it further. Rummaging through the cupboards, she located several steel pots large enough to heat soup in.

"That's all we need, right?" she asked, turning to Tammy.

"Hmm? What's that? Yeah, that's all we need. What do you think about having a sledding social? I think I'm going to have one. We've got the perfect opportunity with all this snow, and I think the church could really use a social. What do you think?"

Sherrie shrugged. "I guess I'm more interested in spiritual get-togethers, but I don't have anything against a social. You're right about the snow. I doubt you'll get a better chance."

"I'm going to do it," Tammy declared, but Sherrie had the feeling that Tammy had decided long before she ever asked for her opinion. "We'll have it on Sunday at the Nasons' farm. I'm sure they'll agree to it. It'll be short notice, but I think we'll get quite a few people to come. I hope the Grants feel like coming."

"Me too. It'll do them some good to have fun. They've been through a lot in the past few weeks. Speaking of the Grants, are we going to take up a collection for them for Christmas?" Sherrie asked suddenly. "I've already gotten them a few things, but I think a collection would be a nice gesture."

"I think it's a great idea. Why don't we do it on Sabbath? But we'll have to keep it a secret."

On Sabbath, Sherrie passed a card and envelope around, watching it closely so the Grants wouldn't discover it. When Tammy made the announcement about the social, Sherrie could almost feel a surge of excitement ripple over the congregation. Maybe the church needed a social outlet even more than she realized. Scott and Caleb had to be told repeatedly not to talk about it until Sabbath was over, but even so, Sherrie was pretty sure they managed to whisper about it in their room after lunch.

"Do you think the social is a good idea?" Sherrie asked Jack that afternoon as he lay on the couch pretending that he wasn't about to slip off to dreamland. Sherrie sat rigidly in the most uncomfortable chair with a worn copy of *The Great Controversy*.

"I don't know. Guess so," Jack mumbled. "Don't see why not."

"I don't know." Sherrie shook her head. "I have a bad feeling about it."

The "feeling" continued to hover over her like an ominous blanket of gloom right up until they pulled into the Nasons' long driveway. Cars were already lined up on both sides of the drive, and by the looks of the snow, some of them were probably going to have to be pulled out. Their owners apparently didn't care, judging from the shrieks of delight coming from a nearby field, where brightly colored figures slid swiftly down a rather steep hill.

"Come on, come on." Scott hopped from one foot to the other in anticipation while Jack pulled some hastily purchased plastic sleds from the back of the car.

"Hold on," Jack said sharply. "Don't you want me to put this rope on your sled so you don't have to carry it?"

"OK," Scott agreed. "But hurry."

Caleb leaned against the side of the car and squinted purposefully out at the sliders, though it was impossible to identify anyone at that distance.

"I think I see the Merrills," he observed.

"You can't see anyone from here," Sherrie snapped, perfectly aware that he wasn't looking for the Merrills but the Peltons. As soon as Jack tied ropes on their sleds, the boys plunged through the snow, whooping and racing each other to the slope.

"Should we go to the house first?" Sherrie asked.

"I doubt anyone's there," Jack replied, waving a hand toward the hill. "I think they're all over there."

"Then you go there. I'm going to check and see if anyone's at the house." She left Jack standing beside the car and plowed her way ungracefully toward the big white farmhouse. It crossed her mind to wonder why a *Listen* literature evangelist had such a big, rambling old house, but she didn't take any time to dwell on it.

She gripped the handrail carefully as she made her way up the stairs. The door suddenly flew open, and Caren Nason bolted through it, her arms full of scarves, hats, and mittens. She stopped short when she saw Sherrie.

"Oh, hi. Did you need to use the bathroom?"

"Uh, yes, yes, I do," Sherrie said.

"It's the first door on the left as you head down the hall. I don't want to go back in," she explained. "I already got heated up finding these things for some of the kids, but you go ahead in. Just don't pay any attention to the mess."

Sherrie turned to watch her make her way toward the screaming, sliding figures; then she went inside the house. Piles of hot-chocolate packets were mounded on the countertop beside a jumble of mugs. Next to them were boxes of doughnuts and cookies.

Sherrie walked over to the counter and stood staring at it in disbelief. *Certainly*, she thought, *people weren't actually going to put that junk in their bodies.* Then she stopped herself. Of course they were. But something had to be done about it.

What about our Adventist health message? What about temperance? she asked herself on the way to the bathroom. *What about caffeine?* she thought triumphantly. It was obvious that one of the very next topics at her women's prayer breakfast should be on the health message.

And in addition to that, she determined, the pastor must be spoken to. He had to be told what was going on. It was very sad that his wife had passed away, but while he was busy grieving, Satan had waltzed into the church carrying a mug of hot chocolate and eating a doughnut.

"Oh, come on Caleb." Trista's voice floated past the closed bathroom door and froze Sherrie's hand as she reached toward the faucet to turn on the water.

"But what if my mother's in here?" Caleb's voice quivered

nervously. "I didn't see her out with the others."

"If she was here, we'd see her. Wouldn't we?" Trista asked. "Be logical. So, now that we're alone, tell me how you liked it."

"It was all right. Good, actually. Yeah, I liked it."

Sherrie sat down on the edge of the bathtub, shaking all over. What were they talking about?

"Want another one? Here, I brought you this one. You can keep it; I've got another copy."

What was it? A book? She wished desperately that she'd taken the time to check out Caleb's notebook to see if he'd written anything about "it."

"Thanks. Here's the other one you lent me last time."

"Do you want a drink?"

"Of what?" Caleb sounded scared.

"Water, silly. What else?"

"I thought you might mean, that is, I thought . . ."

"You mean beer?" Trista coaxed. "You can say it. It's not a dirty word." She sighed. "No, but I wish I had one right now. I think I'll have a smoke before we get back."

"In here?"

"Of course not. I don't mind getting in trouble, but I'm not stupid. I'll go outside on the steps or out in our car if I have to."

"You mean your parents really don't mind that you smoke?" There was awe in Caleb's voice. Sherrie recognized it, and it scared her.

"Nope. My dad used to smoke before he joined the church. I think he still sneaks one now and then. I'm not sure, but sometimes it seems like I go through a pack pretty quick."

"I wish my parents let me do what I wanted."

"Just do it," Trista advised sagely. "That's what I'd do. My parents can't make me do anything, so they leave me alone. What are they going to do to punish you? Kill you? I think not. Come on. I want to smoke this before anyone else decides to come in to get warm. Would you like one?"

"Nah," Caleb replied hesitantly. "No," he repeated, a little firmer.

"Ah, well, your loss. Come on." The door closed heavily behind them. Sherrie continued to sit on the edge of the bathtub, even though she was starting to lose the feeling in her legs.

Part of her cheered Caleb's decision not to join Trista for a cigarette, but it was a very small part of her. The larger part was more worried about his tentative stand. If he was that loosely grounded, he could be convinced to actually try smoking sooner or later.

She stood up slowly and stretched. Surely Trista couldn't be finished with her cigarette yet, but Sherrie was dying to get out of the bathroom to find Jack. She leaned over the tub to the window and pushed back the curtains cautiously. Trista was leaning against the iron railing, laughing as she took a drag on her cigarette. Caleb was watching her, and Sherrie could read envy and approval in his eyes.

She sat back down on the edge of the tub and waited another ten minutes before checking again. The two were gone. She could see them racing toward the slope where everyone else was sledding.

Relieved, she passed through the kitchen, scowling at the offending articles of food, and pushed open the front door. Her mind raced ahead as she trudged through the deep snow, making her way toward the group of people gathered on the hill.

Jack was standing at the top about to go down again with Scott. His cheeks were flushed as he laughed happily. Sherrie was struck by how carefree he looked.

"Jack?" He turned and saw her.

"Come on, Sher! Scott, push over and let your mother go down this time. Get in, Sherrie. I'll give you the ride of your life."

"Jack, I have to talk . . ."

"We'll talk later. Get in." He grabbed her arm and propelled her onto the sled. Before she knew it, Scott gave them a push, and the sled was barreling down the hill. The icy air caught her breath and ripped away the scream that tried to slip past her frozen lips. Finally, they slid to a stop at the bottom. Jack rolled off the sled, laughing, and pelted a snowball at her.

"Wasn't that fun? Come on, we'll do it again."

Sherrie stood up and raced after him as he started back up the hill. "Jack, I have to talk to you about Caleb. He was with Trista. She offered him a cigarette, but he refused. But not adamantly."

Jack stopped and turned around, suddenly sober. "He refused? Well, that's good."

"But I'm worried about him. She gave him something. I don't know what it was, but if it came from her, it can't be any good."

Jack nodded slowly. "I'll make him give it to me."

"No." Sherrie caught his sleeve. "No, don't do that. I'm sure I can find out what it is without his knowing. I think we'll learn more that way. Don't force him, or he'll close up, and we won't find out any more."

"All right," Jack agreed reluctantly. "But I don't want this to continue, so you'd better find out right away."

"I will," Sherrie promised. She followed him back up the hill, but declined going down again. "I'll just watch," she told him.

He went down again with Scott, but by the look on his face, she could tell that most of the fun had gone out of it for him. She looked around cautiously and saw Caleb and Trista with the Merrill kids. They were pretty safe there.

Then she saw Lauren. She looked twice to be certain. It was impossible really. Could this be the same woman whom she'd considered reformed in matters of dress? Tight black ski pants clung to her legs, following every curve as if they'd been custom made. A puffy scarlet jacket hugged her waist tightly, enhancing rather than concealing the immodest leggings.

"She might as well be half-naked," Sherrie muttered to herself. "I can't believe anyone would go out in public looking like that." She spent the next half-hour waiting for Jack to get sick of sledding so they could go home. She was quite certain she would have no trouble talking him out of hot chocolate, doughnuts, and cookies.

CHAPTER
11

The Warning

Christmas flew by in a rush of activity. Although they didn't exchange presents as a family, Sherrie was still busy packing things for the mission in town and preparing dishes for the local soup kitchen. Jack's practice picked up with the onset of flu season, and Sherrie was left coping with the preparations for Christmas by herself.

The boys, who had never been completely happy with the absence of presents beneath the tree, and in recent years the absence of a tree at all, were no help to her. Even Scott, who was normally cooperative no matter what the circumstances, chose that particular time to start getting sloppy in his chores and take forever to do anything she asked of him.

Christmas Day, they banded together with forced cheerfulness and got ready to spend the afternoon serving Christmas dinner at the mission. Jack was called out just before they were supposed to leave, so Sherrie was forced to endure the sullen silence of the boys by herself. A lecture on the importance of giving and the season of joy on the drive over didn't improve the boys' attitude at all. Despite the fact that she had fun at the mission, by the time Sherrie got home, she had a raging headache and went straight to bed.

Later that week, she was annoyed to discover that Caleb had again moved his journal. She'd been patient, biding her time and waiting for an opportunity. On Thursday afternoon, when Tammy asked if the boys could ride home with her and go sledding with her kids, Sherrie readily agreed. It would give her ample opportunity to read Caleb's journal and hopefully discover what had been going on between him and Trista.

As she searched his room, her frustration mounted. It was improbable that he suspected her of reading it. So why had it been moved again? She searched in all the likely places and even a few unlikely ones but turned up nothing except a few dust bunnies. She made a mental note to have the boys clean their room thoroughly.

Absently, she picked up Caleb's Walkman off the floor and set it down on his desk. As she did so, she realized that he might notice it had been moved. Quickly, she placed it back on the floor. She made another quick and fruitless search before deciding that she'd just have to bide her time.

Reluctantly, she went back downstairs to cook supper. As she stirred the soup, her mind kept returning to Caleb's room, wondering if there was any place she might have overlooked. Finally, she decided that it was no use. The missing notebook was going to bother her until she got her hands on it.

It irritated her all the next day, but she had no opportunity to search for it. She spent considerable time wondering if perhaps Caleb had taken to carrying it around with him, but she saw no evidence to support that theory. It was as if the yellow notebook had simply vanished.

Sabbath morning, when it had still failed to turn up, she brooded about it all the way to church. Staring sullenly out the window at the falling snow, she missed Jack's comment and had to ask him to repeat it.

"I said, you're awfully quiet this morning," he chided. "Is your tongue frostbitten?"

Sherrie gave him an icy glare but didn't reply. Since he thought it was silly to read Caleb's journal, she'd stopped telling him anything she read in it. If it was so silly, then he didn't need to know, she reasoned irritably.

Or maybe it's because I'm ashamed of reading it. The thought popped into her head so suddenly that she could feel her heart speed up and a flush of guilt creep up her face. *That's not it at all*, she told herself sternly. *It's for his own good and not as if I were just curious about what he was doing.*

As soon as the car pulled to a stop, she jumped out and stalked into the church, not waiting for Jack and the boys.

"What's wrong with Mom?" she heard Scott ask Jack. But she

was out of earshot when he replied. Charging around the corner, she almost ran into Lauren Pelton.

"Oops, sorry," Lauren exclaimed, reaching one hand out to the wall to steady herself. She smiled shyly when she realized it was Sherrie. "Hi, guess I'm taking up the middle of the road here."

"No, it was completely my . . ." Sherrie began, then faltered, her eyes traveling incredulously from Lauren's head to her heels. She'd done it again. She was wearing a royal blue dress that clung to her body like a surgeon's glove and ended abruptly way above her knee. ". . . fault," she finished, barely able to get the word out.

"Excuse me," she mumbled as she brushed past Lauren. Without even taking her coat off, she hurried quickly to the bathroom and barricaded herself in one of the stalls.

She stood there for a long time, trembling. *What could Lauren be thinking of? Didn't she understand plain English? I thought I made it clear to her about dressing modestly. Why aren't I getting through to her?* Sherrie asked herself over and over.

She pulled her gloves off and folded them neatly before putting them in her pocket. *I've been too vague,* she finally decided. *I've got to go to her and tell her plainly. As head deaconess it's now my place and my responsibility. I won't just be acting for personal reasons but for the good of the entire church, but more importantly for her own salvation. I'm going to talk to her after church.*

After having settled on a plan of action, she calmly hung her coat up in the coat rack and took her place upstairs for Sabbath School.

"I couldn't find any big cans of green beans for the hot lunch menu," Tammy hissed in Sherrie's ear as she slid into the pew beside her. "I got corn instead. Is that all right?"

"I guess it will have to be," Sherrie said. "Everything will be the same color, though. But I guess we're allowed to make a few mistakes."

Tammy wrung her purse strap in her hands. "I'm so nervous," she confessed.

"Why? Are you getting up front?" Tammy had told her how much she dreaded speaking in public.

"Not me," Tammy shuddered. "Anne. She's singing for special music with Lori Wagner."

Sherrie arched her eyebrows. "Really? I didn't know Anne sang."

"Oh, yes," Tammy gushed. "She's got a beautiful voice. She goes around the house singing all the time. This will be the first time she sings in public, though. I don't know if she's nervous, but I am."

"She'll do fine," Sherrie assured her.

"Hope so," Tammy said. "Say a little prayer for her, will you?"

"I will," Sherrie promised. She was tempted to tell Tammy about her decision to speak to Lauren, then decided against it. It would be better to approach Lauren first before she said anything about it.

Tammy slipped out of the pew and went back to the door to greet some newcomers. Sherrie allowed herself a little smile. It was hard to picture outgoing, outspoken, talkative Anne Merrill being nervous about singing in public.

Just before special music was announced, she remembered her promise and sent up a quick prayer for the girls. They didn't look nervous as they made their way to the front. Sherrie looked around for the pianist, but no one came forward. She couldn't believe they were going to sing without accompaniment. They really *were* brave.

Then she noticed something that had escaped her attention before. On the pulpit was a large black box. Lori produced a cassette tape and inserted it. She pushed a button, and the music began. It was twangy, country-style music with a slow beat.

She could see Anne's lips move as she counted out the rhythm. She tore her eyes from them for a moment to look at Jack. Her own astonishment and disapproval was mirrored in his eyes. She couldn't believe the church was going to allow this type of singing for special music!

The girls faltered a little as they began singing, but when they realized they'd come in on the right beat, their voices became stronger. Sherrie was surprised that the song was a well-known hymn . . . and one of her favorites, set to a contemporary country arrangement. She sat rigidly in the pew, her lips pursed tightly together, unable to believe she was being forced to endure the butchering of such a beautiful song.

This isn't right, she told herself. *There's no reason why the pianist couldn't have accompanied them. This type of music has no place in the house of God*, she hissed under her breath. *Especially during the worship service.* But, as she looked around, she realized that she and Jack must be the only two who objected to the style.

The people around her, even the pastor on the platform, seemed to be enjoying it. When Anne and Lori finished, they smiled exuberantly and returned to their seats amid a chorus of Amens.

That was awful. It was wrong, thought Sherrie. In college, she had written a term paper on sacred music. Because of what she'd discovered during her research, she had very strong feelings about what type of music was appropriate during the worship service.

Sherrie resolved to talk about the matter later with Jack. Together, they should be able to figure out a way to tactfully inform the church about the importance of sacred music.

After the service, she got out of the pew with a headache, but firmly resolved that she needed to talk to Lauren Pelton. As she approached the pew where Lauren sat, she was surprised that she felt a little hesitant.

"Lauren? Could I speak to you for a couple of minutes?"

Lauren looked up, startled. "Me? I guess, sure. Mark, would you bring this out to the car for me? I'll be out in a few minutes." She handed a bag to her husband and turned to Sherrie.

"Not in here," Sherrie protested. "Why don't we find someplace where we can talk in private." As Lauren followed her meekly, a wave of guilt swept over Sherrie. She felt like an executioner leading a lamb to the slaughter.

Some lamb, she said to herself. Anyway, it was better to have a clean kill. The old man would die, and a new one would take his place. Lauren would see that her manner of dress wasn't befitting a Christian woman and mend her ways. In the end, Sherrie was sure that Lauren would be grateful. At present, though, she was likely to feel somewhat affronted. That thought was in her mind when she closed the door of a vacant room behind Lauren and turned to face her.

She clasped her hands nervously. "Lauren, there's something that I feel it's my responsibility to tell you, not only as a Christian sister, but as the head deaconess. I had hoped that my talk at the women's meeting would benefit you, that you would come to realize what it means to dress modestly as a Christian woman should. I'm afraid that it failed to have the effect I intended." There, that was tactful.

Lauren seemed puzzled. "What do you mean?"

"Well, just that it doesn't seem to have done any good. I mean, your dress hasn't changed in the least."

"My dress?" Lauren looked down at her dress. "It's new. I haven't even worn it here before."

"Not that particular dress, I mean, yes, that dress, all your dresses, that *style* of dress. Don't you see? It's not modest. Your dresses and skirts all cling to your body, and the length is much too short. As Christians, we're not to draw attention to ourselves by the way we dress," Sherrie explained. "Now, I'm sure someone must have explained this to you when you came into the church and you've just forgotten it, but it can't continue. Think of the kind of witness you present. And what do you suppose men think when they see you dressed seductively?"

Lauren's eyes filled with tears as she began to feel the full import of Sherrie's words. "I don't know," she stammered. "I never think of it. I dress the way I do because it's me, it's what I like."

"But you have to consider the bigger picture," Sherrie insisted. "We're instructed to do nothing that would offend a fellow believer. I can tell you for a certainty that the way you dress offends me and my husband and frankly, I worry about what my boys think when they see you."

"What do you mean 'what they think'?" Lauren cried, red spots appearing on her white cheeks. "They don't think anything about my clothes."

"Come now," Sherrie said shortly, irritation lacing her voice. "Let's not kid each other. They're boys, growing boys; they don't have the ability or the desire to control their thoughts the way grown men do. Even some men have a problem keeping their thoughts pure. Today's society being the way it is, we, as Christian women, have even a greater responsibility to help our Christian brothers instead of giving them another temptation to overcome."

"Are you suggesting that I dress this way to tempt men?" Lauren demanded hotly.

"I am saying," Sherrie said firmly, "that the way you dress will tempt men, whether or not that is what you intend."

"Well, it's not what I intend," Lauren snapped.

"Good." Sherrie almost smiled in relief. "Then you're saying that you'll dress more modestly in the future?"

"I'm not sure I know how," Lauren spat sarcastically. "Do you have a chart on how loose or long clothes have to be before they're considered modest? Or should I just take my cue from you and wear everything so baggy no one can see my figure at all?"

Sherrie sighed. "You're upset. I know it's not easy to accept a criticism, but I'm telling you this because I don't want to see you lost. I also don't want to see others lost through your influence, unintentional though it may be. And I love you enough to confront you about it."

"Love me?" Lauren echoed. "You love me? How can you say that after all the things you just said to me?"

"Look, you're upset, and understandably so. Like I said, it's not easy to change, but you'll see that it's worth it. Heaven is worth any price. Why don't you go home and think over what I've said. I know that once you've cooled off, you'll be grateful that I've brought this matter to your attention. OK?"

Lauren shrugged into the coat she'd been carrying and angrily pulled on her gloves. "I'll go home, all right, and I can promise you I'll think about what you've said. In fact, I can assure you it'll be the only thing I'll think about."

She spun on a spike heel and pushed roughly through the door, leaving Sherrie staring after her.

"Well, I . . . ," Sherrie murmured. That sure hadn't gone well. She bit her lip nervously. Surely Lauren would have to admit that she spoke the truth after she'd calmed down. Then she'd make the proper decisions about what to wear in the future.

"I hope she's got *something* in her wardrobe that can be worn to church," Sherrie said under her breath as she went to retrieve her own coat. "It may be hard for her to find clothes at first."

Jack and the boys were waiting in the car when she finally made her way though the snow to join them. Jack didn't ask her what had kept her, and she didn't offer any information, aware that two sets of ears in the back seat were dying to know.

Jack brought up the issue of the "canned" music at dinner. Caleb's fork stopped halfway to his mouth. He seemed surprised that they didn't approve of the special music.

"What was wrong with it?" he asked.

"Wrong? Everything," Jack replied. "It was far from reverent. If they wanted to sing that hymn, why couldn't the pianist play it, and they could sing it the way it's written in the hymnal? That music was far too upbeat to be played in church during worship service."

"I liked it," Caleb ventured. Jack shot him a withering glance but passed over his remark.

"After dinner, Jack, let's sit down and draw up a sheet of guidelines for music," Sherrie suggested. "We can pass it out at church next Sabbath. And let's list dress guidelines on it too. Maybe we can settle some of these problems before they get out of hand."

Sherrie stared down at her plate as she spoke, moving peas around idly with her fork, and missed Caleb's sudden frown. If he suspected whom she was referring to, he didn't mention it. Had she witnessed his expression, she would have been certain there would be an entry about his suspicions in the elusive journal.

As soon as the table was cleared, she sat down with Jack and helped to draft the guidelines sheet. As Jack read it back to her out loud, she felt a flush of excitement. It was going to be hard to wait the following week before passing it out.

CHAPTER

12

Guidelines

Tammy called three times the next day to ask Sherrie questions about the hot-lunch menu they were serving on Monday. To Sherrie, running the hot-lunch program had seemed like a simple project, but Tammy made it out to be a problem of monstrous proportions.

"Are you sure we've got a pot big enough to cook all that corn?" Tammy was asking. Sherrie could hear her pen tapping against her teeth on the other end.

"I'm positive," Sherrie assured her.

"But tofu? Are you sure the kids will eat it? Just a minute." Tammy made no attempt to cover the phone when she shrieked to the kids. "Brian, leave the dog alone. I said stop. No, you can't go with Dave. Why? Because he's older. I don't have time for this right now, Brian. Go talk to your father. I'm sorry; what was I saying?" she screamed, forgetting to lower her voice.

Sherrie winced and held the phone out from her ear. "You were asking me about the tofu, and, yes, the kids will love it the way I make it. Don't worry."

"Well," Tammy sounded skeptical. "I guess it won't hurt to give it a try," she finally conceded. "Hey, did you hear about what happened to Trista Pelton? Get this; she got caught smoking marijuana at school and was suspended for a week."

Sherrie caught her breath. "Marijuana? Are you sure? That's, that's . . . awful. I'm sure glad I don't have to worry about anything like that with Caleb and Scott." Sherrie's thoughts flew immediately to Caleb. Surely he would never . . . no, of course not. Never.

"What did her . . . parents say?" Sherrie asked.

"Oh, you know, not much. Trista denied it, of course. I really think they believe her. Anyway, I'm sure they want to. Poor Lauren and Mark, as if they didn't have enough to worry about right now."

"What do you mean?" Sherrie's knuckles whitened as she gripped the phone harder. Surely Tammy hadn't heard yet about her conversation with Lauren. She couldn't possibly have that many connections, although it did seem as if she knew things almost before they happened.

"Didn't you hear?" Tammy's voice rose a few decibels in surprise. "Mark's office is making some severe cutbacks, and they're afraid he might get laid off. Lauren will still have her job, but hairstyling doesn't pay that much. They don't know what they'll do. They're praying that he'll get to keep his job, or, if worse comes to worse, that he'll be able to transfer to another job either in that office or somewhere else. But they really don't want to have to move. I don't blame them. Can you imagine living anywhere but Maine?" Her shrill laughter cut through the phone lines. "That's silly, of course you can. Am I dense!"

Sherrie winced. "I'm really sorry to hear about Lauren and Mark. That's really too bad. I'll keep them in prayer."

"Good, great, they'll be glad to hear that. Look, I've got to let you go before my kids rip each other apart." The volume of noise in the background suddenly rose as a scream pierced the air. "I'll talk to you tomorrow. 'Bye."

Sherrie slowly hung up the phone, her thoughts on the Peltons. They certainly did seem to be facing more than their share of problems.

"If they'd only clean up their act," Sherrie mused, "the Holy Spirit would give them the power to overcome their problems. It should seem obvious to them that they're doing something wrong."

"Mom, can I go for a walk?" Caleb's voice startled her and she jumped.

"Walk?" Sherrie scowled. She cast a quick eye toward the window. The sky was gray and sullen, threatening snow at any time. "Where are you going to walk? On the road?"

"Yeah, up the road. I just want to get out and get some exercise." Caleb's eyes avoided Sherrie's.

"Where up the road?" Sherrie probed.

"Just up the road," Caleb insisted.

"Did you ask your father?"

"No, he's out in the garage."

"Well, go ask him, and if he says Yes, then I guess you can go, but don't be gone longer than an hour. Are you taking Scott with you?" Something about Caleb's request didn't seem quite right, but she couldn't put her finger on it.

"No, he's cleaning his half of the room. Mine's all done."

"All right, go." Sherrie watched his retreating back and wondered if his sudden interest in walking was purely innocent. Finally, she shrugged and returned to the bread she'd been making before Tammy's call had interrupted her.

Monday, Sherrie arrived at school in the middle of an uproar. Don was talking to two of the younger boys in the corner, and a group were clustered around Sara, all talking at once. Sara held up her hands in surrender.

"Look," she bellowed, trying to be heard, "I want you all to go to your seats right now, and we'll discuss this in a mature fashion."

As the kids slunk to their seats, they cast worried glances at the two boys sequestered with Don. Sherrie leaned against the wall in the corner and watched. Sara paced in front of the class, her hands on her hips. She chewed her lip nervously.

"Now, one at a time. Raise your hands, please, if you want to speak." She pointed to Brian Merrill. "Yes, Brian?"

"Mrs. Wagner, Jimmy didn't take the money. I know he didn't."

"How do you know, Brian?"

Brian's face was flushed. "I just know. He wouldn't do something like that."

"We need something more than your instinct to go on in this case, Brian. Did anyone see Jimmy take the money out of Mr. Wagner's desk? Jennifer?"

A little third-grader in the corner glanced around shyly. "I didn't see him take the money," she offered.

Sara smiled faintly. "Thank you, Jennifer, but I asked if anyone actually *saw* Jimmy take the money." The kids darted quick glances around the room, waiting for someone to raise their hand, but none went up. "All right. Now, I know that some of you still have to take off your wet things and hang up your book bags. Why don't you do that right now. Quietly," she warned. "Then return to your seats and sit there until Mr. Wagner is finished."

Several kids got up and made their way to the coat racks. Sara sat down at Don's desk and leaned her chin wearily in her hands. Sherrie approached her hesitantly.

"What happened?" she asked.

Sara sighed heavily and motioned toward Don and the two boys. "Ben claims that Jimmy took some book-club money from Don's desk when we were out getting some things in the car. Of course, Jimmy denies it. Don's trying to get it straightened out right now."

"Do you think he really did it?" Sherrie asked.

Sara's eyes narrowed. "I didn't see him do it, so I have no opinion," she replied curtly. "I don't think it's a good idea to speculate about something you didn't witness."

The little party in the corner broke up. The boys returned to their seats. Sherrie guessed the one with the red eyes must be Jimmy. Don walked over and stood near the desk.

"Well? What did you find out?" Sara stared up at him expectantly. *Hopefully*, Sherrie thought.

Don shook his head. "Nothing. Jimmy insists that he didn't take the money. Ben claims that he didn't actually *see* Jimmy take the money but that Jimmy was lingering around the desk while we were outside, and he says he saw him take something out of the desk."

"Did Jimmy admit to taking anything out of the desk?"

"He says he didn't take anything, that he was just sharpening his pencil."

Sara shrugged broadly. "The money *is* gone. Someone had to take it. Do you want to question the rest of the kids?"

"No," Don replied slowly. "But I think I'd better talk to them about stealing and the importance of telling the truth."

"Don't you think you'll be setting a bad example if you don't punish anyone?" Sherrie asked, forgetting that they weren't talking to her.

Don looked up, seeming to be startled to see her there. "How can I punish anyone when I don't know who the culprit is?"

"Someone in this room obviously took the money," Sherrie pointed out. "If that person won't confess, then tell them you'll punish all of them. If the guilty person confesses, you can punish him or her. If not, then punish them all. At least that way, the guilty person suffers in any case."

Don shook his head. "We don't use that method in this classroom. I want to encourage the kids to be honest and mature. I can't do that by arbitrarily punishing the lot of them for something one person did. If the child who took the money doesn't confess, he or she'll suffer from a guilt that will probably be worse than anything I could punish him or her with anyway."

"But what's to prevent the other kids from doing the same thing, since they won't be punished either unless they get caught?" Sherrie hedged.

"Their conscience, I hope," Don replied.

"I still think you're encouraging them to get away with as much as possible as long as they don't get caught," Sherrie insisted. When she received no reply, she turned reluctantly and made her way downstairs to the copy machine. She was standing there running off copies of the dress-and-music-guidelines sheet when Tammy came in to see what she was doing.

The last copy had just fallen onto the growing stack as Tammy walked in. Sherrie scooped the pile up and deposited it into a folder before Tammy could see any of it. There was no sense letting word of it leak out before Sabbath.

"What are you doing?" Tammy asked curiously.

"Just running off some info sheets to pass out on Sabbath," Sherrie replied nonchalantly.

"Oh. Could you come out here and check this tofu? It looks kind of funny to me."

"Sure." Sherrie slipped the folder into her carrying case and followed Tammy out to the kitchen. She checked the tofu and assured Tammy that it always looked like that.

"I heard there was quite a commotion here this morning," Tammy remarked, opening the big cans of corn and dumping them into a huge pot. "It figures I'd pick this morning to let Bob drop off the kids. Then I had to wait until the load in the dryer finished. It isn't safe to leave it alone."

Sherrie quickly filled her in on the details as she prepared the tofu for the kids' lunches. Tammy shook her head ruefully throughout the story.

"I don't know," she muttered. "I tend to agree with you. *Some-*

thing ought to be done. I don't know about punishing the whole lot of them, though. Still . . ."

They debated the topic for the rest of the day but came to no conclusions of their own. From what Sherrie could make out, no one had come forward to surrender the missing money by the end of the day, and the whole school went home that night upset, wondering just who was responsible for stealing the teacher's money.

The rest of the week was filled with tension at the school, and Sherrie was glad when it was Sabbath again. During the week, she had perfected the talk for personal ministries time, when she planned to present the guidelines sheet she and Jack had drawn up. Now, as she waited in the pastor's study to give it, she found that she was nervous.

When she walked out onto the platform, it seemed like every able-bodied member was sitting in the sanctuary, eagerly waiting for her to speak. She briefly recapped the speech she'd given at the first women's meeting and touched on the elements of sacred music before tying them together in the conclusion. Then she asked for two deacons to pass out the guidelines.

After a relieved gulp of air, she made her way back to the pastor's study. She wanted desperately to peek out into the congregation to see their reaction but couldn't bring herself to open the door a crack and look out. There would be time later to see what people thought of her speech and the guidelines, she thought.

But, when Jack was paged just before the end of service for an emergency with one of his patients, Sherrie was forced to leave before she knew what an impact her speech had had. Still, everything they'd written was biblically sound. There was no question about that. So, if people believed the Bible, they had to agree with the guidelines. To Sherrie, it was that simple.

She was surprised the next day to get a call from Tammy, who seemed upset about something. After a few minutes of polite chitchat, Tammy launched herself into the reason for her call.

"You know that sheet you passed out yesterday at church?" Tammy asked. She plunged on without waiting for a response. "This is kind of difficult, but, uh, did you have Anne in mind for the part about singing to canned music?"

The pause while Sherrie collected her scattered wits was long and uncomfortable. "Why, no, it was general. They were general principles. We didn't have anyone particularly in mind for any of them. We just thought it would be a good idea to list a few guidelines to help those who may not be certain in some areas.

"The part on music," she continued, "comes from a study I did on sacred music during college. I certainly didn't mean to target anyone, but it seems to me that there needs to be some specific guidelines."

"I'm glad, for Anne's sake. She bawled her head off all evening, thinking you were referring to the song she sang with Lori Wagner."

"No, no," Sherrie assured her. "I just assumed that no one had ever set any type of guides to determine what style of music is sacred and what isn't. We can't be too careful, you know. Especially during our worship services."

"I know what you mean. We don't want any of that Christian rock in church," Tammy agreed. "I guess I can see your point, though I'm not sure I understand about the canned music. I just wish Anne hadn't taken it so hard."

"I'm sorry if she thought I was pointing a finger at her," Sherrie offered. "Please tell her that I apologize if it seemed like I was."

"She'll be relieved to hear it," Tammy gushed. "I'll certainly tell her. Thanks, Sherrie. I'll talk to you later."

Sherrie hung up the phone and sank into a chair at the kitchen table. She wondered grimly what everyone else thought of the guidelines and wished she'd asked Tammy if she'd heard anything.

"Ah, well," she muttered to herself. "I'll ask her tomorrow. I'm sure she'll have heard something."

CHAPTER
13

Caught!

Sherrie had no opportunity to ask Tammy anything about the guidelines sheet. She battled fiercely with a cold for a week before finally succumbing to it. Feeling miserable, she lay on the couch Friday morning as Jack bumbled around in the kitchen, trying to find something he and the boys could eat for breakfast. She was too sick to care if she ever ate again.

Before he left, Jack popped a thermometer into her mouth.

"What hurts?" he asked, slipping the thermometer out and squinting at it with a practiced eye.

"Everything," Sherrie moaned. "I'm achy and my throat hurts and my head feels like it's going to blow up."

"Congratulations, you're the proud owner of a temperature." Jack shook the thermometer down. "I don't want you to get off this couch today. Here, take these."

Sherrie looked skeptically at the little white tablets he handed her with a glass of water. "What are they?"

"Vitamin C. There are more on the counter. I want you to take some with your lunch, providing you can eat. Drink plenty of liquids, and don't move off this couch until I get back," Jack instructed. "OK?"

He waited until Sherrie nodded reluctantly before giving her a quick peck on the forehead. "All right. I'll drop the boys off at school. Don't worry about a thing."

Scott sidled up to the couch before he left. "How are you, Mom?" The sight of Sherrie, stretched out under the leveling hand of sickness, seemed to strike him with a mixture of awe and fear.

"I'll be fine," Sherrie assured him. The light coming in the window behind him hurt her eyes, so she shut them. Scott's voice floated disembodied toward her.

"Want me to get you some juice before I leave?"

"Sure, Scott." She listened to his footsteps head eagerly for the kitchen, heard him open the refrigerator and pour the juice. The footsteps seemed to pound in her head as he came back and set the glass down with what sounded like a horrendous crash on the end table by the sofa. "Thanks, honey. Have a nice day at school. Where's Caleb?"

"He went out to the car with Dad already."

"OK. You better get going. Don't make your father wait for you. He's got to get to work too."

She sank back onto the couch and listened to him go out the door. Her head throbbed. Sunlight from outside seeped in under the curtains and beat against her eyes. Finally, she pulled the blanket up over her eyes and drifted off into a fitful sleep.

It was over a week before she was back to her old self. She felt as though she'd been out of touch with the rest of the world for months instead of days when she finally returned to school and the hot-lunch program late the next week.

Tammy was quick to tell her that they still hadn't found the culprit in the theft of the teacher's money. She also learned that the women's breakfast had been well attended and the speaker, a child-care professional, had been fantastic. Apparently, Tammy had heard very little talk about the guidelines sheet Sherrie had passed out. Sherrie tried to hide her disappointment at this news.

"You're still coming to the health fair on Sunday, aren't you?" Tammy asked, as if it had suddenly occurred to her that Sherrie might not come after all.

"Of course," Sherrie replied. "Do you still want me to bring vegetarian meatballs and cashew cheese?"

"That'll be great. I'm kind of curious to try that cheese stuff myself. You'll be able to stay and help, won't you?"

Sherrie nodded. "We'll all be there to help out. That will give you four extra sets of hands."

"Good." Tammy sighed with relief. "I'm getting stressed out planning everything. I'm just sure I'll forget something."

Sunday morning dawned bright and clear with just a hint of

spring in the air. When Sherrie went outside for an armload of wood, she heard a bird singing in the bare branches of a nearby tree. It was the first she'd heard since the previous fall. Before Jack and the boys were up, she made the "meatballs" and "cheese," and she half suspected that it was the smell that woke them.

After breakfast, Jack and Scott disappeared upstairs. Caleb wandered into the kitchen and watched her carefully spoon the "cheese" into a plastic tub.

"What's that for?" he asked curiously.

"The health fair we're going to today. You didn't forget, did you?"

"Aw, do we have to go to the food thing with you?" Caleb whined. Sherrie didn't even pause from packing the food into a cardboard box to look up at him.

"Yes, you have to go. Now, go get ready and stop complaining about it."

"But it'll ruin my whole Sunday," Caleb moaned.

"Yes, you do so much on Sunday," Sherrie replied sarcastically.

Caleb didn't answer but stomped up the stairs to get changed. Taking a wet cloth, Sherrie cleaned off the counters and put the dishes away. Then she settled her Crock-Pot gently into the box next to the tub of cashew cheese and filled in the cracks with towels to cushion everything.

"Anything I can do to help?" Jack asked, stopping to peer over her shoulder and sniff appreciatively.

"Yes, you can carry this out to the car for me," Sherrie replied gratefully. "I've got to locate that health literature I promised Tammy. Then I'll be ready to go."

"What about the boys?" Jack hefted the box and headed toward the garage.

"I'll get them going," Sherrie promised. She yanked the closet door open and searched frantically for the box of magazines she had stored there. She located it way in the back and had to move several things before she could finally pull it out in the open. The magazines dealing with health were all on top, bound with string. She grabbed them and hurriedly shoved the box back into the closet.

"Move it, boys," she hollered up the stairs as she grabbed her coat. "If you're not down here in two seconds, we're leaving without you." She had a sneaking suspicion that was precisely what they were hoping for.

Scott bounded down the stairs. "Can I help take blood pressures?" he asked.

"Sure," Sherrie muttered.

"Yes!" He hopped around in a little victory dance.

"You can write them down for me," Sherrie finished.

Scott stopped midhop. "Aw, can't I take them? I know how."

"Caleb!" Sherrie yelled. "No," she told Scott absently. "An adult has to do it."

"Then can I pass out samples of food?" he persisted.

"We'll see," Sherrie promised. She bounded up the stairs two at a time and hustled down the hall. When she wrenched the boys' door open, she was surprised to see Caleb just barely changing his clothes. Shirts and pants littered the floor around his bed.

"Ma!" he shrieked, struggling into his shirt. "I'm getting dressed!"

"I can see that," Sherrie said. "The rest of us are leaving. We'll deal with your punishment when we get back. Is that clear? I want you to stay in your room until we decide just what that punishment is going to be."

She turned abruptly, slammed the door, and made her way back down the stairs. Scott had already gone out to the car. She picked up her bundle of magazines and hurried out to the garage.

"Where's Caleb?" Jack asked when she got in.

"Just go," Sherrie instructed curtly. "He was in the middle of changing. I told him to stay in his room until we get back and decide what his punishment will be."

Jack nodded. "Good. He's always pulling stunts like this. I doubt he'll have more fun spending the next few hours in his room than he'd have at the mall with us."

"I *like* going to the mall," Scott announced.

"And you're always a big help," Sherrie assured him. "It's a pity your brother couldn't have the same attitude."

Tammy was frantic when they arrived, but still smiling. Sherrie couldn't decide if the table looked too big or if there weren't enough dishes on it to make it look full.

"What's that?" Tammy demanded, poking around anxiously in the box Jack was carrying.

"Vegetarian meatballs and cashew cheese," Sherrie replied.

"That's what I told you I'd bring."

Tammy's head bobbed up and down emphatically. "I'm glad someone actually brought what they said they would. I've got two dishes of patties when I only expected one, an Italian stew that was supposed to be lentil, and tofu-salad sandwiches made from mock chicken instead of tofu. And to top it all off, I had to send Bob back home to get the stethoscope."

"I've got one in my trunk. Would you like me to go get it?" Jack volunteered.

"That would be fantastic," Tammy replied. "Would you?"

"I'll be right back," he replied, setting the box down on the table and heading back toward the entrance.

"What a fiasco," Tammy wailed. She squinted up and down the mall hallway, searching for someone. "Have you seen Lauren? She promised me she'd bring some vegetarian chili, but I haven't seen hide nor hair of her."

Sherrie spared a quick glance up and down the hall. She hadn't seen Lauren since the day she'd spoken to her at church. It was starting to worry her. She wondered if she should tell Tammy that it was highly doubtful that Lauren would be coming, then decided that it wouldn't be a good idea.

"I don't see her," she said finally. "Here, let me help you get this table organized."

"Thanks, I'm about at my wits' end."

"Is anyone else coming to help out?" Sherrie opened the tub of cashew cheese and laid it on the table next to a plate of crackers. After searching around, she located a knife to set near it.

"Caren is supposed to come from one to two o'clock, and Lauren said she'd probably hang around all afternoon, but it doesn't look like she's going to show up at all. I can't believe it. It's just not like her. She seemed so enthusiastic about this whole thing when I talked to her a couple of weeks ago."

"Didn't you bring your kids?" Sherrie asked, noticing they weren't anywhere to be seen.

"Nah, they hate stuff like this." She rolled her eyes. "They say they've got more important things to do on a Sunday. Brian and Dave were playing Nintendo when I left, and Anne was practicing the piano. Is that stuff any good?" She pointed at the cashew cheese.

"It's great. Try some." Sherrie spread a little on a cracker for her. Tammy nibbled the barest edge and screwed up her face, anticipating the worst. Then her eyes popped wide open.

"It's not bad!" she exclaimed. "In fact, I think I like it."

"See that," Sherrie chided her. "You could become a regular health-food nut after all."

"I don't know about that, but this stuff I like."

Jack returned with his emergency bag from the trunk of the car just as they finished arranging the table. There were plenty of chairs to go around, and they sat down to wait for their first customers. A woman strolled up to the table and after looking everything over asked to try a meatless meatball.

"Can I get it, Mom?" Scott's voice was right at Sherrie's elbow, making her jump. He'd been so quiet that she'd forgotten he was there.

"Sure, go ahead."

He was so enthusiastic that he almost took over the serving completely. Sherrie was glad because it freed her and Tammy to talk with the people who asked questions. She had a hard time not laughing at Scott sometimes, though. He was so sober, his brow wrinkled in concentration. He looked like some kind of gourmet chef, hovering anxiously over the table, watching the people's expressions for some clue as to whether or not they liked what he'd given them. He got so involved with what he was doing that Sherrie had to tell him when it was all over.

"It's time to pack up."

He looked around in dismay. Other tables were being folded, and people were bundling things back up in boxes. "Already? Can I help pack up?"

Sherrie showed him what to pack. Most of the food was gone, which made the boxes very light when they were loaded. Jack and Bob carried the table out to Bob's vehicle. Tammy, Sherrie, Caren, and Scott followed with the boxes full of empty dishes. Sherrie's entire stack of health magazines had been taken.

"Thanks for coming," Tammy said as Sherrie deposited the box in the trunk and slammed it shut.

"Don't mention it. We were happy to do it," Jack said. "We would have come even if you hadn't asked us. Isn't that right, Sher?"

Sherrie laughed. "We probably would have."

"I don't know what I'd have done without you guys. I'm glad

you came." She gave Sherrie a quick hug, waved, and was gone.

"Affectionate little person, isn't she?" Jack remarked.

"Definitely a hugger," Sherrie agreed. "Makes me a little uncomfortable sometimes. Invades my space, I guess, but she means well."

As they pulled into the driveway, Sherrie suddenly sat as bolt upright as the confines of her seat belt permitted. "Jack! Did you see that? Someone just went in our house!"

"What?!"

"I just saw a flash of red. It happened so fast, but I'm sure it was a person. They were just disappearing in the front door when I caught the movement."

"There's a burglar in our house?" Scott squeaked. "Will he kill Caleb?"

"Nobody's going to kill anyone," Jack said firmly, pulling the car up to a quick halt and getting out.

"Jack, you're not going to go in there?" Sherrie watched him sprint across the lawn as she fumbled with her seat belt buckle. Her fingers were trembling so hard she couldn't get it undone. Scott bolted out of his seat and headed for the door.

"Scott," she screamed hysterically. "Get back here right now." He turned around reluctantly and made his way back to the car.

"I want to see the burglar."

"This isn't a game, Scott." The seat belt came free, and she almost fell in her hurry to get out of the car. "Get right back in that car until we find out what's going on. We may have to go get the police."

Crestfallen, Scott climbed slowly back into the car. Sherrie bit her lip and watched the door and windows for any sign of movement. Was Jack OK? He'd only been in the house for a few minutes, but it seemed like a lifetime.

"Jack?" she called tentatively, then screamed when she got no response. "Jack?! Answer me! Are you all right?"

He reappeared in the doorway, pulling someone behind him.

"Here's your burglar, Sherrie."

"But, it's . . ." Somehow the words wouldn't come out. Caleb all but dangled from Jack's powerful grip that almost lifted him from the ground. His face was as red as the jacket he wore.

The adrenaline that had coursed through her veins like liquid nitrogen now seemed to explode. "What are you doing sneaking in the front door?" she demanded. "More importantly, what are you doing out of your room?"

"I wasn't sneaking," Caleb protested.

"Don't lie," Jack warned him. "You were in such a hurry to get your boots off so you could get back to your room and pretend you'd been there all along that you knocked over the lamp."

"I was . . . it's just that . . . I didn't mean to . . ."

"Let's get inside, and then you better start making some sense, mister," Sherrie snapped.

"Go wait for us in the living room," Jack said, letting go of Caleb's jacket. He got back in the car and pulled it up into the garage. Neither of them said anything as they unloaded the trunk. Scott seemed to sense that this would be a bad time to ask questions and headed up the stairs without saying a word.

Caleb was hunched over in one of the living-room chairs when Sherrie and Jack went in. Now that he'd gotten over his initial scare and the embarrassment of being caught, his face was as white as flour.

"Well?" Jack asked.

Caleb didn't say anything. He just slumped over, looking miserable.

"Why were you out of your room?" Sherrie asked, fighting to keep her voice under control.

"I just wanted to go for a walk," Caleb said in a small voice.

"A walk? When I left I told you to stay in your room until we'd decided your punishment. What made you think it was OK to go for a walk?"

Caleb squirmed. "It was just a little walk. I didn't think you'd mind."

"You knew we'd mind," Jack contradicted him. "Where did you go?"

"Just out. Up the road."

Little bells went off in Sherrie's head. Up the road? Again? Did the Peltons live up the road? "Where, up the road?" She spat the words out like sand between her teeth.

"Just up," Caleb whispered. He seemed to sense that she'd found him out.

"Tell me where right now," Sherrie demanded.

"To Trista's." His voice was barely audible.

Sherrie shot Jack a triumphant look that said "I knew it."

"Sit up," she said to Caleb, "and look at me." When he'd dragged his eyes up to meet hers, she spoke deliberately. "Under no circumstances are you to return to the Peltons. Is that clear? You are not to associate with Trista. Is that also clear? You are grounded for a month, and as for punishment for not being ready on time, you can clean the bathroom, dust the downstairs, and vacuum for a week in addition to your other chores. Now go up to your room. I don't want to see your face again tonight."

Caleb shot out of his chair as if he'd been electrocuted. Sherrie waited until she heard his door slam before she said anything.

"I knew something was funny about his sudden interest in taking walks," she said. Jack had slumped back against the couch.

"We're going to have to keep a close eye on that boy from now on," Jack muttered. "A very close eye."

CHAPTER

14

The Video

Caleb seemed to accept his punishment with a stony kind of patience, but it took Sherrie weeks to get over the flash of anger that jolted through her every time she thought about what he'd done. Each evening she thoroughly went over every area he cleaned, pointing out where he could have done better. Part of her felt petty for doing it, but it wasn't a large part. After all, she reasoned, this was supposed to be a punishment.

One afternoon, the day after Caleb's grounding ended, he asked to go biking with Scott. As Sherrie considered his request, Jack's words flashed through her mind, "We're going to have to keep a close eye on that boy from now on." She wished he were here now so she could consult him.

"I guess you can go," she told Caleb, noting the sudden flash in his eyes. "But I want you to go down the road." She pointed in the desired direction. "Not up toward the Peltons. Understand?"

Caleb nodded solemnly. Sherrie had the feeling that at this point, even though it might be a disappointment not to be able to ride by hoping for a glimpse of Trista, getting out at all was his major objective.

He'd been pretty stoic throughout his punishment period, and she was almost sympathetic. The weather had been beautiful lately, and he'd had to be content with tossing a ball around with Scott in the yard.

"Thanks, Mom," he said, whirling and making a hasty exit.

Sherrie pulled up the kitchen window and watched as they got their bikes. Whooping excitedly, they pedaled down the driveway and onto the road. A gentle breeze blew in through the window, brushing the chimes. She could hear them tinkling on the porch.

It was one of those lazy late spring–early summer days that was just right. The breeze kept mosquitoes away, and she decided that it would be a good day to clean out the old dead plants from her flower garden.

Later. Right now was the perfect opportunity to search again for Caleb's journal. She'd seen it in his possession a few times lately and was pretty sure it wouldn't be hard to locate.

She was right. A quick search of his room disclosed it back in its original place behind the dresser. She flipped it open quickly to where she'd left off. He'd written a lot since then. The first entry that snagged her eyes was about Trista. Bingo!

"I sure wish Trista went to our school. She doesn't always come to church, so I don't get to see her very often. We had fun sledding together, though. Mom doesn't like her, but I think she's radical. I wish I had her freedom. Her parents are great. They let her do all kinds of things. Even smoke. I don't think I'd ever smoke even if I could, but it would be nice to know that I could if I wanted to."

Sherrie's breath sucked in sharply. What was that supposed to mean? That he would smoke or wouldn't? What was it about Trista and her freedom that was so irresistible to him? Why couldn't he see that she and Jack had his best interests in mind? Why couldn't he understand that if there were no rules for him to guide his life by, he would be miserable in the end?

Rules and boundaries make children feel secure, she remembered hearing. And it was true. Why couldn't they see it? All this pulling against authority was beginning to wear her out. It was only for Caleb's sake that she endured it at all. It certainly wasn't for fun that she and Jack enforced their rules. It was for Caleb' and Scott's good, present and eternal. After all, if they couldn't abide by a few simple house rules, they'd sure have a hard time keeping God's laws.

Another entry at the end of the page caught her eye.

"I walked by Trista's house today. At first I didn't think Mom was going to let me go; I think she suspected something. I don't know why she doesn't trust me. She told me I had to get back in an hour. Man, did I have to walk fast. When I went by one way I didn't see anyone at their house, so I went farther up the road;

then I turned around and started back. Trista must have seen me go by because she was waiting for me at the end of her drive-way. We only got to talk for about ten minutes before I had to head back. She said she'd been having trouble in school. I offered to help her study, but she just laughed."

"I'll bet she did," Sherrie muttered. So, she'd been right. Caleb had been headed for Trista's house the first time he went out "walking." And he wondered why she didn't trust him? It should be obvious. Her eyes rapidly scanned the next few pages. There was a lot about school, Scott, and the Merrill kids. Finally, she found one she was interested in.

"Today at church Anne and Lori sang a really nice song. Nobody played the music for them, though. They used a cassette recording of the song that was just the music part. Mom and Dad hated it. They said it was like Christian rock music. I didn't think it was bad at all. It was even a hymn. I know why they didn't like it, though. It's because it wasn't the same old boring thing they're used to. It sounded kinda country. They don't like anything new, but I liked it."

That hardly surprised her. His opinion of her was somewhat irritating, though. It wasn't true. She liked new things, as long as they conformed with her religious principles. He made it sound like she objected to the music simply because it was new and not because it wasn't sacred. She made a mental note to clear up that point for him later in a casual sort of way.

Finally she found the entry that most concerned her. She could almost feel his anger pulsing on the page as she read it.

"I hate them! I hate them! They left me here on purpose just to get back at me because I wasn't ready to leave the second they were. Mom said I had to stay in my room, but I'd told Trista that I would meet her halfway between her house and mine so we could talk for a while. I couldn't just let her wait there, so I met her. We had a good time too. She brought some beer and let me take a little taste. It was awful! I don't know why she likes it. Before I could get back in the house, Mom and Dad drove in. They didn't let me explain or anything. All they had to hear was 'Trista,' and automatically I was guilty just because they don't like her. They said I'm grounded for a whole month, and I've got to do lots of cleaning. I've got to find a way to call Trista and let her know because I'm supposed to meet her at the old tree on

Tuesday. I can't wait until I'm eighteen."

Sherrie sat limply on the edge of the bed, the journal falling onto her lap. What had he done? Why had he even tried Trista's beer? Should she tell Jack? No, she'd better not. She expected to feel angry or disappointed or something, but she didn't. Instead, everything just felt numb—her body, her mind, and her heart.

She reread the part about Trista and felt a stab of something she couldn't identify. It sure sounded like Caleb and Trista were getting to be pretty good friends. Her thoughts ran ahead in a morbid fashion—Trista his girlfriend, Trista his fiancée, Trista his wife. She shuddered. She wanted the best for Caleb, and Trista was not it. He needed a good Christian girl, someone who would anchor him.

She thought about what Tammy had told her about Trista being expelled for smoking marijuana. Caleb had tried her beer. Would he also try marijuana if she offered it to him? *Surely he wouldn't,* she assured herself. *Surely he wouldn't go that far.*

She wondered again if she should tell Jack. He had a right to know. But, then, no real damage had been done yet. Caleb himself said he didn't like the beer. Maybe it was best that he had tried it and wouldn't try it again. If she told Jack, he would insist on punishing Caleb. Then they'd have to tell him how they found out. That would be the end of the journal and the end of her source of information.

She replaced the journal with trembling fingers. Better to wait. She had a terrible feeling that the worst was yet to come. So strong was the feeling that she went immediately to her bedroom, fell to her knees, and prayed for both Caleb and Scott for a half-hour without even being aware of the passing of time. The pattern on the rug was imprinted on her knees when she finally rose and went out to weed her flower garden, but she felt better than she had in weeks.

With the onset of spring and some truly beautiful weather, the kids in Don Wagner's class were a restless bunch. Sherrie could almost feel the electricity in the air each morning. One particularly beautiful day, Don announced that they were going to have a surprise. He suspended classwork at midmorning and let the whole school out for some gymnastics and games.

Sherrie and Tammy watched the kids whooping and hollering around the parking lot as Don got up a game of basketball. Sara's team was ahead, and Sherrie was startled into a laugh when Sara outmaneuvered her husband and landed a beautiful basket for her team.

"The kids really needed this," Tammy commented.

"They sure did. They've been working hard all year," Sherrie replied. "I think it was nice of Don to let them blow off some steam."

After lunch, Sherrie and Tammy decided to clean the kitchen cupboards. Although there wasn't much demand for hot lunches anymore, they continued to make lunches for the kids. Usually it was a sandwich and vegetable sticks. They compromised twice a week and offered a healthy cookie as a dessert. At first the kids hadn't been very enthusiastic about the food, but lately Sherrie had heard fewer negative comments about it.

She and Tammy were both surprised when they went upstairs after they finished in the kitchen and found the lights out in the schoolroom. Subdued excitement all but sparked in the air. Tammy nudged the door open to check it out.

"They're getting ready to watch a video," she reported to Sherrie, who was anxiously trying to peer around her.

"What video?" Sherrie asked, immediately suspicious.

"Looks like *King David*. I saw it before, a long time ago. Do you think they'd mind if we watched it too?" Tammy was so excited that she was having a hard time keeping her voice down. A loud "Shhhh!" issued from the darkened interior of the room.

Sherrie pushed past her, and Tammy followed. She didn't care if they minded or not. If her kids were seeing a video, she wanted to be sure she knew what it was about. After all, how did she know that some director in Hollywood knew the biblical account well enough to represent it clearly?

She found a place in the back of the room where she could see the television they were showing the movie on. Tammy settled in next to her and immediately became engrossed in the movie. A quick look at her now and then told Sherrie that the roof could cave in, and Tammy would probably not notice.

She shifted uncomfortably. She hadn't watched TV in so long that the very format made her edgy. The bright moving pictures grated on her nerves, and she made an effort not to get so engrossed in the movie itself that she wasn't paying attention to its accuracy.

Right from the beginning, the clash with the biblical account was apparent. So was the violence. As she watched David hold up Goliath's head, she winced, swallowing hard, and had to remind herself that it had really happened. She glanced quickly around the room at the kids. Most were engrossed in the action, two little girls in the corner were covering their eyes during the violent parts, and little Jimmy had fallen asleep at his desk.

A kind of raw panic began to build inside her chest. Why was Don showing this movie? Granted, the basic account really happened, violence and all. But what about the errors and semi-shaded nudity? Children were watching this. *Our children*, she thought.

And then it happened. It was so sudden and so shocking that it drove every other thought from her mind. She had expected they would skip over the bathing scene with Bathsheba, but they didn't. It was only a few seconds, darkened by shadows, but it was seared into her mind for all time. A hot flush swept over her, and she realized that her mouth was hanging open.

She closed it with a snap and looked over to catch Tammy's reaction to the scene, but Tammy didn't appear to notice anything wrong. She was still so absorbed in the movie that Sherrie had to nudge her twice before she broke her concentration and turned around, her irritation hastily disguised.

"Did you see that?" Sherrie hissed in a loud whisper.

"What?" Tammy was still keeping one eye on the movie.

"That's the second nude scene in this movie, and they're showing it to our children."

"My kids have seen this movie before," Tammy replied, as if that made it all right. "Besides, it was only for a second. Anyway, it's pretty accurate."

"Not that accurate," Sherrie snapped. "It's totally unnecessary."

Tammy ripped her eyes from the screen and gave Sherrie her full attention. "You're really steamed about this, aren't you?"

"Yes, I am," Sherrie replied, hardly able to keep her voice down. "This movie isn't appropriate for our children to watch, and we don't even have a say in it. That's wrong."

"I don't know what we can do about it," Tammy pointed out.

"I do," Sherrie said darkly. She sat back, quietly seething, to watch the rest of the movie.

Calling an emergency school board meeting wasn't as easy as she had first thought. Pastor Hawley didn't need to hear much to be convinced that a meeting should be held, but some of the people were hard to reach. Finally, at nine o'clock, the school board gathered in the basement of the church, where the board meetings were held.

Don and Sara Wagner were seated at the head of the table right beside Pastor Hawley. Don looked weary, but Sara's face was void of all emotion. Her dark features cast shadows beneath her eyes and gave her a sinister appearance.

The rest of the members eyed each other somewhat nervously, silently questioning what was so important as to drag them out at this hour. Tammy was present, although she wasn't a member of the board. Sherrie had asked her to come as a witness, a position Tammy wasn't entirely comfortable with.

Pastor Hawley cleared his throat before he began. "I asked you all here this evening to discuss something that has come to my attention. During school today a video was shown that has sparked some, shall we say, controversy. Mrs. Raines, who was at the school today and saw the movie, would like the school board to determine a course of action if we should so deem it necessary."

He's starting to sound like a lawyer, Sherrie mused. *Get on with it.* He obliged her by giving a brief recap of the points she'd discussed with him and then opened the floor for discussion.

"I would just like to say," Sherrie spoke up, "that it's not my intention to criticize the teacher or his choice of viewing material. My entire contention is that the content of the video was unsuitable for the audience. If our children are going to be subjected to nudity, violence, and false accounting of a biblical story, then we should have some say in the matter. Mrs. Merrill was present when the video was shown and can attest, for those who haven't seen the film, that the scenes I am most concerned about were very graphic and should not have been shown to our children without our consent."

Tammy squirmed uncomfortably. "Well, the movie *was* violent and there were two very brief nude scenes, but the account was pretty accurate."

"Pretty accurate is not the same as accurate," stated a woman known to Sherrie as Mrs. Morgan. "It sounds like this movie did just what Satan is trying to do, mix truth and deception. Anyway, accuracy is hardly a motive for showing anything like that. Lots of terrible things happen in the world every day, but we don't feel compelled to allow our children to view them."

"Children are impressionable," a man in the corner said. "Images that might pass through an adult's mind without a thought can stay with children for a long time. When I was a kid, my father let me stay up for a scary movie one night. I had nightmares for a week, but I'm sure it didn't affect my father at all."

"That's hardly the point," contended Duncan Grant. "We're told clearly that as a man thinketh in his heart, so is he. We're influenced by what we see and hear. Paul tells us to think only on good things, uplifting things. We don't have a television, and my kids aren't missing anything. I agree with Mrs. Raines. If a video is going to be shown at school, it should be previewed by the school board first. I don't want my kids watching something like that even if it is true."

Don Wagner cleared his throat. "It wasn't my intention to present this picture as a documentary. It was for the children's entertainment. They've been working hard in school, and I thought it would be a nice treat."

"But the content," sputtered a red-faced mother across from Sherrie. "How can you defend the content?"

"We're not defending it," Sara replied. "We didn't create it, and we don't defend it."

"You showed it to our children," the woman pointed out.

"Yes, because we thought that despite its flaws, it was worthy as *entertainment*," Sara stressed.

Silence settled around the table for a few minutes. Pastor Hawley searched each face, waiting to see if there were any more comments.

"I don't think it was the teacher's intention to present something that would upset parents," Tammy ventured in a small voice. "We're losing sight of the fact that the kids worked hard all year, and this was supposed to be a fun day for them. I mean, the video was biblical."

"That's not the question," insisted Mrs. Morgan. "The question is, do we want our children viewing such material?" The shaking of heads that rippled around the table indicated that no one did. "Then to prevent such a thing from happening in the future, I think we should follow Mr. Grant's suggestion of having videos previewed by the school board. That way, we all have input and say into whether it is something we want our children seeing."

Discussion seemed to be at an end. Pastor Hawley called for a vote, and Mr. Grant's suggestion was unanimously approved. Don and Sara didn't say anything but stayed behind to talk to Pastor Hawley as everyone filed out.

Sherrie followed Jack to the car. He hadn't said much the entire evening, but she knew he agreed with her 100 percent. She slumped into her seat, feeling limp and drained.

"I'm glad that's over," she sighed. Having run on nervous energy since that afternoon, she suddenly felt completely empty. Although the outcome of the school-board meeting could be viewed as a victory, she wasn't the least bit happy about winning. She was, however, glad that she would be given a say in what her children viewed from then on.

CHAPTER

15

The Meeting

After supper one evening, Sherrie laid out brand-new note pads and freshly sharpened pencils at every place setting around their table. Jack had called a meeting of the personal ministries committee to discuss upcoming plans. She was surprised to find herself a little nervous and was glad that Jack was leading and she was only the assistant. She went over the list of names comprising the committee in her head. A few of them were familiar, but some she still couldn't place.

The first people to arrive were no surprise. Don Wagner and his wife were quickly followed by Tammy Merrill and Josh Nason. As they were settling themselves around the table, the doorbell rang again, and Sherrie left Jack with the guests while she answered it.

A short, pert woman with jet black hair stood on the doorstep. "Hello," she said, her voice high and squeaky. "My name is Jill. Jill MacCulkin. I'm here for the meeting."

"So am I," called a voice as footsteps pounded up the walk. A disheveled young man rushed up out of breath and grabbed Sherrie's hand, pumping it vigorously.

"Terry," he panted. "Terry Knoll."

"Come right on in. You're not late," she assured Terry, who looked around a little wildly. "Everyone is just arriving." Sherrie took their coats and led them to the dining room, where they were greeted by the rest of the members already seated.

"Can I get anyone anything?" Sherrie asked politely, feeling that her smile was just a little strained. "Herbal tea? It's no bother. The water's already warm." A few tentative hands jabbed the air for tea, and she busied herself filling cups.

"Are we waiting for anyone?" she heard Jack ask.

"Ben Tarden is supposed to be here," Jill volunteered.

"And isn't the pastor coming?" Tammy asked.

Jack waited impatiently for Sherrie to distribute cups among the people who had requested tea. "I guess we can start," he said finally. "They can jump in whenever they join us. Now as you all know, the purpose of this meeting is . . ."

Before he could finish, Caleb bounded down the stairs and exploded into the middle of the meeting. At the last instant, before he could correct himself, he seemed to remember that a meeting was in progress. Red flames shot up his face, and he ducked quietly into the kitchen.

"What are you doing down here?" Sherrie hissed, following him into the kitchen. "You knew we were having a meeting tonight."

"I forgot," Caleb mumbled. "I came down to see if I could have some whole-wheat graham crackers."

"No, you can't," Sherrie replied, straining to keep her voice civil. She was positive everyone in the adjoining dining room could hear every word they uttered. "You know we don't allow any snacking between meals."

"But, Mom, I'm really hungry," Caleb pleaded, not caring that his voice rose in volume.

"Then I guess you should have eaten more for supper," Sherrie observed with thinly veiled sarcasm. "Back to your room, please, and don't come down again tonight. Thank you."

Caleb turned sulkily and slunk back up the stairs. Sherrie took a moment to compose herself before returning to the dining room. She positioned herself by Jack's elbow and braved a glance around the table to see if anyone might have overheard her conversation with Caleb. She intercepted a glance and smile between Jill and Terry, but she wasn't sure if she was the cause.

Jack handed her a stack of papers to pass out. "This is a schedule of the activities that we'd like to do for the remainder of the year," he was explaining. "We've divided them up by months and further divided them up by responsibility. We'll need volunteers for each of the areas of responsibility. Now, I realize that most of you don't plan a year in advance, so we'll only commit to a month at a time. Do I have any volunteers for the first activity? The Daniel Seminar?"

He paused, but no one spoke. "I'll be teaching the seminar, so that will be my responsibility," he offered as if he hoped to prompt them into following suit. "Sherrie will take care of the communications department... placing ads, getting it mentioned in the paper, advertising, and all that."

Sherrie heard the masked frustration in his voice building. "Do I have any volunteers to prepare a mailing list? Someone to welcome people and register them at the door? Someone to take care of setting up each night? Someone to take care of securing supplies for the seminar?"

The people seated at the table snuck looks at each other, as if daring someone else to go first. As Jack waited, Sherrie could sense his irritation rising.

"First things first," he said with forced patience. "I need someone to prepare a mailing list." He stared at them as if daring them *not* to speak up. "Sara?" he prodded. "How about you?"

Sara looked up, meeting his gaze steadily. "I suppose I could take care of that," she agreed. *Reluctantly*, Sherrie thought. She wondered if it had anything to do with the meeting last week about the video. But, then, Don and Sara hadn't seemed the type to hold grudges.

"And someone to welcome people and register them at the door? Tammy? Did I see you volunteer? You'd be perfect for that."

"I would?" Tammy asked, startled. "Well, I guess, I could, sure. Why not?"

"We need someone to set up every night. Don? Do you think you and Josh could manage that?"

Don took his time answering. "I suppose I could."

"Josh?"

"Whatever you want me to do is fine with me," Josh replied, as if he'd been waiting for an assignment all along.

"Terry or Jill, do you think one of you could manage to get the materials we'll need for the seminar? I can give you the catalog to order from."

"I'll do it," Jill ventured timidly.

"We'll both do it," Terry said quickly. "No problem."

Jack sighed with relief. "There, that's all taken care of then. We'll be starting in a few weeks. That doesn't give us much time, so you'll want to get right on the ball. I'll warn you right now that I plan to be actively involved in every step of this project. I'll be calling each one of you once a week to get a progress report."

Sherrie caught the same glance and smile pass between Jill and Terry. It was almost as if they were smirking, she thought. She pushed the thought from her head and paid attention to Jack.

"That's all for tonight, but I would ask you to look over the projects that are scheduled to come up next month. I hope that at our next meeting, there will be more volunteers. This is the Lord's work we're doing here. There's no need to be ashamed to take part in it. Thank you all for coming."

Jill was the first one out of her chair. She handed Sherrie her empty mug and glanced appreciatively around the spotless room. "You have such a beautiful home," she gushed. "It's like something out of *Better Homes and Gardens*. Really, I'm serious," she added, as if Sherrie might think she was joking.

"Thank you," Sherrie murmured.

"And not a piece of lint anywhere. How do you do it? My, it's so quiet here. Did the boys go out?"

Sherrie glanced at her watch. It was five minutes past seven. "No, they're in bed by now."

"Bed?" Jill exclaimed. "But it's just after seven."

"We all go to bed at seven," Sherrie informed her, trying to quell the irritation that she felt at the grilling.

"My goodness, I couldn't go to sleep before eleven if I was going to be lined up and shot for it," Jill shrieked, in her high, peculiar voice. "I guess I'd better scram and let you get to bed, then. Good night. Thanks for the tea. That's OK, I can find the door myself."

Sherrie watched her retreating back with a feeling of relief. The other guests, except Terry, lingered a little while longer, and it was twenty of eight before she closed the door behind the last one. Sinking against the cool wood, she sighed, whether from relief or exhaustion, she wasn't sure.

"Glad they're gone?" Jack asked wryly. "I can't believe that from a whole roomful of people, I couldn't get a single one to volunteer. It was like pulling teeth from a chicken. What's the matter with those people?"

"They seem to think the world is going to bang down the church door and beg to come in without the slightest bit of prompting," Sherrie observed wearily. "But right now, I don't care. I'm tired, and all I want is my pillow and my pajamas."

She followed Jack's rigid back up the stairs, flicking off the lights as she went. *Hopefully*, she told herself, *the meetings will get better as people get used to volunteering for things. Hopefully.*

Sherrie noticed, over the next several weeks as they hustled to get everything ready for the Daniel Seminar, that Don and Sara tended to avoid her. She mentioned it to Jack one evening and learned he was getting the same impression from them himself. Still, it didn't actually dawn on her that they were making a conscious effort to do it until one week when they planned a field trip.

"Are you going with the school?" Tammy asked as they made lunch the day before the big event.

"Of course," Sherrie replied without hesitation. "Aren't you?"

"I can't. I've got a dental appointment tomorrow."

"Reschedule it," Sherrie said simply.

"How? They make those appointments months in advance. Besides, if I cancel now, they'll charge me because I can't give them a two-day notice." She was about to stick a humus-covered finger into her mouth when she caught Sherrie's disapproving look and decided against it. "Anyway, there will be other field trips."

"Don't you want to keep an eye on your kids?" Sherrie asked curiously.

"Why? Don and Sara will watch out for them. How much trouble could they possibly get into on a field trip?"

Sherrie shrugged. "I don't know, but I want to go . . . to help out."

Don and Sara had different ideas when she approached them to find out which kids would be riding with her.

"We really don't need the help," Don insisted, careful not to look her directly in the eye. "Honestly, we'll be fine. Sara's mom is in town, and she'll be driving a carload of kids herself. I really can't see the sense in your coming."

"But I want to come." Sherrie tried to maintain a smile and keep her voice as firm as possible.

"Take the day off. Enjoy yourself for a while," Don urged. "You and Tammy have been working yourselves pretty hard all school year. Take advantage of the break to do something you've been putting off."

"I don't want to take the day off," Sherrie said. Why was he doing this? To punish her for the movie incident? She did think it was rather odd that he hadn't proposed another movie since.

"We really don't need you," Don repeated. Sara glared at Sherrie from under her bushy black eyebrows.

"No sense taking an extra car for nothing," Sara said flatly.

"You're telling me I can't come?" This was impossible! They couldn't *make* her stay home.

"We don't need you." A wan smile accompanied Don's words.

"If I don't come, then the boys won't be going," she ground out, clenching her teeth.

"We're sorry they won't be able to make it," Sara said.

Sherrie looked from one to the other. Neither flinched. They weren't going to back down. "I'm sorry too," she managed, trying not to cry in front of them. "I can't believe I'm such a problem to have along. I only wanted to help."

"But we don't need the help," Don maintained.

"My help, you mean," Sherrie whispered under her breath.

She spent the rest of the afternoon sitting out in her car alternating between anger and tears. There was no doubt in her mind that the reason they didn't want her along was because of the movie incident. She wondered idly if they could really prevent her from accompanying the school, then decided it was a useless cause. What could she do? Complain to Pastor Hawley?

"Pastor Hawley," she could hear herself say, "Don and Sara won't let me go on the field trip with them." She'd sound like some kind of thwarted child. Still, it was hardly fair that the boys had to miss out.

It was the principle of the thing, she decided, after reasoning that there really was *no* reason the boys couldn't still go. *If I let the boys go, I'll be caving in to them. I'm not going to do that*, she told herself firmly.

She stared out through the windshield at the pine trees lined up like rigid soldiers guarding the property boundary of the church. When the kids began pouring from the interior of the school, she tried to put on a smile. Caleb and Scott were at the tail end of the pack.

Scott was bouncing up and down with suppressed excitement. He jumped into the car and slammed the car door exuberantly. Sherrie winced at the noise and realized she was getting a very rotten headache.

"Must you?" she asked him.

"Sorry, Mom, but I'm just so happy." It was like he was filled with helium. Caleb, more subdued, got in on the other side.

"About what?" Sherrie turned the key in the ignition and backed the car around.

"The field trip. Did you know we even get to go out on a boat?"

"I'm afraid that you don't," Sherrie ventured, loathe to tell him outright. "We'll be staying home tomorrow."

Scott's face fell. "Why?"

Sherrie bit her lip. *Why? What was she supposed to say? Because I can't go?*

"I don't feel that it will be properly supervised." That sounded reasonable.

"What about all the other kids?" Scott wailed. "There are going to be adults there."

"In the first place, I'm not responsible for the other kids," Sherrie told him. "And in the second place, I don't feel like arguing about it."

Scott sank down sullenly in his seat. One look at Caleb told her that he had expected something of the sort and wasn't as disappointed. Then she had an idea.

"I know. Why don't we go on a field trip ourselves? Just the three of us?" Her voice sounded bright, even to her own ears.

Scott perked up a little. "Where to?"

"Oh, I don't know, uh, where would you like to go?"

"To the marina with the other kids," Scott said flatly.

"Scott . . ." Sherrie's voice held a subtle warning.

"How about a museum?" Scott suggested.

"Sure," Sherrie agreed enthusiastically. "There must be a good museum around here. Maybe in Portland. Leave it to me. I'll find us the best museum in the state."

The boys didn't say anything the rest of the way home, and Sherrie wondered what they were thinking. She knew they weren't all that crazy about the museum idea, but it was better than nothing, which was all she had without it. Well, they'd get over it. After all, it was only one crummy little field trip.

CHAPTER
16

Heavy Metal

The next day, it rained. Scott was thrilled, if for no other reason than that the kids going to visit the marina weren't going to have much fun.

"At least if I can't go, I'm glad it rained," he confided to Sherrie as she frantically searched for a museum they could go to.

"That's not a very Christian attitude, Scott." It startled her to hear him talk like that. Usually Scott was able to see the humor in any situation. It wasn't like him to wish rain on his friends just because he couldn't go with them.

"You know what I mean, Mom," Scott protested. "I mean that as long as it had to rain, I'm glad I couldn't go. I mean, I'm not glad that I couldn't go, but . . . well, I'm glad I'm not going out on a boat and getting soaked."

Sherrie stabbed the yellow pages with one finger, ignoring Scott's stumbling explanation. "Here's one."

I've done it, she thought to herself. The trip to the museum would be a great substitute for the marina. In fact, it would be better . . . more educational. Everything was going to be fine, rain or no rain.

She realized later that she hadn't counted on Caleb blanketing the entire trip with a dark and gloomy silence. It pervaded the entire car and soon even rubbed off on Scott, who had just begun to show a measure of enthusiasm for the trip.

While they waited for Scott to get back from the restroom at the museum, Sherrie pulled Caleb aside. The hostile look on his face did nothing to encourage her, but she didn't let it daunt her either.

"All right, Caleb. What's your problem? Are you trying to spoil this trip for Scott and me?" She studied his face. His eyes flashed momentarily before he could lower them. He clenched and un-clenched his jaw.

"What difference does it make?" he asked belligerently.

"It makes a lot of difference. This trip is supposed to be fun for all of us. You're not having fun, and that's affecting Scott and me. Are you upset about not going to the marina?"

"Yes," he snapped, "but you don't care about that."

"I care," Sherrie began, then he cut her off.

"You do not. You just say you do. There wasn't any reason we couldn't go to the marina. Was there?" His voice challenged her, goaded her to tell him the real reason she had pulled them from the trip.

"Look, Caleb, we are here today because I think this is more important than a trip to the marina."

"It was so important that you had to ask us where to go?"

Sherrie wished she could wipe that smug grin off his face. "It's important for us to be together, to do things together. That is more important than going on a field trip with your school."

"Why couldn't we do both?"

"Because we couldn't. Look, this isn't getting us anywhere." Out of the corner of her eye, she saw Scott approaching them. "I want you to be civil for the rest of the day. Do you understand? Scott is having a good time even if you're not, and he deserves the right to learn without you hovering over him like a storm cloud."

Caleb nodded as if he understood what she was saying, but she could still sense that, like an iron rod, he would bend only so far. It irritated her that she couldn't do something more to get him to cooperate. Instead, she radiated as much enthusiasm as she could to counteract his lack of it.

By the time they left the museum, Sherrie felt drained. Even the sun, which had come out while they'd been inside and was shining fiercely, did nothing to lift her spirits. Being enthusiastic was hard work!

She couldn't wait to get home to spend a few minutes on the porch watching the birds come to the feeder. A few deep breaths of fresh air and a tall glass of cold lemon water would do her a world of good.

The idea was so appealing that as soon as the car stopped moving, she told the boys to go ride their bikes. She followed that with a strict admonition about *where*, exactly, they could ride. Then she scooped up everything they'd brought with them, the boys' Walkmans, empty lunch bags, some museum pamphlets, and her purse and headed into the house.

Cleaning could wait. She dumped everything on the kitchen table and went upstairs to change. When she came back down, Scott was rummaging through the stuff she'd put on the table for his Walkman. He put one on and headed for the door. Before Sherrie made it to the kitchen, he stopped dead in his tracks, a look of horror on his face.

"What's the matter? Walkman broke?"

Scott removed the headphones slowly, his face a pasty shade of white. "Mom, I think you're going to want to hear this."

Sherrie was only vaguely concerned. Scott was prone to dramatize things. Besides, the porch was calling. She took the headphones and put them on. Vulgar words poured into her ears. Instruments screamed like they were in pain. The cacophony of sound was exactly what she imagined a pit full of demons at full cry would sound like.

Fingers trembling in anger, she ripped the cassette from the Walkman. "This isn't yours?" Scott shook his head solemnly. It was Caleb's, of course. "OK, go outside. Tell Caleb to come in, please."

Scott crept out as if he was afraid even the sound of his footsteps might spark the powder keg of tension that filled the room. Sherrie's knees felt weak, but she refused to sit down. This wasn't something she could talk about sitting down.

She doubted that Scott would tell Caleb why she wanted to see him, but he seemed to pick up some premonition of impending peril. He entered the kitchen the way some people enter a dentist's office. His eyes went immediately to the cassette in Sherrie's hand.

She held it out, trying to get the words out past the anger, hurt, and pain constricting her throat. "Wha . . . what is this, and where did you get it?"

"It's a tape." Caleb shrugged.

To Sherrie, it seemed as if he hoped his simple, obvious answer would trivialize the question. She refused to play his little game and waited, staring at him. The silence stretched and became painful. Caleb's eyes wandered uncomfortably around the room.

"OK," he blurted out. "So it's a heavy-metal tape. So what? I can listen to whatever I want."

Sherrie neatly sidestepped the implications of that statement. "Where did you get it?"

Caleb screwed up his face stubbornly. "I can't tell you that."

"You can, and you will."

"I don't want to get anyone else in trouble."

"I know who gave you the tape, Caleb," Sherrie said quietly, too quietly. Suddenly the conversations she'd overheard between Caleb and Trista made sense. *This* is what Trista had loaned him. "I want to hear you say it."

"It's not fair," he yelled. "You always blame Trista. For everything! What did she ever do to you?"

"It isn't what she's done to me that bothers me, Caleb," Sherrie said sadly. "It's what she's done to you."

"She hasn't done anything to me. Trista is my friend. Her parents at least respect her and let her do what she wants."

"That's not respect, Caleb. And it's not close to love. Would you say I loved you if you wanted to jump off a bridge, and I let you? No, you'd say I didn't love you enough to stop you."

"Yes, I would," Caleb contradicted her, but his voice lacked his earlier conviction. "If that's what I wanted to do. At least it would be my decision."

"I don't think you really believe that, Caleb. I hope you don't." Sherrie sighed wearily. "I want you to go up to your room now. We're going to have a family meeting about this later. We'll decide your punishment then. You don't need to come down for supper."

Caleb's back stiffened as he turned without another word and went up to his room. Sherrie sighed again and laid the offensive tape down on the counter. Her fingers felt dirty just from touching it. She washed her hands before squeezing half a lemon into a big glass of ice water.

The bright sunshine seemed to mock her as she sank onto the bench on the porch. Who would believe this was the same day she had begun with such high hopes? Maybe it would have been better to have let the boys go on the field trip. Then she would have avoided this ugly confrontation with Caleb.

Don't be stupid, she told herself fiercely. *Playing ostrich isn't going to help Caleb. You have to confront issues like these head on, even if they are painful and even if they don't come at convenient times. Life couldn't be planned so you could endure your toughest trials on the days you were the most rested.*

That's what relying on God was all about. He isn't going to let you walk through a storm alone, she reminded herself. *He's going to be right by your side through the whole thing. All you have to do is rely on His strength rather than your own.*

She laid her head back against the porch rail and closed her eyes. Just knowing God was there, supporting her, was enough for the moment. She poured out the anger, frustration, and betrayal she felt to Him and could feel it dissipate. Instead, a love and pity for Caleb filled her.

He was growing, struggling to find his own identity separate from hers, separate from Jack's. And he had stumbled on a bad influence in Trista. Certainly, he was responsible for his choices, and he should pay the consequences for his actions, but he was just testing the waters, after all. He wasn't engaged in active rebellion simply for the sake of rebellion.

Sherrie's thoughts were interrupted when she heard the door slam. She pulled herself up reluctantly and went into the house. Jack looked tired, and she hated to burden him with what had happened, but it couldn't be avoided.

He listened quietly but refrained from listening to the tape when she offered it to him. She could see the pain and hurt she'd felt earlier in his eyes and wisely didn't say more. It would be better for him to have time to come to the same conclusions she had come to.

As Jack went upstairs to change, Sherrie busied herself in the kitchen making supper. She had planned to have something nice but found that she didn't have the heart for it. Instead, she made a simple dish of couscous and vegetables, then tossed a green salad.

Supper was eaten in almost strict silence. Neither Jack nor Sherrie felt much like talking, and Scott, who well realized the cause of their silence, had no intention of being the one responsible for breaking the silence. He ate methodically, quickly, and asked to be excused the moment his plate was clean. Sherrie waved him away.

"Tell Caleb we want both of you in the living room in about twenty minutes," Jack informed Scott abruptly, startling him. Scott nodded and scurried up the stairs.

With Jack helping her, Sherrie had the kitchen cleaned and the dishes put away inside fifteen minutes. They went into the living room to wait for the boys to come down. Jack set the Walkman and the tape on the table in front of the sofa where they sat. The significance of the evidence being in plain view wasn't lost on Sherrie, and she doubted it would be lost on Caleb either.

Here we go again, she thought as the boys came down and sat in the two chairs Jack had set up directly opposite the sofa. It hardly seemed any time ago that they were confronting Caleb about sneaking out of the house. Would it ever end?

"You both know why we're having this family meeting," Jack stated in a quiet voice that had an edge to it. "Your mother tells me, Caleb, that you feel you should be allowed to listen to any type of music you desire. Is that right?"

Caleb nodded curtly, his eyes fastened on the floor.

"And what kind of guidelines do you use to choose your music?"

Caleb looked up quickly, then averted his eyes again. "I don't know," he muttered. "I guess if I like it."

"What have we taught you about choosing entertainment?" Jack asked, pressing him. When Caleb didn't reply, he answered his own question. "You know that entertainment should be chosen for its uplifting quality, that it should draw the mind of the listener toward God. Now, why don't you explain to me how this tape," he gestured towards the heavy-metal tape on the table in front of him, "does that."

Caleb maintained a stoic silence. There was no way he could defend the tape, and he realized it. Instead, he waited patiently for his father to finish and get on with his punishment.

"Can you do that?" Jack prodded. A shake of Caleb's head was the only response he received. "Then, until such time as you can demonstrate the ability to choose edifying music, your Walkman is off limits. You want us to trust you, to give you responsibility, yet you trample the very trust you want. Why is that?" Jack didn't wait for Caleb to respond. "We trusted you with your music, and you betrayed that trust. Now, you're going to have to earn any trust you receive from us."

Jack picked up the tape, and Caleb's eyes followed it worriedly.

Jack noted his concern. "Don't worry. I'll return this tape for you. At the same time, I'll inform Mr. and Mrs. Pelton that Trista is forbidden to loan you any more tapes of this kind."

Caleb squirmed with embarrassment. Sherrie could tell he wished heartily he could snatch the tape from Jack's hands and disappear from their lives forever, free of their restraint. The thought frightened her.

"As for your punishment," Jack continued. "You will be grounded for a month, and during that time, the lawn mowing will be your responsibility." Caleb's restraint cracked, and a low moan issued from his lips. Sherrie couldn't really blame him. They had a big lawn, and it was a lot of work to mow it. "That's all, boys. You can go back up to your room."

When they'd gone, Jack slumped against the back of the sofa and rubbed his eyes. "I think I know a little of how God felt toward Israel." He glanced up the stairs. "I want to protect them even from my punishment, but I can't, because they'll never learn that way."

Sherrie laid her hand on his arm but didn't say anything. She understood. Exactly.

CHAPTER
17

Exposed!

As spring ended and summer began, the dismal museum trip became a dim memory. Occasionally something would remind Sherrie of it. Today, it was the purr of the lawn mower; sometimes it was the sight of Caleb's grass-stained sneakers that usually sat by the door. She knew he would be grateful next week, when his month of mowing was finished.

As she mixed the tofu mayonnaise she was making, the phone rang. Sherrie wiped her hands quickly on a towel before answering it.

"Sherrie? It's Tammy. I just had the greatest idea!"

Sherrie smiled faintly. Tammy's ideas were always great. At least, according to her. "What kind of idea?"

"How would you like to help me run a Vacation Bible School this summer?" Tammy's voice held an excitement she seemed barely able to contain. "Isn't that a super idea? Our church hasn't had a VBS in years."

"Sure, I'll help." Sherrie wrapped the phone cord around her finger absently. "But I should warn you that I haven't done anything with VBS for years."

"That's OK. We won't be in it alone. Hey, have you seen Lauren lately?"

Sherrie yanked her finger free of the cord. A shiver chased up her spine. She'd only seen Lauren a few times since the day she'd spoken to her, mostly from a distance. Jack had returned the tape to her and said she'd been cool about it. "Do you mean to talk to?" Sherrie asked tentatively.

"Well, yeah. I'd like her to be part of this. I think she's really good with crafts and stuff. She'd be perfect to help out with VBS. Did you hear they're staying? Mark's company didn't end up laying him off. Isn't that great? I've been praying for them."

"Yes, that's wonderful," Sherrie agreed, embarrassed to remember that she had said she'd pray for them also. There had been so much going on . . . no, that wasn't true. She'd just forgotten or simply blocked it out of her mind.

"Anyway," Tammy was saying. "I'll get in touch with her somehow. Talk to you later. OK?"

Sherrie hung up the phone and stared at it blankly for a few minutes. She felt like praying for the Peltons. But now, the crisis was over. Still, she didn't need a crisis to prompt her to prayer. She bowed her head, standing there at the counter, and said a prayer for Lauren, Mark, and Trista. When she finished, she felt much better.

A quick look out the window told her Caleb was only half-finished with the lawn. Suddenly, she decided to run upstairs and see if his journal was around. She'd been curious to read what he had to say about the tape incident.

She found it quickly enough, beneath his mattress. Her eyes scanned the pages until she found the entry she was looking for.

"Mom and Dad found the tape Trista loaned me. Trista told me it would only be a matter of time. I don't care. I'm glad they found it. They think they can control me, but they can't. I'll do whatever I want. I don't care what they say. I hate them. As soon as I'm eighteen, I'm getting out of here. Then, even they can't make me stay."

Sherrie cringed. No, they couldn't make him stay. But why did he want to leave so badly? Why did he want his freedom more than the salvation of his soul? Her eyes wandered to an entry farther down the page.

"Trista's been asking me to go to a keg party with her, but I haven't been able to get away from the house. Either Mom or Dad is always around. There's one in a couple weeks, when school's out. Maybe I'll try to go then. I'll just have to think up a really good excuse."

For a few minutes, the only emotion Sherrie felt was a numb kind of shock. It spread over her whole body. The pages in front of her eyes became blurry. Finally, a piercing scream penetrated the angry haze that had settled into her brain.

"Mom! What are you doing?!"

It was Caleb, standing at the door, his face livid with rage. "That's my private property." In one lunge, he reached out and grabbed the notebook, clutching it close to his chest.

Sherrie fought with the sluggishness of her mind and body to adjust to what was happening. "Caleb," she whispered, as if just becoming aware that he was standing in front of her.

"What are you doing?" he repeated, his face blotchy with anger, unspilled tears in his eyes.

Sherrie rose unsteadily to her feet and held out her hand. She shook her head to clear it. "Give me the notebook, Caleb."

Caleb's jaw dropped. His grip on the notebook tightened, whitening his knuckles. "No way. It's not yours. It's mine. My property. You had no right to read it. No right."

"I said give me the notebook, Caleb, and I meant it." Sherrie struggled to keep her voice level.

"I won't." He was weakening, and Sherrie could tell parental authority was kicking in. "What do you want it for? To show Dad?"

Sherrie nodded. "Yes. And because you won't be needing it anymore. I've let you keep it for quite some time because I thought maybe it would help you with the struggles you seem to be having. Unfortunately, I can see now that it was a mistake. You're only using it to strengthen your rebellion."

"You mean you've been reading my journal all along?" He obviously wanted her to deny it and give him some shred of dignity to cover the nakedness of his soul as it lay exposed within the pages of the yellow notebook.

"Yes, I have. It was for your own good."

"My good?!" Caleb shouted, his face twisted in anguish. "It's always for my own good, isn't it? How do you know what's for my own good? Here, you want it, take it."

He flung the notebook at her and fled. Sherrie heard his feet pound down the stairs. They were cut off a few seconds later by the slam of the door. Funny how she didn't really care where he was going. Right now, it didn't seem to matter.

She picked the yellow notebook up off the floor and returned to the kitchen to finish making lunch, fully aware that there might not be anyone to eat it. Scott was at the Merrills, she was too sick at heart to even think about food, and she didn't expect

Caleb to come back for a while. At least it gave her hands something to do while she waited for Jack to get home.

She heard Jack's car drive up just as she finished making lunch. She steeled herself to go over the ugly incident with him. Her fingers reached out automatically for the notebook that lay on the counter. She heard him speak to someone before he came in. As the door closed behind him, the sound of the lawn mower starting up drifted in the open window.

"Hey, Sher, what's for lunch?" Jack gave her a quick hug, but Sherrie's arms stayed pinned to her sides. "What's wrong?"

She held out the notebook to him without saying anything. He took it, almost reluctantly. "Not again?" She nodded.

Jack sighed deeply and sat down in one of the kitchen chairs. When he'd finished reading the sections she'd pointed out to him, he closed the book thoughtfully.

"I told him he couldn't keep a journal anymore," Sherrie said.

"Good," Jack replied. "And I think he can retain the lawn mowing for another month, too, as well as continuing to be grounded. That should keep him busy enough to miss these parties he's so determined to go to. I don't think, with his schedule, that he'll have time."

Sherrie didn't think so either. And with only two weeks left of school, she wondered how he was going to feel tied down for the first part of his summer vacation. If things didn't go well, she could see Jack keeping him grounded for the rest of the summer too. Just the thought was almost a relief. At least they'd be able to keep an eye on him.

Things had just begun to settle down at home when Sherrie received an odd phone call from Pastor Hawley asking her to meet with him and the Wagners after school. It was the very last week of school, and she couldn't possibly think of what it might all be about.

On the appointed evening, after school, she sent the boys out to wait in the car. Don and Sara had been pointedly ignoring her all day, but now they found her a chair, arranged theirs across from her, with Pastor Hawley next to them.

Sherrie's smile was strained. "So, what exactly did you want to talk to me about?" She tried to keep her voice light.

Sara glanced at her husband, waiting for him to say something. He cleared his throat nervously. Pastor Hawley just smiled.

"It's just that, well, after speaking to Pastor Hawley, we feel it might be best, for all of us, if you were to spend less time at the school." Don seemed relieved that he'd gotten the mangled sentence out of his mouth in one piece.

Sherrie shook her head slightly. "I'm not sure I understand what you're saying. This is the last week of school."

"Oh, we understand that," Don agreed emphatically. "But, you see, we didn't want to let this go until next year. Maybe we should have said something a little earlier, but we really didn't see the need until just recently."

Sherrie stiffened. "And may I ask just when that was?"

"Mrs. Raines," Pastor Hawley said gently. "Sherrie, please don't feel that this is any reflection on you or your presence here at the school."

"Then, exactly what is it?" Sherrie demanded.

"It's just that we don't feel things are working out well. We'll be asking Mrs. Merrill to spend less time here also. It isn't just you," Don assured her, as if that made a tremendous difference. "But this year has been hard on Sara and me. You and Mrs. Merrill were very helpful with the hot-lunch program and all your other help, but we've discussed it, and we'd prefer to keep the running of the school just between the two of us. There is less chance of hurting anyone's feelings that way. Do you understand what I'm trying to say?"

"Mr. Wagner," Sherrie said, emphasizing the *mister*. "All I understand is that you no longer want my presence at the school. Whether or not I have been helpful doesn't seem to make much difference to you."

"Mrs. Raines, I'm sure the Wagners appreciate your help, as does the rest of the church. But I'm sure you can see Don and Sara's point. It's hard for them to conduct school properly with additional adults present."

Sherrie's eyebrows shot up. "Especially those who complain about movies, isn't that right?"

"I assure you that that incident had nothing to do with wanting you to spend less time at the school," Don protested vehemently.

"I'm sure you'll understand, Mr. Wagner, if I say that I find that hard to believe. Are you also aware that there are other schools in the area where I can enroll my children?"

Don shrugged. "That would be entirely your choice, Mrs.

Raines. I would certainly hate to see the boys leave."

Sherrie stood. "Is that all?"

Pastor Hawley jumped to his feet. "Why don't we have prayer before you leave," he suggested.

Sherrie obediently bowed her head while Pastor Hawley prayed, asking God for understanding and love between Christian brothers and sisters. A wry smile tugged at Sherrie's lips. *How very appropriate*, she thought. *Maybe he should have prayed for that* before *their meeting*.

That evening, when the boys had gone up to their room, she told Jack about the meeting. He listened sympathetically.

"There are only a few more days of school left," he reminded her.

"I know that, Jack, but they mean next year too."

"We'll put the boys somewhere else."

"Could we?"

Jack shrugged. "You're the one who will have to deal with the driving. It's up to you."

Sherrie thought about what he'd said for the rest of the evening. What did she care how far she had to travel? The Wagners had no right to bar her from the school.

Tammy called right after supper. She was hurt and confused by their firm request that she spend less time at the school also.

"I've been going to that school every day for years," she told Sherrie. "Why are they just coming to the realization that they don't want me there so much now? I mean, it isn't like we're a bother," she said indignantly. "After all, we work like horses for that school."

Sherrie agreed with her. Still, in the back of her mind, the thought that it was her fault nagged at her. Like Tammy said, she'd been going there for years, and nothing was ever said about it before.

When Annette Grant called later, she was angry about the incident too, having heard about it from Tammy. She called to lend a sympathetic ear and support. She promised that she and Duncan would speak to the Wagners about how they felt. She assured Sherrie that if she were able, she'd love to spend time at the school herself, helping out. That way she could see more of her kids.

Her call soothed Sherrie's feelings a little. It helped to know that she had the support of people she liked and admired. Many of the parents were grateful for her help at the school; why weren't Don and Sara?

As Sherrie listened to the rain outside her open window that night before falling asleep, she wondered how the boys would feel about changing schools so soon after just moving. Damp night air brushed in under the window and across her cheek.

Who knew? Maybe by next year Don and Sara would have changed their minds. Especially if some of the parents came forward to complain. She couldn't see them holding out against mass opposition. As she drifted off to sleep, she wondered what, exactly, would constitute mass opposition.

CHAPTER
18

Confrontation

Summer was half over before Sherrie even realized it. Tammy kept her busy planning for the Vacation Bible School. They plastered posters everywhere and got a spot under community events in the local papers and even on one radio station. Sherrie was very surprised that Lauren agreed to help them.

Her surprise turned to shock, however, when Lauren showed up the first day in lace-edged, skin-tight, bike shorts and a tank top. Sherrie wasn't sure if she was more concerned about what the kids thought or what their parents must have thought as they dropped their kids off. Lauren's clothing was certainly a far cry from Christian.

She mentioned it to Tammy, who just shrugged her shoulders as if to say, "What can you do?" Sherrie wasn't sure, but she was starting to think something had to be done.

The idea cemented in her mind the Sabbath following the VBS, when she saw Lauren at church wearing a short skirt and tight sweater. Lauren acted as if she hadn't seen Sherrie and hustled by her without stopping to speak. Not that Sherrie was surprised at that. Lauren hadn't spoken to her at VBS unless it was absolutely necessary.

"Did you see that?" she asked Jack in a loud whisper.

"See what?"

"Lauren. Did you see what she was almost wearing? She dressed even worse than that for VBS, if you can believe it. I can just imagine the impression those kids' parents had of us. I'm really surprised no one yanked their kids out."

"Oh, that. She hasn't changed, if that's what you mean." Jack's eyes narrowed.

"I really think I should do something," Sherrie mused. "Something more than I've already done. Apparently my talk did nothing to convince her, although I was sure she'd see my point after she had time to think it over. I've been praying so hard for her and this issue."

She couldn't get Lauren out of her mind for the rest of the day. After lunch, when the boys were upstairs reading, she sat down on the couch beside Jack.

"I'd like your opinion on something," she told him, her eyes studying the pattern on the rug. "I'd like for us to go to the Peltons house and talk this over with them."

Jack looked up from his Bible. "Do you think it's necessary?"

Sherrie nodded. "Yes, I do. I've tried the roundabout way, and I've tried being direct. Now I think it's time to bring a witness and confront her directly. And I really think we'd be doing her a disservice if we didn't do it. I can't believe no one in the church has done it before now."

"If you think we should, then we should. Why don't you give them a call and find out when it would be convenient for us to come over."

"All right," Sherrie agreed. "But I'd like to wait until after Sabbath." She spent the rest of the afternoon praying for Lauren and Mark and their upcoming talk. As the sun sank slowly into the mountains, she searched her Bible for inspiration and then gathered her courage and dialed their number.

"Hello?" It was Lauren's voice.

"Lauren? It's Sherrie Raines."

"Oh, hi, Sherrie." Lauren's voice cooled a few degrees.

Sherrie tried to sound cheerful. "Jack and I were wondering if we could come over and visit with you and Mark for a little while. We have something we'd like to discuss with you."

"Something to discuss?" Lauren sounded skeptical, but curious. "Sure, I guess. When did you want to come?"

"Is this evening good for you?"

Lauren hesitated. Sherrie could hear her cover the receiver and mumble something to someone in the background.

"Yeah, I guess. That will be OK. How about eight?"

"Eight sounds fine," Sherrie agreed. She took down the directions Lauren gave her and hung up. "She says eight o'clock," she hollered to Jack.

"Then we'd better get going," Jack said, closing his book and getting up off the couch. "Do you have directions?"

Sherrie waved them in the air. "It's the fifth house up the road," she told him. "White with black shutters."

She rubbed her palms on her baggy slacks. "I think I'll get changed before we go," she decided. It would look better if she were in a skirt, she thought. "A nice, long, loose skirt," she muttered as she searched her closet.

Sherrie was surprised at how close Lauren and Mark's house actually was. No wonder it was easy for Caleb to walk there. Her anxiety made the short drive seem even shorter. Too soon they were pulling up the driveway, gravel crunching under their tires. They walked up the path to the front door of a small, prim little white house. A profusion of roses tumbled over an arbor that spanned the walkway, and Sherrie stopped to admire them. As much, she thought, to stave off the inevitable as for appreciation of their beauty.

Lauren answered Jack's businesslike knock. She looked nervous. Sherrie noticed that she had a big, baggy sweater on over a pair of faded jeans.

"Come on in," she invited, holding the door open for them.

Sherrie looked around and was surprised to discover that Lauren had a positive genius for decorating. Most of the furnishings were simple enough, but the colors and textures Lauren had used to decorate the rooms gave them a French flair.

Lauren directed them toward the couch, and they sat down tentatively. Sherrie kept to the edge instead of leaning back, afraid to relax until they'd gotten through what they'd come to talk about.

"Can I get you something to drink?" Lauren asked, twisting her hands nervously. The diamond on her left hand sparkled in the light. Too late, her hands moved to cover it.

"No thanks," Sherrie replied politely, unable to pry her eyes from Lauren's hands. Jack declined also.

"Mark will be here any minute," Lauren said apologetically. "He's changing a light bulb in Trista's room." She laughed tensely. "She was trying to study when it blew. I'll go see what's taking him so long."

She disappeared down the hall, and Sherrie allowed herself to relax for a minute. "Beautiful house, isn't it?" she murmured. Jack only had time to nod in agreement before Lauren and Mark emerged from the hallway.

"Hello, hello." Mark smiled heartily. "How are you folks tonight? Fine, fine, that's fine. I can probably save you some time tonight."

"Oh?" Jack and Sherrie exchanged startled glances.

"Yup. If you're here to ask me to be a deacon, I accept."

"That's actually not why we're here," Sherrie ventured hesitantly.

"No?" A frown creased Mark's forehead. "I'm sorry, I guess I've jumped the gun. Maybe I ought to ask you why you *are* here. Lauren, honey, aren't you going to sit down? No, take the comfortable chair. I'll sit here."

He stationed himself closest to Jack, and Lauren sat uncomfortably in the plush armchair off to one side. She tucked her feet up under her and looked very small against the cushions. As she watched them, she chewed nervously on her bottom lip.

"We're actually here to discuss a subject that my wife spoke to Lauren about a while back," Jack explained. "We thought that maybe it hadn't been presented in the best light, and we were hoping there could be a successful resolution."

Sherrie kept a close eye on Lauren as Jack spoke and saw the color drain from her face. Mark looked confused.

"What topic would that be?" he asked, shooting a quick, questioning glance at Lauren.

"Sherrie spoke to Lauren about her manner of dress," Jack began.

"Wait, hold on." Mark raised his hands irritably. "What do you mean 'manner of dress'? Are you talking about what she wears?"

"Yes, what she wears," Jack agreed. "In the Bible, we're taught to dress modestly and not for show. Some of Lauren's clothes are, well, suggestive."

"Suggestive? Of what?" Mark's voice rose in volume as his anger grew.

"Suggestive," Sherrie said firmly. "In a sexual way, Mr. Pelton. Clothing that clings to our bodies and emphasizes every curve has no place in our worship service."

"So you're saying *I* have no place in your worship service,"

Lauren cried, almost coming out of her chair. "Is that what you're saying?"

"No," Sherrie explained patiently. "Just as Jesus loves the sinner but not the sin, we love you, not your clothes."

"And my clothes are sinful?" Lauren demanded, angrily blinding back tears.

"Yes. They are. Any garments that tempt our brothers to think unholy thoughts are sinful. Surely you can see that."

"I don't see it," Lauren hissed. "I don't see anything wrong with my clothes. No one ever said anything to me about them before."

"We're aware of that, but it doesn't cancel out our responsibility to you," Jack said. "If we were to remain silent about this and it were to ultimately cost you your soul, we would be responsible for that if we made no attempt to bring you into an awareness of your sin."

"I'm not aware of any sin," Lauren retorted, tears coursing down her cheeks. "All I'm aware of is that you won't leave me alone about my clothes."

"I think it would be a good idea if you left," Mark said coldly. "I can't believe I thought you were here to ask me to take an office. We've been at that church for a year and a half, and no one has asked us yet to do anything important. I guess now I know why. Anyway, it hardly matters anymore. We wouldn't grace the doorway of that church again if you were to pay us. So, now that you've done your spiritual and moral duty and upset my wife too, please leave. You can go back and tell the rest of them that you've done your job and you're well rid of us."

"But you're not taking this in the spirit in which it was intended," Jack said, attempting to smile as if he thought it might lighten the sudden eruption of tension in the room. Lauren sobbed quietly in the corner, her face in her hands. "We didn't come here tonight to chase you out of the church. We love you, and we value you as people and as a brother and sister in Christ. If we didn't care, we wouldn't be here. It's just that morality is a very important issue, and we felt that you weren't as aware of it as you should be."

"Personally, I don't care what you thought," Mark said frostily. "I just want you to go." He got up, crossing the floor to the front door and opening it.

Jack and Sherrie stood slowly. Jack walked out without a word. Sherrie paused as she passed Lauren's chair and laid a hand on her shoulder.

"I'm sorry, Lauren. I was hoping it wouldn't end this way. The church will be happy to have you back whenever you feel up to coming."

Lauren shook off her hand. "When I'm good enough for all you saints, you mean," she sobbed.

"Lauren," Sherrie tried again softly, feeling pity for Lauren's pain. "I love you. I really do. Don't stay away too long."

"Don't say things you don't mean," Lauren snapped. "If you really loved me, you'd accept me the way I am. I thought Jesus took people where they were at. What good does it do to grow in Christ if people are always hacking you down at the roots?"

"Lauren, I . . ." Sherrie could think of nothing to say. Turning quickly, she made her way out to the car, where Jack was waiting.

"I guess that wasn't such a good idea," Sherrie sighed.

"What do you mean?"

"It didn't do any good, and now they won't come back to church," Sherrie said. "And on top of that, our relations are strained."

"So you're saying that comfort is more important than Christian responsibility?" Jack pressed her.

"No," Sherrie protested. "I mean, I didn't say that."

"Look, Sher, living the Christian life isn't always easy. It requires sacrifice. Sometimes that sacrifice is other people. We had no control over the way the Peltons responded to us. We prayed about it, but the outcome is up to Jesus. We were just doing His work. He'll see to it that it turns out all right in the end."

"You're right," Sherrie murmured. "My spirit just feels so rumpled up."

"Pray about it," Jack suggested. "He'll give you peace."

Sherrie leaned her head against the car window and closed her eyes in prayer. Her lips moved silently as she prayed. Soon a quiet peace filled her.

CHAPTER
19

The Pastor's Visit

Sherrie knew she was right. Jack agreed with her. The Bible backed her up. As she tossed and turned, trying to find a comfortable position, she couldn't understand why sleep seemed so far away. The sheets beneath her were soaked with sweat. Not a breath of fresh air blew in through the open window. Beside her, Jack snored quietly.

Finally she threw off the covers and crawled out of bed. Her head throbbed, and her eyes felt red and irritated. She made her way down the stairs and got a glass of water from the faucet. The cool water refreshed her a little. She found her Bible by the light of the moon, which glanced in through the living-room windows and illuminated the house with a silvery glow.

The moonlight was intense enough on the porch that she probably could have read her Bible by it. Instead, she clutched it to her middle. She knew what it said. There was no need to look.

The scent of freshly cut grass clung to the muggy air, hanging around her, stifling her. Sherrie closed her eyes and turned her face up toward the gray sky.

" 'I also want women to dress modestly,' " she repeated softly. The crickets chirping noisily in the meadow across the street almost drowned her out. " 'With decency and propriety, not with braided hair or gold or pearls or expensive clothes, but with good deeds, appropriate for women who profess to worship God.' "

Suddenly an image popped into her head. It was one she had pushed aside, not wanting to remember. She saw herself in a skimpy cocktail dress at a bar with a friend. Her head was thrown back in loud laughter, her face painted heavily, a drink sloshing in an unsteady hand. A wave of shame enveloped her as she firmly buried the memory one more time.

That had been a long time ago. Her heart was much different then in those rebellious days following high school. Now it was surrendered to God. Now she knew what was right and what was wrong, and she was obligated to pass on what she knew.

"I believe Your Word, Lord," Sherrie whispered. "I believe it with my whole heart. But Lauren doesn't. I've tried to show her, Lord. I spoke to her privately. Then I brought a witness, just like it says in Matthew eighteen. Still she wouldn't listen. Now I'm afraid she'll never come back to church again."

Sherrie buried her face in her hands as sobs shook her body. "That's not what I wanted, Lord," she cried. "That's not what I was trying to do. Why didn't she respond to me? Did I do something wrong? I followed what You said in Matthew. What went wrong?"

Sherrie crumpled into one of the deck chairs and wept for what seemed like ages. Finally, as her sobs subsided, she wiped her face and laid her Bible down on the chair beside her. Hugging her knees to her body, she rested her chin on them and stared out at the shadows in the woods, thinking.

"If I'm really going to follow the advice in Matthew," she mused, "then I'm going to have to finish it. I have to tell the church." She shuddered. "This is not going to be easy."

She sat for a while longer, contemplating this. The sound of the crickets was putting her to sleep, and her eyelids drooped heavily. When her head nodded violently, she got up quickly and went back into the house. She left her Bible on the kitchen table and returned to bed. Tossing fitfully, she finally fell into a restless, exhausted sleep.

Jack shook her awake the next morning. Sherrie rolled over and groaned, feeling like she'd slept on a bed of rocks.

"Are you OK, hon?" Jack's forehead wrinkled with concern.

Sherrie rubbed her eyes. They felt swollen. "I'm fine," she managed. "I had a bad night, that's all. What time is it?"

"It's eight. I'm just ready to leave for the office for a while. I've got some work to catch up on. I was worried about you. You never sleep in. Still thinking about last night?"

Sherrie nodded. "I'm so afraid we did the wrong thing."

"Do you believe in the Bible?" Jack asked.

Sherrie glanced sharply at him to be sure he had a straight face. "Of course, I do. Don't be silly."

"Then how can you think we did the wrong thing?" Jack asked pointedly. "You know what the Bible says, every bit as well as I do. Don't let Satan mess with your head, Sherrie," he warned. "Are you going to be OK?"

"I'll be OK," she repeated. "Where are the boys?"

"Outside tossing the ball around. I already told them to weed the garden this morning and pick whatever needs picking. Get up, and I'll pray with you before I leave."

Sherrie stood, and Jack wrapped his arms around her. "Lord, please go with each of us today. Give Sherrie the assurance that we've done the right thing in regards to Lauren Pelton, Lord. Please be with Lauren and Mark and impress them with the truth of Your Word. Convict them of their error. Thank You for this beautiful day. Amen." Jack gave Sherrie a light peck on the cheek. "Feel better?"

Sherrie smiled wanly. "Yes. Have a nice day."

"You too."

After he'd gone, Sherrie straightened the room and made the bed. A quick look in the mirror told her that her eyes were indeed red and swollen. "It's because I was crying last night," she muttered to herself as she splashed cold water on her face. It didn't help with the redness very much, but it made her feel better.

She was tempted to call Tammy and beg off on their plans to hit a local rummage sale that morning in search of clothes for the Dorcas room. The Dorcas room was Caren Nason's brainchild, but since Caren worked every Sunday, she'd asked Tammy and Sherrie to attend the rummage sale and see what they could find in the way of bargains. Sherrie's thoughts were interrupted as Scott barged in the side door, slamming it noisily.

"You sick, Mom?" he asked. The wrinkled frown that creased his brow reminded Sherrie of Jack. Scott was looking more like his father every day.

"No, I'm not sick. Just a little tired, I guess."

"Are you going to be around this morning?"

"No, I'm going to a rummage sale with Mrs. Merrill," she replied before she had a chance to give the idea any additional thought. Well, now she was committed. "Why do you ask?"

"No reason," Scott answered vaguely. "Just curious. Caleb and

I were going to weed the garden this morning. Can we go for a bike ride after?"

Sherrie's eyes narrowed into little slits as she observed him. Scott squirmed uncomfortably under the scrutiny.

"What?" he asked defensively.

"Did Caleb send you in here to ask me that?" Sherrie demanded.

"No." Scott shook his head emphatically. "He didn't say a word."

"Just because Caleb isn't grounded right now doesn't mean that he's not still on restriction, but . . ." Scott's eyes lighted up as Sherrie wavered. ". . . I suppose as long as you go *down* the road, and you aren't gone long, you can go."

Scott beamed. "Thanks, Mom."

"But," she warned, shaking a finger at him. "Make sure the weeding and picking are done *first*. And don't do anything to make me regret my generosity."

"Absolutely," Scott assured her, racing for the door. *Anxious to tell Caleb, no doubt*, Sherrie mused.

Sherrie hurried to be ready by the time Tammy drove into the driveway. As they pulled out, she waved to the boys, who were busy in the garden. Plants and dirt flew in all directions.

"I hope those are weeds," Tammy commented. "I don't think my kids could tell the difference."

"Don't you ever have a garden?" Sherrie asked absently.

"Oh, sure. But the kids don't work in it. Bob and I take care of it. Of course," she observed, "it isn't nearly as tidy as yours because Bob and I don't have much time to spend in it. Maybe it would be worth educating the kids."

"What do your kids do all summer?" Sherrie asked curiously.

"Not much," Tammy replied. "Play sports, mostly. I guess I hate to see them work during their vacation."

"But they get three whole months off," Sherrie protested. "Surely they can do a little work in that time."

Tammy shrugged. "I guess. But they complain so much that it's almost not worth it. In the end, I have to go behind them and do everything over anyway. Why bother?"

Sherrie bit her tongue. She knew from experience it wasn't worth arguing with Tammy about things like this. For some reason, Tammy couldn't see the logic of instilling her children with a sense of responsibility and good old-fashioned work ethic. They ran roughshod over her.

Bob didn't seem to be able to do much with them in that respect either, though Sherrie suspected that he pretty much stayed out of their lives altogether. From what she'd seen of him, he was a shadowy father figure, completely overpowered by the more colorful and boisterous characters of Tammy and the kids.

The rummage sale proved to be the bargain-hunting ground Tammy had claimed it would be. They came away with garbage bags stuffed with clothes and Sherrie's particular victory: a wooden playpen for three dollars. They divided the clothes and agreed to wash them all before bringing them to the church and hanging them up in the Dorcas room.

Sherrie was folding the last load of laundry that evening when the sound of a car pulling up in the driveway startled her. Jack looked up at her over the top of his glasses.

"Were you expecting someone?" she asked. The look on his face answered her question. A moment later the doorbell rang. Sherrie whisked the folded clothes back into the hamper to make room on the sofa while Jack answered the door.

Josh Nason and Pastor Hawley followed Jack into the living room. Sherrie nudged the hamper over and waved them to the couch.

"Please, have a seat," she murmured, her heart racing triple time in her chest. What could they possibly want? The memory of her meeting with Don and Sara Wagner popped back into her mind, followed by a guilty flush. Had she offended someone else?

"Well, this is a nice surprise," Jack observed warmly, sitting in the chair opposite the two men. "Can we get you anything? A glass of milk? Herbal tea? Water?"

"No, no," Pastor Hawley held up one hand, declining the offer. "We're not planning to stay long."

Silence fell over the room and hung awkwardly. Pastor Hawley's broad smile tightened, and Josh shifted nervously in his seat. Finally, Jack cleared his throat and broke the ice.

"So, what brings you here tonight? This isn't just a social visit, is it?"

"No, I'm afraid it's not," Pastor Hawley agreed. "We, that is, I, received a disturbing phone call from Mark Pelton last night. First, let me ask you folks if you visited the Peltons last night."

Sherrie felt her hands and feet go numb. Part of her wanted to deny it, like a child frightened of the consequences of his actions. She stifled the feeling and sat up a little stiffer in her chair.

"Yes," she admitted. "We did visit Lauren and Mark last night. I had planned to talk to you about what transpired there, but I guess you beat me to it."

"Mr. Pelton . . . Mark, was very upset," Pastor Hawley said. "He claimed that you accused his wife of dressing in such a way as to, well, seduce men. He said some other, rather vicious, things that I'll spare you. I'll be very frank with you. I told him that I had no previous knowledge of your visit. He informed me, in no uncertain terms, that it didn't matter. He also told me that they would not be returning to church.

"I have to admit that I'm very disturbed about this. I wish you'd spoken to me first." Pastor Hawley gazed sorrowfully at Jack and then at Sherrie.

"Pastor Hawley, I appreciate your concern, but it is unfounded," Sherrie stated firmly. "Jack and I were very careful to follow biblical counsel on this issue. Lauren Pelton was most certainly in the wrong. I approached her personally and privately. That did no good. So, I brought Jack with me as a witness. My next step was to bring the matter before the church."

"But Mrs. Raines," Josh interrupted, "do you really believe this 'matter,' as you call it, is worthy of the attention you've given it? Do you realize that Lauren and Mark are brand-new baby Christians? No one expects them to have the same convictions as a lifelong member."

"I hardly think that's a valid point," Sherrie returned. "Even if you can excuse sin by ignorance, how can you condone it after it's been brought to someone's attention? Maybe Lauren didn't know she was dressing immodestly at first, but what about after I educated her about it? She was at the women's meeting. She heard the evidence. Then I spoke to her personally. How can she say she didn't know?"

"Maybe she did know, but that doesn't mean the Lord convicted her on the point of dress just because she knew," Josh replied. "It's possible, in fact, probable, that she didn't realize her dress standards were that different from what is advocated."

"That seems to be a very liberal point of view to me," Sherrie observed. "Are you saying that even though I know eating pork is wrong, I can still have ham and bacon and sausage because it's not exactly pork?"

"Mrs. Raines, I believe you are missing the point," Pastor Hawley broke in. "You are convicted in the matter of dress. I am convicted, your husband is convicted, Lauren Pelton is *not* convicted. Only God can convict her. Isn't it possible that He knows what He's doing and that maybe He's working on more important issues in her heart than what she wears on her body?"

While Pastor Hawley was speaking, Jack took his Bible off the table and flipped it open. He handed it to Josh.

"Would you mind reading chapter seventeen, verse three?" he asked politely.

"If your brother sins, rebuke him, and if he repents, forgive him," Josh read.

"Which is what we did," Jack said.

Pastor Hawley sighed deeply, a look of pain on his face. "I understand what you did and why you did it. Please, before you do something of this kind again, I would appreciate it if you would speak to me first. Will you do that?"

"Certainly," Jack agreed. "We never meant to keep you in the dark, Pastor. I'm sorry you didn't hear this from us first. Next time, we'll speak to you beforehand."

"I would appreciate that," Pastor Hawley replied. "Shall we have prayer before we leave?"

The four knelt on the living-room floor as Pastor Hawley prayed.

"Lord, we are only broken vessels, with many flaws and inconsistencies. Give us tolerance in our dealings with our brothers. Keep us from judging them by outward appearances. Fill us with Your love for them. Amen."

After a quick goodbye, Josh followed Pastor Hawley out the door. Sherrie sat on the couch and stared into space.

"What are you thinking about?" Jack asked.

"His prayer," she replied. "I don't think he agreed with us."

"He didn't," Jack said simply. "But he was right about one thing. We should have told him first. Then he could have come with us last night. We were too hasty."

"Umm," Sherrie mused. "I guess."

Jack held out his hand and pulled her up from the couch. "Come on. What's done is done. Besides, it's past our bedtime."

Sherrie followed Jack upstairs, flicking the lights off behind her. Jack was right. It was done. Now it was up to God to make something good of it. They had done all they could.

CHAPTER
20

The Board Meeting

Monday evening, right after supper, Jack and Sherrie sat down at the kitchen table with a pad of paper and the list of items to be addressed at the church board meeting later that night. Caleb and Scott had hustled upstairs to their room as soon as they'd helped clean the kitchen, and the quiet seemed almost unnatural. Sherrie could hardly believe that school would be starting again in only a few short weeks.

"First things first," Jack was saying. "The hymnals have to go. Don't you agree?"

"Absolutely." Sherrie nodded. "They're shabby and old. I can't believe they haven't been replaced before this."

Jack wrote *hymnals* on the pad and put a series of stars beside it. "All right. The next thing I think we should bring up for discussion is the junk-food element that seems to have seeped in. Maybe we could get a policy passed that would limit what kinds of food and drink would be allowed at church gatherings."

Sherrie's head bobbed vehemently as Jack scratched *junk food* onto the pad just below *hymnals*. He underlined it so hard the tip of his pencil broke.

"Is there anything interesting on the agenda?" Sherrie asked, leaning over to scan the list by his elbow.

"This item on missing and former members looks like it might be interesting," Jack grunted. "If this church doesn't watch out, there will be a lot more missing members. How much time do we have before the meeting?" He rubbed his wrist where his watch usually was. "Strap broke," he explained in response to Sherrie's questioning look.

"Just half an hour," she replied. "Maybe we should have prayer here before heading over. Are you sure it will be OK to leave the boys alone?" Ever since the incident with Caleb sneaking out, Sherrie was hesitant to leave the boys alone.

"Of course," Jack said, pushing his chair back and kneeling beside the table. "Besides, they'll be in bed soon. I just hope this meeting doesn't last too long."

Sherrie slipped down to her knees. Jack offered prayer, asking God to guide them at the meeting and to lead in each of the items they discussed on the agenda, blessing their discussion and bringing the church closer together.

"Amen," Sherrie said when he was through. She opened her eyes and stood up. "I'm going to run up and let the boys know we're leaving now."

"Go ahead. It's a little chilly out. I'll get your coat."

When Sherrie pushed the door of the boys' room open, Caleb glanced up in surprise from the book he was reading. Scott pulled off the headphones of his Walkman.

"We're leaving now," she informed them. "I expect you to be in bed at seven, even though we won't be here."

"We will, Mom," Scott assured her.

"All right, I'll see you both tomorrow morning. Good night, boys." She closed the door softly and stood for a moment in the hallway. Hearing nothing, she turned and went down the stairs, to where Jack waited.

"All set?" he asked, helping her into her coat.

"All set," she repeated.

There was a full turnout, and she was pleasantly surprised that she knew everyone attending. Sometimes it seemed like they had lived in Maine and been a part of this church forever. Except for the few recent unpleasant incidents, she was happy to be there. It was a nice feeling to know she was a contributing part of the church body, a driving force for change.

Someone was reading aloud in a droning voice, and Sherrie realized with a start that she'd daydreamed through the reading of the last meeting's minutes and had no idea what was being discussed.

She nudged Jack with her elbow, and he pointed to where they were on the agenda. The lively discussion centered around development of the historical room Tammy had told her about. The one that was supposed to house the antique furniture she'd inadvertently thrown away soon after they'd moved. For a second, she wondered if the topic would come up, but a quick glance at Tammy led her to doubt it.

Tammy, who had arrived late, was sitting with uncharacteristic silence, her eyes glued to the tabletop. Sherrie wondered briefly what could be wrong with her, then dismissed the thought. If there was something wrong with Tammy, she'd hear about it sooner or later. Probably sooner.

The discussion moved on to the next topic, which centered on missing and former members. Jack sat up straighter as he listened to the dialogue but added no comment. It sounded to Sherrie as if there were quite a few, and no attempt had been made to contact them since they'd left. The secretary read a list of names that were considered the most critical. Lauren's and Mark's names weren't mentioned. Sherrie wondered how long it would be before they were considered "missing" and an attempt was made to bring them back to church. She made a mental note to speak to Pastor Hawley about it.

After Pastor Hawley agreed to visit each of the names on the list with the head elder, the board meandered down the rest of the list, dragging each item out into a twenty-minute discussion. Sherrie watched the hands of the clock creep past nine and wondered why each meeting followed the same pattern. It was as if short, succinct discussion was an impossibility. Finally, they came to the end.

"Does anyone have something to discuss that wasn't on the agenda?" Pastor Hawley asked, closing his folder. He swept his notes to the side and went on without a pause. "Then we'll just close with . . ."

"I have a few items," Jack interjected, clearing his throat.

"Mr. Raines." Pastor Hawley smiled. "Go ahead."

"There are two items that I, that is we, my wife and I, would like the church board to address," Jack began. "The first is the condition of the hymnals. Frankly, they're very shabby and old. They create a poor impression on visitors. I propose that we purchase a set of the new hymnals."

"OK," Pastor Hawley said slowly, letting his eyes touch briefly on each face. "Is there any comment on this item?"

"I agree with Mr. Raines," Caren Nason offered. "But I think you're going to have trouble convincing some of the old members to switch to the new hymnal. Furthermore," she pointed out, rattling her copy of the budget that they'd all been handed at the onset of the meeting, "I don't see how we could possibly cover the cost of new hymnals, even if you were able to persuade everyone to accept them."

"I'm afraid I agree with Caren," Sara Wagner said. "There isn't a single place to take that much money from."

"Shall we vote on it?" suggested Pastor Hawley.

"Before you do," Jack interrupted, "could I just say that my wife and I are prepared to pay for the cost of the new hymnals. That will take the burden off the church."

Pastor Hawley's eyebrows shot up. "The entire cost? Are you certain?"

Jack nodded. Pastor Hawley called for a vote, and the board members decided unanimously to replace the hymnals, with a big thank-you to Jack and Sherrie for their generosity. While the secretary entered the vote in the minutes, Jack brought up his second point.

"And next, I'd like to address the issue of junk food. It seems that this insidious health thief has slithered in under the door and is infiltrating our church. Doughnuts, cookies, sugared muffins, and hot chocolate should not be the kind of fare we offer our members and visitors during church functions. What are we saying to people about health principles? That we advocate them but can't abide by them ourselves? I would be ashamed to ask someone to one of our functions and offer them such unhealthy refreshments while trying to uphold the image of a healthy lifestyle."

Sherrie watched the faces around her as Jack pounded the table for emphasis. He was standing now, his face flushed. All around him people squirmed in their seats and avoided each other's eyes. *They're uncomfortable*, Sherrie thought. *Well, someone needs to shake them out of their complacency.*

"You can't just tell people what kinds of refreshments they can serve at their homes during socials," Tammy protested. "How can you say, 'I'm sorry, but you'll have to serve things like carob and honey-sweetened cookies and drink nothing but water.' People aren't going to go for that. Not everyone lives strictly by the health message."

"Isn't that just the point?" Jack asked. "Shouldn't we be? We are, after all, the church with a message for the end times, and part of that message is one of health. How can we call ourselves Christians and not do what we know to be right? That's like saying, 'Do what I say, not what I do.' "

"But it isn't that simple," Tammy insisted. "I'm sure everyone is trying, but living the strict health message is a hard thing. We're all at different places. You can't rush people just because you don't have a problem with it yourself."

"Health foods are one thing," Jack argued, "but what we're really talking about here is eliminating sugar and caffeine from refreshments served at church functions. You may not realize it, but both are addicting, and we've become an addicted church. Technically, what I'm proposing isn't even part of the actual health message, since both sugar and caffeine are an abomination to the body."

"In the book *Temperance*," he continued forcefully, "Ellen White tells us that 'tea and coffee are neither wholesome nor necessary. They are of no use as far as the health of the body is concerned. But practice in the use of these things becomes habit.' I believe we can apply this principle to hot chocolate, or any chocolate, since it contains the drug caffeine just as coffee and tea do. And when Mrs. White said, 'All this is false strength that we are the worse for having. They do not give a particle of natural strength,' she was referring to tea and coffee, but I believe we can apply that statement to sugar just as easily."

Caren Nason lifted her hand tentatively. "I agree. There have been times I've felt pressured by popular demand to serve things that go against my conscious. Things that aren't a regular part of the diet Josh and I eat."

"That shouldn't be the case within our church," Jack exclaimed. "Of all places, we shouldn't see that in our church."

Sherrie noticed that most of the members had switched their attention from Jack to the clock. She could feel her own eyelids getting heavy.

"Mr. Raines?" Pastor Hawley interrupted. "I believe that this topic will bear quite a lot of discussion, and since we are closing in on ten o'clock, I suggest we table it until the next meeting."

Sherrie watched Jack struggle to downshift, feeling his frustration as he attempted to halt the flow of thoughts supporting his point. He shuffled his notes irritably, trying to redirect his attention. Then he sat down abruptly. Sherrie grabbed his knee under the table and squeezed it. The closing prayer was short, but Sherrie couldn't keep her mind on it. She was more concerned with Jack and the feelings he was struggling with. She wondered how he was going to react.

She didn't have long to wait. As soon as the car door closed, Jack grabbed the wheel and squeezed until she could see the white of his knuckles even in the semi-darkness.

"What did I do wrong?" he demanded. "What did I say that was wrong? Was I right or not? Tell me."

"Yes, you were right," she assured him. "I really think, Jack, that the only reason we were put off tonight is that the meeting lasted so long, no one really wanted to hang around and discuss the issues, no matter how important they are. But I believe we were right in raising them."

Jack's shoulders relaxed slightly. "I can't believe they spent so much time talking about nothing, and then when it came to the important issues, everyone wanted to go home. And what was Tammy advocating? She seems to think that everyone ought to be able to do whatever they want, no matter the consequences to others."

Sherrie waved a hand in front of her face. "She's not really like that. She just doesn't want to be hemmed in by standards, I think. She's trying to be in the world but not of the world, and the lines have become blurred to her.

"I think we also have to realize," she continued, "that some of these people aren't all ready for the kind of changes we're talking about. We're going to have to work hard to convince them that this is something they need to do, that they *have* to do."

"Well, we've got our work cut out for us," Jack grumbled as he started the car and pulled slowly out of the parking lot. "I get absolutely panicky when I realize where this church is standing. We've got to wake these people up. They don't realize how close to the end we really are, and they're not going to be ready."

"We'll do it," Sherrie promised. "Slowly, but surely. We'll do it." She watched the street lights flash past and slowly drifted off to sleep, gently rocked by the motion of the car.

CHAPTER
21

Pastor Hawley's Sermon

After a long debate one evening, Sherrie and Jack came to the conclusion that it would be best to forget what was past and put the boys back into the church school. Sherrie wasn't entirely comfortable with the idea. In the back of her mind was the thought that if things didn't work out, she could always move them later on.

She felt funny driving them to school the first day and then just leaving them there. Ever since Scott had started first grade, she'd volunteered at the schools the boys attended. The teachers appreciated the extra set of hands, and she'd been able to spend more time around her kids. As she drove home alone, she felt as if a bond had been broken.

On impulse, she stopped by Jack's office on her way home. She was greeted by the receptionist/nurse, a young graduate named Carrie, brimming with enthusiasm.

"Do you have an appointment?" Carrie asked brightly.

Sherrie smiled. "Hello, Carrie. No, I don't have an appointment. I'm Mrs. Raines. Remember?"

The girl blushed. "Mrs. Raines, I'm sorry. I didn't recognize you. How stupid of me."

"Don't be silly," Sherrie said. "I haven't been in as much as I should, I guess. Is Jack busy?"

Carrie glanced quickly around the waiting room and lowered her voice. "He can see you for a few minutes. Go on in."

Sherrie dropped her voice conspiratorially. "Thanks, Carrie."

Jack was dictating into a microcassette recorder when she tapped on his office door and hesitantly pushed it open. He flicked the machine off and turned to her with a smile.

"Hi, hon. What brings you?"

Sherrie closed the door quietly behind her. "Lonely, I guess. I just dropped the boys off at school." She twisted her hands in the straps of her purse. "It felt weird, like I abandoned them."

"You know better than that," Jack chided her. "We had this all settled, remember?"

Sherrie nodded. "I know. I just feel so empty and strange inside. What am I going to do with myself all day?"

"Why don't you go out to lunch with Tammy? She must be home too. She'd probably welcome the company."

Sherrie's eyes widened. "You think so?" Her voice sounded small, like a lost child. "Maybe I will. That's a good idea."

Jack crossed the room and gave her a peck on the cheek. "You'll feel better soon," he promised. "After a while, you'll wonder how you had any time at all to spend at the school."

Sherrie tried to smile. "You're probably right."

"I'm *always* right," Jack corrected her. "Don't forget that I've got a Bible-study group tonight, so I won't be home until late."

"All right. I'd better go. You've got patients waiting." Sherrie managed a genuine smile before slipping out the door. People in the waiting room eyed her quizzically as she said goodbye to Carrie and left.

She decided to walk to Tammy's house because it was so close. Before she had finished knocking, Tammy wrenched the door open and pulled her inside.

"I'm so glad you're here!" she exclaimed. "I never knew life could be so cruel. I've been sitting here trying to decide between dusting and vacuuming, and I'm so bored I can't even make up my mind!"

The look on Tammy's face made Sherrie laugh out loud in spite of herself. "I think I know how you feel. Even school vacation was better than this. Then at least the kids were home, and we could keep busy picking up after them. Now that they're at school, there's no one at home to mess anything up."

"Tomorrow, we'll have the women's prayer breakfast to keep us occupied. But what are we going to do for the rest of the week?" Tammy wailed.

Sherrie shrugged. "I don't know. I feel as lost as you do. Jack had a good idea, though. Why don't we go to lunch today? It'll give us something to do, and maybe between the two of us we can figure out some productive way to spend our free time."

"That's a great idea! I feel better already. Where do you want to go?"

"What do you think about the bagel cafe?"

"Sounds great. I've been dying for a garlic bagel with garlic cream cheese for weeks. Think you can stand my breath?"

Sherrie laughed. "Sure. I'll meet you, OK? I think I can keep busy until noon anyway. I've got some laundry I could do."

"All right," Tammy agreed. "Just don't be late. My thumbs are all twiddled out."

Sherrie returned home and started the laundry. It wasn't really that she wanted to get it done. Although she was looking forward to lunch with Tammy, she wanted to be alone for a while.

In a way, she felt like she was in mourning. Part of her life was ending. *This must be what it feels like when your kids leave home*, she thought with a sniff of self-pity. After a short cry on the couch, she sat up and shook herself.

"This is no way to behave," she said out loud. "The boys aren't gone. They're just at school. It isn't as if they've left home or anything. In a week or two, once I adjust, I'll have so many things to do, I won't even think about it."

By the time she met Tammy at the bagel cafe, she felt much better. Tammy seemed hyper, her eyes shifting constantly. After ten minutes, she began to make Sherrie nervous.

"Are you late for something?" Sherrie asked finally.

Tammy took a big bite of garlic bagel. "Uh-nuh," she mumbled, chewing furiously and swallowing twice before she could speak clearly. "No, I just feel so lost without something to do. To tell you the truth, I think my kids are happy about it. They keep telling me that it makes them feel like 'mama's kids,' you know, special privileges and all that, to have me hanging around the school all the time."

She mimicked her kids, "Maaaa, nobody else's mother stays at school all day." She rolled her eyes. "What difference does that make, I ask you? I don't know. I guess I just always centered my activities around my kids and ignored my own interests. Now, I'm not sure what my interests are."

"Doesn't it kind of seem like they've left home?" Sherrie asked, scraping cream cheese off her bagel. She had eyed the inch-thick pile helplessly for a full five minutes before finally deciding what to do with it.

"Yeah, that's exactly what it feels like," Tammy agreed vehemently. "Oh, well. I guess we've got to start letting them go now, or we'll really be in trouble in a few years. Hey," she continued, changing the subject. "Have you seen Lauren and Mark lately?"

Sherrie froze, her bagel halfway to her mouth. "No. Not lately."

"That's really funny. I've been kinda bugged about this whole school thing lately, and I haven't called Lauren. Guess I should. Maybe I'll wait until tomorrow to see if she comes to the women's meeting."

Sherrie bypassed the comment with a mumbled agreement. She had a feeling that Lauren was as likely to be at the women's meeting as she was to fly to the moon. Still, she couldn't help holding the vague hope that maybe Lauren *would* show up.

She took special pains the next day with the way she looked. Her hands fluttered nervously as she got dressed, and butterflies careened around in her stomach. What if Lauren did come? What if Lauren ignored her? Should she make a special point to speak to her anyway?

She decided that she should. As she drove the boys to school, she changed her mind a half dozen times. Finally, as she actually walked into the fellowship room, she decided firmly that she *would* talk to Lauren. No matter what.

Her gaze darted quickly around the room. Lauren wasn't there. She resented the rush of relief that flooded over her. Tammy approached Sherrie, her lips tucked down into a worried frown.

"Lauren's not here," she said, stating the obvious. "You know, I heard some of the women talking, and they said she and Mark have been offended by someone in the church. That's why they haven't been in church lately. I can't imagine who could have offended them. They don't really have many friends here. What do you suppose happened?"

Sherrie bit her lip before replying. She had no doubt that whatever she said would be repeated throughout the entire church body by the following Sabbath. She chose her words carefully. "Jack and I visited with them to discuss her clothes," she said

finally. "They didn't take it in the best way, but we didn't set out
to offend them."

Tammy's mouth dropped open in surprise. "You? Did what?
Does the pastor know?"

"Yes," Sherrie replied, suddenly defensive. "He knows everything."

Tammy's mouth closed with a snap. "Well, I'm sure it wasn't
something intentional," she agreed. "It's just too bad they took it
the wrong way."

Sherrie watched Tammy's face closely. She wasn't the type
of person who could keep a secret. Her eyes belied what her words
were saying, but her instinctive loyalty forced her to say them.

That look haunted Sherrie for the rest of the week. She had
plenty of time on her hands to wonder what people in church were
thinking about them and what they had done. A thousand times,
she reminded herself that what they had done was based on
biblical counsel.

On Sabbath, she sat uncomfortably in church. All around her
a dull rustling swept over the congregation before the sermon
started. It seemed as if everyone was whispering. She flushed
guiltily and tried to look around without being obvious. Many
people were looking at their programs, but she did catch an angry
look or two. Hastily, she looked away. Was it her imagination?

Finally Pastor Hawley began speaking. Sherrie sighed in relief and listened intently. He started telling the story about an
ambitious young man who was responsible for the deaths of
many people. *Probably a Nazi*, Sherrie thought. A hush had
settled over the congregation as they became engrossed in the
story.

As he neared the end, Sherrie found herself hoping that the
vicious young man met with an unkind end. Pastor Hawley drew
the story out a little longer before telling the detail that revealed
the identity of the young man.

"On the road to Damascus," he continued, "Paul came face to
face with his Saviour. I'm sure we're all familiar with the rest
of Paul's story. Can I ask how many of you judged Paul harshly
for the things he did in his life before he met Jesus?"

A few tentative, embarrassed hands poked the air. Mostly,
people avoided each other's eyes. Pastor Hawley's voice became
sober, as if he'd reached the most important part of the story.

"Each one of us has our own road to Damascus," he stated. "For some of us, it comes before baptism. For others it may not come until they've been in the church for a time. Then they are convicted, and as a result, their lives begin to change. Some, sadly, never reach the road to Damascus. They are turned away by people standing by the side of the road."

He paused to look earnestly out at the congregation. His next words were filled with pleading. "As Christians, mature Christians, it's our duty to guide new lambs on their journey to the Damascus road. We have a solemn responsibility to our Shepherd to do everything in our power to encourage them, rather than reject them.

"No one in this room probably has a history as darkly stained as Paul's, but each of us has things in our past, and probably in our present, that we're not proud of. Rather than pointing these faults out to each other, we should be loving one another in spite of all our faults. None of us is perfect. And only a perfect man can cast the first stone."

As they stood to sing the closing hymn, Sherrie couldn't identify her feelings. Part of her was sure Pastor Hawley's sermon was directed at her and Jack. The other part of her didn't believe he would be so blatant, rifling up what were sure to be mixed feelings throughout the congregation.

She shuffled out into the aisle when her turn came, following the line that was moving slowly past the pastor. Ahead, someone stopped to ask him something, and the line came to a standstill. As she shifted from one foot to another, Sherrie heard someone behind her whisper her name in connection with Lauren Pelton.

She tried to glance back nonchalantly but couldn't make out who had spoken. An amused titter followed the comment, and Sherrie had the distinct impression that several people were talking about her. She searched Jack's face to see if he'd heard anything, but he seemed oblivious.

Pastor Hawley's hand engulfed hers as he greeted her. "It's so nice to see you this morning, Mrs. Raines."

Sherrie scrutinized his face. His eyes held nothing but warmth. "Thank you, Pastor, for that wonderful sermon. You had me stumped until the very end."

Pastor Hawley threw back his head and laughed. "Good, good.

That's the sign of a true storyteller, I'm told."

Sherrie followed the crowd down the stairs. Before she turned the corner at the bottom, Tammy's voice floated up to her, as distinct as if she were standing right beside her.

"I'm telling you that's not the way it was," Tammy insisted. "They didn't mean to come across the way they did. I'm sure it's all just a big misunderst . . ." Her voice trailed off abruptly as she caught sight of Sherrie coming around the corner.

Sherrie forced herself to smile but didn't stop to talk. What could she say? Her legs felt like wood as she willed them to propel her out to the car. If she hadn't been so preoccupied with what she'd just heard and the general bad feeling she'd gotten from the members, she might have noticed the scowl on Caleb's face and the dangerous glint in his eyes. If she had, she might have been worried.

CHAPTER
22

The Party

Caleb didn't think too much about it the first week Trista and her parents weren't at church. The second week, he wondered if maybe they'd gone on vacation. It was too risky to try and call Trista from his house, so he'd had to bide his time. But when he heard that they weren't coming because his parents made a big deal out of what Mrs. Pelton wore, he knew he had to see Trista.

All the way home from church, he sat seething in the back seat. His mother and father were quiet. *Hopefully, they were ashamed of themselves*, he thought viciously. *What made them think they were God? It wasn't enough that they had to control him—they had to control everyone.*

When Sherrie called him down to lunch, he told her he was sick, too sick to eat. It was true, sort of. He sure felt sick. Sick of them, sick of living under their controlling hand, sick of being powerless to get away.

"Are you sure you don't want to eat a little something?" Sherrie hollered up the stairs. She sounded worried. Good.

"No thanks," he called back. Scott gave him a funny look before going down to lunch himself. As soon as Caleb was sure Scott had gone down the stairs, he scooted over to his closet, rummaged around for a while, and pulled out a battered notebook. It wasn't the yellow one, but it served the purpose.

He flipped it open to where he'd left off. Fear gripped his stomach, thrilling him with the knowledge that he was doing precisely what his parents had forbidden. It gave him a sense of satisfaction to know that there were parts of his life they couldn't control. At the same time, he was afraid they'd find out, even though he'd been very careful not to write in the notebook around anyone, even Scott.

He poured out his anger onto the page, his hand cramping as he furiously scratched out what he thought of his parents. His pencil dug into the paper, cutting through in places. The more he wrote, the madder he got. Finally he slammed the notebook shut, tucked it under his mattress, and rolled onto his back.

As he'd written, he'd slowly come to a decision. Now, it was all he could think about. He was going to see Trista. It might take a while, but he was determined. Several plans ran through his mind.

As it turned out, all his planning was a waste of time. A few days later, Sherrie and Jack had to attend a school-board meeting. Caleb realized the opportunity was custom-made. He waited impatiently until seven and pretended to settle down for the night. It seemed like an eternity until Scott's breathing settled into a steady, even pattern.

Quietly, he slipped out of bed. He was sure that he'd end up putting his shirt on backward in the dark, but it didn't matter as long as he got out of the house undetected. Clutching his shoes, he crept out of the room, down the stairs, and out the door.

The moon was full, and the temperature had dropped. Puffs of his breath preceded him down the road. He tried to ignore the shadows around him in the woods, especially the ones that looked as if they were moving. He shoved his hands into his pockets and quickened his steps.

As he walked up the darkened walkway at the Peltons' house, he hesitated in the shadows. Behind the shade, he could see someone moving. Suddenly the door opened, and Trista came out.

"OK, Mom. Don't worry. I'll be back by midnight." She closed the door behind her and started down the steps before she caught sight of Caleb, half hidden in the darkness. "Caleb? Is that you?"

Caleb stepped out onto the walkway, where the light over the door confirmed his identity. "Hi, Trista." He stood awkwardly shifting from one foot to the other, not sure what else to say. "Are you going somewhere?"

"Yeah, I'm going to a party. Want to come with me?" She hastily scanned the road in front of the house. "A friend of mine is picking me up. You're welcome to come with us."

Caleb could feel his heart thudding in his chest. Every fiber of his being knew he should decline. What would his parents do if they found out? At the thought of his parents, a flush of anger flooded over him.

"Yes," he said loudly. Then he repeated himself. "Yes, I'll go."

Trista looked at him quizzically. "You sure? You sound like you're worried about getting caught. Don't your folks know you're here?"

"No, they don't. Actually, I came over to say that I'm sorry for what they did to your parents."

Trista waved a hand in front of her face as if she was brushing away a fly. "Aw, my folks don't care. I'm glad, really. Now, I don't have to go to church anymore. I know my mom will be a lot happier not having to worry about the stuff she wears."

"It's just . . . they're so . . ." Caleb stopped, frustrated. He clenched and unclenched his fists, trying to put his feelings into words. It was so easy on paper. "They've got to control everything. Especially me. I can't stand it."

A car driving by slowed down and whipped into the driveway, screeching to a stop. The horn tooted loudly. Caleb could feel the bass beat of the music from the speakers inside. The car window rolled down, spilling the squalling music into the still night air.

"Come on, Tris, we're late. Everyone will already be bombed by the time we get there." The girl inside leaned out and studied Caleb, squinting. "Do I know you?" she asked bluntly.

"I don't think so," he mumbled, beginning to have second thoughts.

"Let's go," Trista said, grabbing his arm and propelling him toward the car. He let her lead him and scooted into the back seat, where an older boy was slumped against the door. He looked half-asleep. Trista got in front beside the driver.

"So, who are you?" the girl in front asked, as she peeled the car out of the driveway, slammed it into first, and spun the tires.

"Caleb Raines," Caleb managed. He grabbed the handle on the door and hung on. Trista saw the movement and laughed.

"Kelly's a wild driver. She's the fastest clutch in the East." Trista gave Caleb a reassuring smile and followed his worried look to the boy in the shadows near the other door. He hadn't changed positions. "That's Spaz," she informed Caleb.

"Spaz's had too many already," Kelly said. "That's why I'm driving. It's better this way. This is his car and he hates my driving, but as long as he's passed out he doesn't care. See? Just watch out he doesn't puke on you."

Caleb pressed his body harder against the door and eyed Spaz cautiously. Soon Kelly pulled off onto a dirt road. They bounced along for what seemed like ages before coming to one house lighted up like a Christmas tree. Kids were everywhere. Almost all had paper cups in their hands.

It didn't take long for Caleb to find out what was in them. He hung next to Trista's elbow as she made her way through the crowd to the keg. A tall boy handed her a cup and turned to Caleb.

"Wanna beer?" he asked, sloshing his on the tops of his sneakers. Caleb glanced around, but Trista wasn't paying any attention to him. She seemed to have found some friends and was laughing at something they told her.

"Yeah, I guess so," he told the boy. He took the cup and tasted it. The first time he'd tried beer it had tasted like warm dishwater. Trista had told him that beer really needed to be cold to taste good. This was plenty cold, but to him it was still reminiscent of something you'd find in the septic tank. He choked a little down and maneuvered his way over to Trista.

"You found the beer," she observed. "Like it any better this time around?"

He nodded, wondering if that constituted a lie, and tried to smile. The kids she was talking to were looking at him funny. Self-consciously he checked out his clothes to see if he'd put something on wrong in the dark, but he couldn't find anything that was obviously wrong.

"I've got a dead soldier," Trista said, indicating her empty cup. "Want a refill?"

"I'm not done yet," Caleb stammered.

"Well?" she said impatiently. "Drink up. You're not going to nurse that thing all night, are you?"

Caleb downed what was left in three gulps and concentrated on not letting it come back up while Trista went off to fill the cups up again. By the end of his fourth or fifth glass, he decided that beer didn't taste so bad after all.

Several times, he felt a wave of shame and guilt when he realized what he was doing, but he forced the feelings aside. He was on his own, doing what he wanted to do. No one could stop him. Not his parents or his teacher or Pastor Hawley or even God.

Thinking about God sobered him up a little. He knew he could never please his parents, but God? For a while he'd thought it was possible. Then, when he saw how much it took to make God happy, he decided it was useless and gave up. He wasn't like Scott, who seemed to be able to please their parents and God, too, without hardly trying.

For Caleb, it was difficult, and no matter what he did, it wasn't good enough. Just when he thought he'd gotten all the rules straightened out, they changed, or new ones were added, and nobody informed him until he'd broken one. After a while, he decided it wasn't even worth trying anymore.

His thoughts stopped abruptly as he scanned the crowd for Trista. She was over by the pool in the backyard. As he moved toward her, he realized with a jolt that things around him seemed to be moving.

"I'm drunk!" he murmured incredulously. "I'm actually drunk."

Trista laughed at him as he approached. "Hey, you better go light on that stuff. I don't want you tossing your cookies in Spaz's car. Maybe I should have given you a limit."

"I donneed a limit," Caleb slurred. Trista wove back and forth in front of him, and he stuck out a hand to steady her.

"Are you going to fall?" She sounded worried. "Do you need to go home?"

"Aw, don't baby him, Tris," sneered a boy at her elbow. "Can't the baby hold his liquor? Hey, baby, maybe a little water'll sober you up. How 'bout a swim?" He motioned to several other boys nearby, and they converged on Caleb, hoisting him over the rim and into the pool.

"Stop! Stop! What are you doing?" Caleb heard Trista shriek as he hurled through the air and landed in the half-drained pool. The frigid water shocked him, and he struggled to get his feet under him, but the floor of the pool was too slippery. Half his body was submerged before he was able to pull himself out.

"What did you do that for?" he asked, shivering. The boys

laughed and slapped him on the back, sending water spattering in little showers.

"Get away from him," Trista demanded. "Caleb, are you OK?" She grabbed his arm. "You're freezing. You better go home. I'll go find Kelly. Don't move."

Caleb wrapped his arms around himself and stood shivering while he waited for Trista to return with Kelly, who looked none too happy about having to leave early.

"Look, we can come back," Trista was saying. "But we've got to get Caleb home before he dies of cold."

"I'm s . . s-sorry to b . . b-be such a bother," Caleb chattered as he followed them to the car. Suddenly, he didn't feel the least bit drunk, but he felt very sorry about what he'd done. Knowing that he was going to have to face the wrath of his parents when he got home did little to cheer him up. Earlier, he'd looked forward to it. Now, he dreaded it.

Kelly pulled up to the side of the road in front of Caleb's house, where Trista directed her. Caleb mumbled a quick Thanks and got out. Every light in the house was on, and he could make out the form of his father pacing in the living room.

He stood by the side of the road as long as he could stand the cold, before approaching the house. His mind raced ahead, wishing there was some way to avoid what was about to happen. His stomach churned violently, and before he knew what was happening, he found himself hunched over in his mother's flower garden, his stomach heaving.

When it was all over, he pushed himself up off the ground and wiped one grimy hand across his face, leaving a thick black smudge. He rubbed his hands briskly up and down his arms, trying to warm them. In the moonlight, he could see steam rising off his body and melting into the air around him.

It was now or never. If he stayed outside much longer, he was likely to catch pneumonia. He forced his legs to carry him to the door, felt his hand reach out and grasp the knob, turn it. He blinked in the bright light as the door opened, and he lurched inside.

Sherrie was sitting at the table, her head buried in her arms, but he didn't notice her. The first thing he saw when his eyes adjusted to the light was his father. Jack stopped and watched him walk in the door as if he were seeing a horrible vision.

Caleb saw shock, dismay, and finally anger flit across his face as each emotion struggled to dominate the others.

"Sherrie," Jack said, his voice sounding hoarse, as if he'd been yelling for hours. Sherrie picked her head up off the table. The moment she laid eyes on him, she let out a cry of relief that was choked off in a low moan.

"You smell like a brewery," Jack said quietly. "Go." He jerked his head toward the stairs. "Get changed, and then get back down here. And don't waste time talking to your brother."

Caleb avoided their eyes as he sidled past and went upstairs. He was almost surprised to see his brother awake. Scott sat on his bed with his knees pulled up under his chin and eyed Caleb with wide eyes as he got changed.

"Where were you?" Scott whispered.

"I'm not supposed to talk about it," Caleb replied gruffly.

"I woke up, and you were gone. I got scared, and I told Mom and Dad when they got home. You aren't mad at me. Are you?"

Caleb shook his head. "Forget about it." He threw his wet clothes in the hamper and left. At the top of the stairs, he took a deep breath before going down to face his parents.

CHAPTER
23

Awakening

When Sherrie and Jack returned home from the school-board meeting, the first sign they had that something was wrong was the house. Lights were on in the living room and kitchen that shouldn't have been. The second sign was Scott's pale, anxious face, which met them at the side door.

"What? What is it?" Sherrie demanded, heedless to Scott's quivering jaw. "What's wrong?"

"I don't know where Caleb is," Scott said, sounding shaky. "I got up to go to the bathroom, and he was gone." His voice sank to a hoarse whisper. "Do you think he was kidnapped?"

"No," Jack said firmly. "I don't think he was kidnapped. Go back to your room, Scott. Thank you for waiting up."

Scott made his way slowly up the stairs, stopping every now and then to glance back. When he was finally gone, Jack set his Bible on the kitchen table and sat down, tapping the tabletop with the tips of his fingers in an irritating staccato rhythm. Sherrie sat down next to him.

"Do you think he's with 'her'?" It was a question she hardly dared ask. Surely it wasn't possible. Still, her mind flitted back to the notebook. Parties, he'd wanted to go to parties. He'd just been waiting for the right opportunity. Who else would he go with?

"Yes, I do," Jack answered. "He deliberately disobeyed us. I just don't see how he thought he'd get away with it. Does he think we're stupid?"

"I don't think he cares anymore," Sherrie said.

"Well, he better start caring," Jack spat, slamming his hand down on the table and making Sherrie jump. "We've spared the rod too much, Sherrie. Apparently the punishments we've been giving him aren't enough. He needs something stronger."

"You don't mean spanking?" Sherrie asked, aghast.

"I mean spanking," Jack repeated.

"But isn't he just a little old for that?" Sherrie struggled to remember when it was that her parents had stopped spanking her. Had they ever spanked her? She had a brief recollection of her mother hitting her with a hairbrush, but she could hardly call that spanking.

"He's still our child, isn't he? Spare the rod, spoil the child. He's getting spoiled. We have to make him see that he can't get away with unacceptable behavior in this house."

Now, as Sherrie watched Caleb walk slowly, deliberately down the stairs toward them, she wondered again if he was too old for a spanking. The look on his face frightened her. When had he developed those hard, angry lines around his eyes?

"I'm going to give you a chance to explain your actions tonight," Jack informed Caleb when he had reached the bottom of the stairs. Caleb tensed. The fearful, almost contrite look that had stolen over his face as he had begun to descend the stairs vanished. Sherrie watched as his eyes hardened and became dull.

"Does it matter?" he asked, his voice emotionless.

"What's that supposed to mean?" Jack snapped.

"You've already made up your mind about what I did and what you're going to do to me," Caleb replied flatly. "Does it really matter if I explain it? It won't change your mind."

"No," Jack yelled. "No, it won't change my mind. What you did is wrong, no matter how you look at it."

"But you don't even *know* what I did," Caleb sputtered.

"I have a pretty good idea," Jack retorted. "You went to a party with that little tramp up the street, got soused, and thought you'd come home, and everything would be fine. Well, it's not. This time you're going to answer for your actions, mister."

"Tramp?" Caleb's face registered disbelief. "Who are you calling a tramp? And by whose standards are you judging her? I thought the Bible said, 'For God so loved the world,' not 'For God so judged the world.' If God's like you, then I hate Him!"

"Caleb!" Sherrie whispered hoarsely. "Never say that. Never."

"Why not? I mean it," Caleb shouted, his face contorting in anger. "I can't make you happy; how can I ever make God happy? I'm sick of trying. I don't care if I rot in hell. I'd rather do that than spend my whole life doing stuff to make God happy."

"You don't mean that," Sherrie said. "I can't believe you mean that."

"Yes, I do," Caleb said quickly, swiping a sleeve across his eyes. "I hate everything, every stupid little thing: no junk food, in bed by seven, up at four, do your lesson every day, go to church, go to all those stupid church things, don't eat between meals, no desserts, finish your shower with cold water. I've eaten junk food. I've even watched TV a couple of times, and God hasn't struck me down with lightning yet."

"You're being ridiculous," Jack retorted. "God doesn't strike people down with lightning for disobeying Him. But you'll be rewarded for your deeds, good or bad."

"Oh, so what? I'll get a little shack on the back forty instead of a mansion in the holy city like you and Mom?" Caleb asked sarcastically. "God's gonna boot me out for a few chocolate-chip cookies? I don't even see anything wrong with cookies, and I don't see anything wrong with staying up until eight either. Or nine. Seven isn't some magic number. God's not going to let me into heaven just because I go to bed at seven o'clock religiously. You sound just like the Pharisees to me." Caleb's voice rose in pitch as he said mockingly, "Can't work your way into heaven, Dad."

Jack blanched. "That's enough," he choked as he began removing his belt. "Turn around. You're getting the strap, young man. Your mother and I have been patient, trying more subtle means of correction. I can see now that I've been wrong. It's time for the biblical method."

"You're not touching me with that thing," Caleb shrieked as Sherrie cringed. "I'm fifteen, not five! Ground me all you want, but you're not going to hit me." In one bound, he reached the stairs, taking them two at a time. Jack leapt after him, catching just a handful of air. Caleb pounded up the stairs, Jack just behind him. Sherrie heard the boys' door slam. A quiet click told her that he'd locked Jack out.

Dazed, she wandered over to the sofa and collapsed. She wasn't even aware when Jack came back down the stairs and sat brooding in his chair opposite her, twisting the belt absently in his hands. Caleb's words echoed in her ears, "Can't work your way into heaven, can't work your way into heaven, can't work . . ."

But that wasn't what they were doing.

Was it?

Thoughts swirled and collided around in her brain, making her weary with their activity. Works, faith, works, faith. Where did they separate? Where did they meet?

Sherrie laid her head on the back of the sofa. Her whole body felt numb with fatigue and stress. Pharisees. People who tried to work their way into heaven. It wasn't them. Not them. It couldn't be.

Sherrie jerked her head up. "We're not Pharisees. Are we?"

Jack stared at her blankly. "Of course not," he replied finally, but Sherrie detected some self-doubt in his eyes that hadn't been there only a few moments before. Was he questioning too? "Pharisees are self-righteous, puffed up with their own importance. That's not us."

"Oh." Sherrie let her head fall back on the sofa. When she closed her eyes, pictures of Lauren Pelton accosted her. Lauren crying. Lauren's hurt look when they talked to her. Lauren defending herself against their attack. Attack? They hadn't attacked Lauren.

Had they?

Jack's words drifted around in her head, disjointed, repetitive. "Pharisees are puffed up with their own importance, puffed up, puffed up . . ."

She shook her head, trying to clear the pictures, the voices. Without realizing it, she slipped into a fitful sleep. When she awoke early the next morning, her neck was stiff. She turned her head carefully and saw Jack sprawled out in the chair, his mouth hanging open.

Everything came rushing back at her with the speed of a locomotive and crashed into her consciousness. With it came the unshakable conviction that Caleb was right. Lauren was right. Pastor Hawley and Josh Nason were right. She struggled with an overwhelming feeling of panic as guilt washed over her like a tidal wave.

Judge not, or you will be judged. With the same measure you use for others will it be measured to you. Don't look at the speck in your brother's eye before taking the beam out of your own.

Writhing in shame, she slipped from the couch onto the floor, burying her head in her arms on the sofa. Loud, wrenching sobs shook her body. With every remembrance of the things they'd done, her sobs became more and more violent. Her hand clutched at the empty air, reaching for God, as she felt the peace that was always present slip out of her grasp.

False peace, false security. In her agony, it seemed like God had turned His back on her. She could feel His displeasure as a damp, smothering blanket. Rather than clawing at it in desperation, she let it settle around her, knowing it was just punishment for what she'd done. "Judge not, or you will be judged," a voice in her head mocked.

A soft hand on her shoulder startled her. She looked up, her eyes as tortured as her conscience. Jack, rumpled and uneasy, shook her shoulder.

"Are you OK?" he asked gently.

"Oh, Jack," Sherrie wailed, sucking back a wrenching sob. "We've been wrong. So wrong. We've been playing God for people, standing in His place. We can't do that. No one can be God except God. I think . . . I think we've misrepresented Him."

Jack sank down on the floor next to her. "I know," he said, his voice shuddering. "I've been afraid. I didn't want to believe it. I don't want to now."

"How? How did it happen? Where did we go wrong?" Sherrie begged. "What are we going to do?"

Jack shook his head helplessly.

"I keep thinking of Lauren. I was so sure I was doing the right thing, so sure it was biblical. Now I can't help but ask myself if maybe it was something that would have been better overlooked. I'm supposed to be the mature Christian. I should have nurtured her, not condemned her." She took a long, gasping breath. "But I didn't realize what I was doing. All I could see was that she was wrong. It wasn't my job to convict her; it was God's. I was playing God, and I didn't even know it."

Jack rubbed his hand absently in circles on her back. "You're not the only one. I agreed with you. I'm still not sure we were wrong." They sat in silence for a few minutes. Jack chewed his lip, thinking. Deep furrows lined his brow.

"It's just that when I look at my motives, they seem skewed. The lines have become blurred. Where does faith become replaced by works? *Am* I really trying to get to heaven by works?" Jack's hands covered his face. "I don't know anymore. I just don't know," he moaned.

Sherrie cradled her head in her arms. Her own crisis of faith was frightening enough; Jack's really scared her. What were they going to do? For years, they'd been upstanding members of the church. Now what?

Worse, would God ever forgive them? What they had done came close to blasphemy. Had they completely alienated God? Sherrie felt guilt pressing down on her that was almost literal pressure. She didn't have the strength to fight against it. Instead, it overwhelmed her.

The ringing of the doorbell shot through her like a knife, sending adrenaline coursing wildly. Her head jerked up, and she looked around dazed, trying to orient herself. Life was going on in spite of what was happening to them. It didn't seem possible. Jack didn't even bother to look up from where he sat next to her on the floor. It was as if he hadn't even heard the bell. When it rang a second time, Sherrie rose unsteadily to her feet. She didn't quite take in the fact that it wasn't really early, though there was no sound from the boys' room upstairs. The passing of time had ceased to exist for her.

Had she given any thought to her appearance, she might not have answered the door. Her clothes were rumpled from sleeping on the couch all night, and her eyes were red and swollen. Red streaks stained her face following the path her tears had taken. She pulled the door open a crack and peered out, squinting in the morning sunlight.

Josh Nason stood on the doorstep. If he was shocked by her appearance, he gave no indication. Instead, he smiled broadly as if everything in the world was all right.

"Good morning, Mrs. Raines. I stopped by to see if maybe I could talk with you for a little while this morning."

Sherrie stared at him blankly. "I don't . . . what did you . . . about what?"

"Oh, this and that. Just a little chat, really. Is your husband home too? Wonderful! I wasn't sure I'd catch him before he left for work."

"I don't think he's going to . . . that is, something happened last night . . ." Sherrie's voice trailed off. Inadvertently, she let the door open wider. Josh had a clear view of Jack slumped on the floor in the living room and her own mussed appearance.

"Mrs. Raines, is everything all right? What happened?" His tone was so full of concern that it brought tears to Sherrie's eyes instantly. She buried her face in her hands, weeping quietly. How could she tell him? What could she say? Worse, what must he think?

"Mrs. Raines, I can see that something is desperately wrong. I'd like to help. What can I do? May I come in and talk to you both?"

Sherrie nodded. Maybe he could help. She wiped desperately at her eyes and nudged the door open wider. Josh patted her awkwardly on the shoulder as he followed her into the living room. Jack rose unsteadily to his feet, anticipating that Sherrie would invite him in.

Jack sat down on the couch. Sherrie perched next to him, unwilling to relax against the cushions. Josh's expectant gaze rested on them, but Sherrie found she couldn't look directly at him as she related what had taken place the night before.

CHAPTER
24

Rejected

Josh listened patiently, nodding now and then, but not saying anything. When Sherrie finished, she braved a glance at him. His face was an impartial mask, eyes closed as if he were contemplating something or praying. When he opened them, Sherrie could see a deep sadness in them.

"We were wrong, weren't we?" Sherrie asked quietly, dreading the answer, but knowing it already in her heart.

"We're all at different places in our walk with the Lord," Josh said slowly, weighing each word carefully. "What I believe may not necessarily be what you believe . . . right now.

"God works on our characters every day," he continued. "I believe that when the time is right, He will convict us of the things in our lives that aren't up to His perfect standard. My job is just to work with Him and pay attention to the voice of His Holy Spirit when He speaks to me."

"But what about our responsibility to our brethren?" Sherrie protested. "Certainly God holds us accountable for not making them aware of their sin."

"Sin, yes. If you are aware of one of the brethren who is committing a serious sin, then, yes. I believe you should confront that individual. However, you should do it in a kind yet firm manner and have an established relationship with the person before you do it.

"But," Josh said, his hands waving around as he tried to make his point, "if God has convicted me on, say, mixed swimming or dress or the health message, it doesn't necessarily follow that everyone I know must conform to my understanding of what

God has convicted *me* about."

"What you're trying to say," Jack interrupted, "is that God convicts each person in His time and in different degrees."

Josh nodded emphatically. "Exactly. We receive justification immediately after we surrender our lives to God. He replaces our sinful characters with Jesus' perfect one. Jesus stands in our place. Because of that, to God we are as perfect as Jesus is. *Sanctification* is God working out His righteousness in us. It takes a lifetime. We're all unique individuals, so with everyone it's different. And we aren't on some kind of schedule. God may be working on one person's drinking problem at the same time He's working with someone else on their gossip problem."

Josh took a deep breath and eyed them carefully. "Do you understand what I'm saying?"

Jack nodded. "I understand what you're saying, but what I can't understand is that it's so *clear*. Why can't people see it? All they have to do is read the Bible and Ellen White, and God will convict them."

"But there are many interpretations of the Bible and Ellen White," Josh protested. "There are some statements that are almost certainly intended to be cultural and not to stand as the law for all time."

"How about the things that *are* perfectly clear? Like music, jewelry, dress, sugar, and things like that?" Jack demanded.

Josh took a deep breath before answering. "I believe that they have more to do with our personal preferences and the way we were brought up than they do with actual biblical morality."

"I never meant any harm," Sherrie interrupted, swallowing hard against the sudden lump in her throat. "I really thought my actions were motivated by love. I still think they were. But now I can see that my love was warped. It was more a 'do what I say so I can love you' kind of love. Not an 'I'll accept you wherever you are and love you anyway' kind of love. It wasn't Jesus' kind of love."

She wrapped her arms around herself, feeling cold. "And the boys . . ." Her voice trailed off, cracking. Josh waited patiently for her to regain control, not attempting to fill in the silence with sound. "I think maybe we were too hard, tried too hard to fit them into the molds we made up ourselves for good Christian kids. I guess it comes down to the issue of control. I'm not sure I'm ready to let go, but I think it's time."

Josh nodded. "Change is always hard. The best thing to do is to start small. From what you've said, Caleb and Scott have been pretty restricted. I would suggest beginning by letting them make age-appropriate decisions."

Sherrie cringed and eyeballed Jack. She wasn't at all sure she was ready to do that. He looked skeptical too. "Are you sure? I mean, we haven't been having too much success with the decisions Caleb's been making on his own even without our approval."

"There can and should be limits, of course," Josh agreed readily. "But, if you continue to make all the boys' decisions, when they finally have to make one on their own, they'll fail, and it will be harder for them. The consequences may be much more serious too. Now is the time for them to test their decision-making skills. If they make a wrong decision, it won't be fatal. You'll be here to help them out and hopefully to give them advice.

"But," he cautioned. "you'll have to restrain yourself from catching them before they fall if you see it coming or from bailing them out. Let them learn from their mistakes. We can't live our children's spiritual lives for them. The only way to teach them to make responsible spiritual choices is to stand back and let them make them without interference. Do you think you can do that?"

Sherrie surprised herself by chuckling. "I don't know. I guess we can try. I know it will be hard for me."

Jack nodded. "Me too. My father was very demanding with me when I was growing up. He was a perfectionist, and he wouldn't settle for anything less than perfection. He told me exactly what to do, even when to breathe, until I was eighteen years old. I guess I've carried that with me. It will be hard to accept failure or a less-than-perfect job in Caleb and Scott."

"Pray about it," Josh suggested. "That's the best thing you can do. Pray that God will help you release the boys into His care. After all, who can take care of them better than God? Pray for the ability to trust Him with your children.

"May I suggest something else? I think you would both benefit from counseling." He looked at them frankly, with no hint of amusement in his voice or manner.

Sherrie and Jack exchanged shocked glances. "Counseling?" Jack asked. "That's just for people with really bad problems. We don't really need something like that, do we? I mean, we know what we've done wrong now. We don't know how to fix it, but we acknowledge it."

"Counseling is for anyone," Josh assured them. "It would be very beneficial for you to be able to talk to Pastor Hawley and discover the reasons behind some of your attitudes and actions. In the meantime, there are some apologies you may consider making."

At that, Sherrie panicked and quickly cut him off. "Apologies? To whom?" Shameful pictures of groveling invaded the peace that had begun to replace the chaos in her mind. She writhed at the thought. She couldn't do it. It was impossible.

"To Caleb and Scott," Josh suggested. "And to Lauren and Mark . . . and a public apology to the church."

Jack leaned his chin on the tips of his fingers. "You're right, of course."

Sherrie straightened with a jerk. He couldn't be right! Jack couldn't agree with him. She'd die before she'd be able to face Lauren and Mark and ask for their forgiveness. Facing the boys would be hard enough. And the church? It was unthinkable.

"But I don't think we should go alone," Jack continued. "I realize we got into this ourselves, but . . ." His voice trailed off, and he eyed Josh hopefully. "Would you set up the meeting and come with us? We'd appreciate the moral support and encouragement."

"Yes," Josh agreed. "Yes, I will. Shall we pray before I go?" The three knelt together on the living-room floor as Josh offered a simple prayer. "Lord, we thank You for helping Jack and Sherrie understand themselves and their attitudes. Give them wisdom, Lord, that they may fully see what their actions and words do to others. Change their hearts. Make them kind, loving, accepting Christians who will win people to Jesus. Amen."

Sherrie offered a timid Amen before wiping her eyes and rising to her feet. "Thank you," she said shyly. "Thank you very much for caring and for taking the time to help us."

"You'll let us know about meeting with the Peltons?" Jack asked.

"As soon as I know myself," Josh promised. "Take care, both of you. God bless." He let himself out the front door as Jack and Sherrie sat back down on the couch to discuss what they were going to say to the boys.

"This is going to be hard," Sherrie moaned.

"Hard?" Jack exclaimed. "My father never apologized to me once, even when I knew beyond a shadow of a doubt that he was wrong. For me, this is going to be next to impossible."

"But we have to do it," Sherrie stated firmly. "We can't back down now. Do you want to call the boys down, or should I?"

Jack glanced at his watch. "I'm surprised they're not up. They're going to be late for school. Maybe we should wait until tonight?"

Sherrie shook her head emphatically. "No. This is more important than school."

Jack shrugged. "You're right," he admitted. "Why don't you go get them? I'll call my office and the school and let them know we'll all be late this morning. Have them come down to the living room."

For Sherrie, it went better than she had thought possible. When they began to explain their position to the boys, Caleb's face registered skepticism, a rather hostile skepticism. *He doesn't believe us*, Sherrie thought. But, as Jack spoke and she struggled to keep from crying, the look slowly changed to amazement.

"Your mother and I are sorry for the way we treated you boys," Jack said. Sherrie could tell from the tone of his voice that he was struggling with the words. "From now on, we're going to try to let you make your own decisions. That doesn't mean that there are no rules of the house anymore, but we won't be making all your spiritual decisions as we have in the past.

"We've brought you up by the Bible. You have your own relationship with Jesus. You are responsible for your choices." Scott glanced sideways at Caleb and tried to hide a smile. Caleb looked stricken.

Sherrie felt a flash of panic sweep over her body. Were they doing the right thing? They had prayed about it, but maybe they should have waited for some kind of sign.

Be reasonable, she told herself firmly. *You know this is right. You know it's truth. Face it; change is scary. Letting go is scary. Lord*, she prayed silently, forcing her lips not to move, *help me to accept this. Help me to let them go into Your hands.*

The boys didn't say much after Jack finished his speech and Sherrie had added her own choked apology. They stiffly accepted a hug and then went back up to their room to get ready for school.

It was going to take some time to sink in, Sherrie rationalized. This was new to them too. There was sure to be some testing to follow, just to see if she and Jack would fall back into their old pattern. It was just as sure that there would be mistakes made on both sides.

But God will be with us, Sherrie reminded herself. *He'll help us to keep our promises and strengthen us. And He'll watch over the boys and guide them.*

She spent a quiet day alone with her Bible and her thoughts. Until the phone rang and Josh told them that Mark and Lauren had agreed to see them that evening, she wondered if the past twenty-four hours had been a bad dream.

Now, as they made their way up the walkway at the Peltons, she allowed herself to believe that it was real. She couldn't block it out any longer. Josh's rap on the door sounded too loud, as if it would wake up the whole neighborhood.

Lauren answered the door, her expression deadpan. "Come in." It was hardly an invitation. Sherrie had the distinct impression that she had not wanted them to come at all.

They seated themselves on the couch as Mark came in. He looked them over with a hint of a smile. Lauren sat down opposite them in a straight-backed chair, and he stood behind her, rubbing her shoulders.

"Well, well, you've come back to apologize, I hear," he observed. Sherrie shifted uncomfortably in her chair. He didn't sound as if he was in any mood to accept an apology, just to hear one, so he could laugh them out of his house.

"Yes," Jack began. "We've come to apologize to you and to Lauren." He nodded his head at Lauren. "We're very sorry for the things we said. Your relationship with Jesus is just that. Your relationship with Him. It isn't with us and Him. We had no right to violate that relationship and judge your Christian experience. We're very sorry.

Will you," Jack hesitated, swallowing hard. "Will you forgive us?"

Lauren stared at the floor, her mouth tightened into a belligerent pucker. She acted as if she hadn't heard a word Jack said. Mark's eyes flitted from Jack to Sherrie and back again.

"What? That's it? Just an 'I'm sorry,' and you figure we'll just forgive you and forget the past?" He laughed, a short, humorless bark. " 'I'm sorry' just doesn't cut it. You've completely demolished my wife's 'Christian experience,' as you call it. And frankly, you crushed the last spark of interest I had in that church."

Sherrie felt a sob rising in her throat. It escaped before she could catch it, and she buried her face in her hands, weeping uncontrollably. Mark appeared not to notice, although a smirk tugged at the corners of his lips.

"Mark, Lauren," Josh pleaded. "I realize how hurt you both were, but the Raineses have made a sincere attempt at reconciliation. Won't you accept it?"

Mark shook his head with determination. "No, we won't."

Jack brushed hastily at his eyes. "I'm sorry. What more can I say? I wish I could take back what happened, but I can't. I hope that at some point, you'll be able to forgive us for what we did. We'll be making a formal apology at church this Sabbath. I hope you can be there."

Mark looked smug. "Oh, we'll be there, all right. This I've got to see. It's about the only thing I'd go back to church for."

Josh rose to his feet. "We'll be praying for you," he said softly as he turned to go. Jack took Sherrie's arm and led her to the door.

"Don't bother," Mark quipped cheerfully as he followed and closed the door, leaving them alone on the walkway with their thoughts.

CHAPTER

25

The Apology

For Sherrie, the rest of the week crept by. She tried to keep busy, tried to forget what she was going to face on Sabbath, but the specter of their humiliation loomed ahead of her like execution day. A dark cloud of depression settled over her, making each day seem stale and endless.

Friday evening, before Jack came home with the boys, she wandered into her bedroom and slumped dejectedly on the bed. Out of the corner of her eye, she saw her Bible. She jerked her gaze away guiltily. She hadn't opened it since the evening they'd gone to the Peltons. Now, it drew her like a magnet.

She reached out and picked it up off the night stand. She flipped through the pages idly, waiting for something to catch her eye. Red highlighting leapt off the page at her, stopping her hand. It was Psalm 91. She had memorized it over a year ago, shortly after they had first moved to Maine.

"He who dwells in the secret place of the Most High shall abide under the shadow of the Almighty. I will say of the Lord, 'He is my refuge and my fortress; My God, in Him I will trust.' "

Her eyes skimmed the words again. Anguish gripped her. "If only that were me," she whispered softly. "I need a refuge. I need a fortress. I'm afraid."

"God," she said, raising her voice, "if You're still listening, if You still care about me, be my shelter. Hide me in Your secret place, under Your shadow."

She bowed her head and closed her eyes. Peace fell over her like a light spring rain. In her mind's eye, she could see a giant bag slip from her shoulders. Jesus walked up to the bag and lifted it.

Staggering under the weight, He slowly made His way to the foot of the cross and dropped it there.

Tears squeezed out from between her closed lids. "Thank You, Jesus," she murmured. When she opened her eyes, everything looked brighter. By the time Jack arrived with the boys, she was able to greet him with a genuine smile.

Sabbath morning dawned bright and clear. Sherrie rose an hour before her usual time to prepare herself mentally for the day ahead. It wasn't going to be easy, but Jesus would be there. He would hold them up through the trial they faced, the trial of their own creation.

Sherrie sat on the couch and looked out the big picture window, watching the sky turn blue. Most of the leaves had already fallen from the trees, carpeting the woods with a pungent cushion. Maybe they'd go for a short hike later up one of the nearby mountains. They could pack a picnic lunch and have worship at the top. She began to get excited about the idea.

Her daydream was interrupted by the sound of an alarm going off upstairs. She glanced at her watch and giggled. As part of their new responsibilities, the boys were supposed to get themselves up and be ready on time for school and church. Where before they complained about getting up, they now rose even earlier than she would have woken them. She wondered if the novelty would wear off eventually.

By the time Jack and the boys came downstairs, she had breakfast ready and on the table. They would need extra time this morning to talk and pray before they left for church. Sherrie wanted to be sure they weren't rushed.

After breakfast, the boys listened solemnly as they explained again the change in their attitudes and how the Lord had convicted them that they had been wrong. Scott threw his arms around Sherrie's neck as soon as Jack stopped talking. Caleb held back, watching.

"I'm behind you, Mom," Scott assured her, then looked at his father. "You, too, Dad. I know you didn't mean it. Jesus will forgive you. I'll ask Him to."

Sherrie searched Caleb's face over Scott's shoulder. She read mistrust in his eyes, but he looked uncertain, as if he desperately wanted to believe that things were going to be different now.

"Can I tell Trista you're sorry?" Caleb asked hesitantly. "I mean, when I see her again."

Sherrie shook her head. "No. I'll tell her myself. But that doesn't mean that I want you going to any more beer parties with her," she warned.

Caleb grinned self-consciously. "Don't worry, Mom. I hate the stuff."

"Good." Sherrie sighed with gratitude. "Do you both think you'll be able to hold up today? It's not going to be easy, you know. We want you to realize that right up front. We have no idea how people are going to react to what we have to say."

"We'll be OK," Caleb said firmly, reaching out and mussing Scott's hair. "But," he added worriedly, "we don't have to sit up front, do we?"

Jack laughed. "No, I guess this is one time it'll be all right for you to sit toward the back."

They joined hands and stood around in a circle while Jack led out in prayer. When he was through, Sherrie and then each of the boys offered a brief prayer. Sherrie squeezed Caleb's and Scott's hands before letting go.

She tried to smile at them, hoping it didn't look too much like a grimace. Even though she was prepared for what was going to take place, butterflies of every imaginable size fluttered in her stomach. She tried to push them aside and concentrate on retaining the peace that had been with her since the previous evening.

When they pulled up in the church parking lot, the first thing she noticed was the Peltons' red car. So, they *had* come. The reality of their presence shocked her into a temporary panic. Caleb and Scott followed Jack out of the car, but Sherrie stayed glued to her seat.

"Coming?" Jack inquired, poking his head back in and frowning at the look on her face. "You all right? You're a little green around the gills."

"I'm . . . I'll be fine. I just need to sit here for a few minutes. You go on ahead with the boys. I'll be right along," Sherrie said, wondering if she looked as scared as she felt.

"If you're sure," Jack agreed hesitantly. "But don't stay out here all day. I'm not sure I can go through this alone."

Sherrie smiled. "I won't," she promised.

When he'd gone, she took several deep breaths. This was going to be OK. Jesus was here. He was with her. "I'm abiding under the shadow of the Almighty," she reminded herself. Then she realized that she wasn't really worried about herself. It was Lauren and Mark.

"Lord, they came here to witness our humiliation. And that's OK. But, Lord, touch their hearts. Our confession and apology to the church will be so hollow if it doesn't draw Lauren and Mark back to You. Send Your Holy Spirit to speak to them as we speak to the church. Show them that though we are imperfect vessels, You are perfect. You can help them turn loose of the bitterness and forgive."

Her lips stopped moving as her prayer ended. The peace had returned. She drew a deep breath and got out of the car. It was going to be OK. God was leading.

As she walked in the door of the church, Jack beckoned her from the pastor's study. When she entered, she found him sitting with Pastor Hawley and Josh. Pastor Hawley motioned her to a chair as she glanced at each of their faces for some sign of what had taken place before her arrival. Josh answered her unspoken question.

"We've been trying to decide the best way to approach the service today in light of what you and Jack would like to do this morning," he explained.

"Before we really get into that," Pastor Hawley interjected, "I'd like to apologize myself for not being available this week when you both needed me. I understand, though, that you are interested in counseling, and I'd be happy to set something up with you later."

Jack nodded in agreement. "Thank you. We'd appreciate that."

"As far as the service goes," Pastor Hawley continued, "I feel the best way to conduct this is for you both to sit in the front pew until after the worship service. At that time, we'll call you up front, and you can speak to the congregation. I feel that would be better than your sitting on the platform through the entire service. How do you feel about that?"

"I think that will be fine," Sherrie agreed, speaking for both of them. "There is something I'd like to ask you, though."

"Yes?"

"May we walk out with you and stand in the receiving line?"

Sherrie asked. "Personally, I would like the opportunity to face the congregation one on one afterward. Otherwise, I'll feel uncomfortable the first time I have to talk with them later."

"Certainly," Pastor Hawley agreed. "I can understand your position, and I don't see any difficulty with that. I think it will be a very strengthening experience for the members also. I find your courage in this matter admirable."

Sherrie shook her head. "No. The only admirable thing in this entire situation is God's mercy in forgiving us and His strength that will enable us to face the people we've wronged and ask for forgiveness."

Pastor Hawley glanced from Sherrie to Jack. "Then, if we have everything settled, I'd just like to have a short prayer before we leave."

He offered a brief prayer before ushering them into the sanctuary. Sherrie hadn't realized how late it was. Sabbath School was just breaking up, and people were filtering into the sanctuary from different areas of the church.

She followed Jack to the front pew and sat down beside him. Just before the service started, she braved a glance back to locate the boys. They were sitting toward the back. Scott gave her an encouraging grin, and Caleb flashed her a thumbs-up signal. She smiled before turning back around.

The service seemed to fly by. She found herself wondering if the sermon had been short or if it just seemed so to her. Suddenly, the pastor was explaining that she and Jack had something to share with the congregation and invited them up front. She gripped Jack's hand so hard that she was afraid she'd leave an imprint.

Facing the congregation, her mouth went dry. She tried not to notice how nervous Jack looked. What if he couldn't speak? What would she say? And then he was talking, explaining, apologizing.

She lifted her eyes and hesitantly scanned the congregation. Lauren and Mark sat bolt upright in their pew. Trista was not with them. Sherrie expected them to be gloating over their victory, but they weren't. She recognized pity in Lauren's eyes and was shocked. Mark's face was an unpenetrable mask, his eyes sober.

Jack nudged her. He had finished, and now it was her turn.

She tried not to look at anyone in particular, afraid her nerve would desert her at the last instant. She licked her lips and began to speak.

"As Jack explained, we feel that we owe this congregation a public apology." She faltered, and then saw Tammy. She was white as a sheet, but she smiled encouragingly at Sherrie. "There are some people to whom I will apologize personally. The first thing I'd like to say I'm sorry for is throwing away some antique furniture when I helped Mrs. Merrill clean the church. I didn't realize they were antiques, but I wouldn't have cared. To me, they were old and ugly. I really hoped when we moved here to make this church more modern. Mrs. Merrill was very kind about the whole thing, but I've been hiding behind her silence for too long."

She took a deep breath before going on. "I am also sorry for the dissention I've caused about issues that I've come to realize are personal choices.

"Some of you have heard me say derogatory things about Lauren Pelton, and I'm very sorry for that." Sherrie caught Lauren's eyes and held them. "I've already apologized to Lauren, and I hope the rest of you can forgive me for the harsh, judgmental things I've said."

Sherrie allowed herself to study each face as her gaze slowly swept the congregation. "I'm sorry. Please forgive me. I'm sure that I won't change overnight, but with Jesus' help, I will change. Thank you."

She followed Jack blindly down the aisle behind Pastor Hawley, Josh, and the other deacon as tears filled her eyes. As she took her place beside Jack in the receiving line, she brushed her tears away quickly. One by one, people in the congregation filed past. Most shook her hand; some ventured a self-conscious smile.

Scott threw his arms around her neck. "I'm proud of you, Mom," he whispered in her ear.

Caleb gave her a hug, a genuine hug, waiting for her to break away before letting go. The action brought fresh tears to her eyes. He turned and followed Scott down the stairs to the fellowship room. That's when she saw them.

Mark and Lauren hung back, waiting at the end of the line. Finally, they reached Pastor Hawley. He shook their hands, and they murmured something about a wonderful sermon. Sherrie didn't need to ask if Lauren had forgiven her. She could see it plainly in her eyes.

Mark stepped up to Jack, and Lauren clung close to him. Mark didn't say anything, but it was obvious that he had been cheated of any triumph he had expected to feel over their public humiliation. Instead, his face reflected pity and sympathy.

Jack held out his hand, and Sherrie held her breath. Would he take it? She prayed fervently, her eyes closed, unaware that her lips were moving. When she opened them again, she saw Mark reach out and grasp Jack's outstretched hand. As if in slow motion, she saw him allow Jack to pull him into an embrace.

As the two men stood there, she took a good look at Lauren. She was crying. The barriers that had been between them crumbled. Although no words were spoken, Sherrie sensed that their relationship was on the mend. Old wounds would heal with the help of Jesus, the "Balm of Gilead," and there was hope for the future.

It would take time, counseling, and prayer, but she was ready to face the growth process. She offered Lauren a smile and took her hand as they followed Pastor Hawley, Josh, Jack, and Mark down the stairs to the fellowship hall.